The
Lost
Husband

The
Lost
Husband

A Novel

Katherine Center

Ballantine Books
New York

A Ballantine Books Trade Paperback Original

Copyright © 2013 by Katherine Pannill Center

Published in the United States by Ballantine Books, an imprint of The Random House Publishing Group, a division of Random House, Inc., New York.

BALLANTINE and colophon are registered trademarks of Random House, Inc.

Library of Congress Cataloging-in-Publication Data
Center, Katherine.
The lost husband: a novel / Katherine Center.
pages cm
ISBN 978-0-345-50794-5
eBook ISBN 978-0-345-53891-8
1. Widows—Fiction. 2. Single parents—Fiction. 3. Psychics—Fiction.
4. Country life—Fiction. I. Title.
PS3603.E67C46 2013
813'.6—dc23
2012046345

Printed in the United States of America

www.ballantinebooks.com

Book design by Diane Hobbing

For my sweet children,
Anna and Thomas,
who have given me
a whole new understanding
of love.

The
Lost
Husband

Chapter 1

My husband had been dead for three years before I started trying to contact him.

By then, our house was long sold, his suits were donated, and his wedding ring was in a safe-deposit box. All I kept with me was a shoebox full of meaningless stuff: a button from a shirt, an old grocery list, his driver's license, his car keys, a doodle he'd drawn on a Post-it. That was everything of Danny's I'd held on to: a box of junk.

That, and, of course, his children.

Piece by piece, I had left our old life behind—though I suppose you could argue that it had left me first—and now I was in the final stages of starting over, which meant, for my little lopsided family, leaving town. And so on this Texas-warm New Year's Eve morning, I was following a ribbon of asphalt out to the countryside, checking and rechecking my directions while my kids poked each other with magic wands in the backseat of our minivan.

"Hey!" I said, catching their eyes in the rearview mirror. "Those are for spell casting only. No poking! Or else."

This was about the tenth time I'd threatened to confiscate the wands. Weak parenting, I knew. I should have taken them away ten exits back—no second chances. But I didn't want to have to take them away and go through all the drama that would follow. I wanted the threat to be enough.

We were approaching the town square of Atwater, Texas. A town two hours from Houston at the edge of the hill country that I'd never visited or even thought much about. The speed limit downshifted as we drew closer, and the rolling fields that had surrounded us since we left the interstate now gave way to barn-sized feed stores, cinder-block motels, and fast-food joints. I glanced down to review my next step: go around the courthouse, then a right on FM 2237, known to locals, apparently, as Broken Tree Road.

We were beginning, I kept telling the kids in a voice that sounded false even to me, "an adventure." Though the truth is, moving to Atwater was much less about starting something than about ending something. Because there were many hardships in the year after my husband's death—finding out he'd spent our savings, for example, and cashed in his life insurance—but the hardest hardship by far was having to move in with my mother.

Since then, we had stayed at her condo for two passive-aggressive years as I endured judgments on my parenting, my figure, my wrinkles, my grieving process, my haircut, and my "joie de vivre" with no end in sight until, unexpectedly, I'd received a letter from my mother's famously crazy sister offering me a job and a place to stay. On her goat farm. In Atwater. Somewhere southeast of San Antonio.

Now, less than a week later, we were trading one kind of crazy for another—hoping against hope it was an upgrade.

And so the morning's drive from Houston was not just the pavement between towns. It was the shift between our old life and our new one. All morning I'd felt it—the big-dealness of it—as a nervous flutter in my chest, and I was sitting straight up in the driver's seat, gripping the wheel with both hands like a student driver at attention.

That is, as *at attention* as you can be with two children bapping each other in the backseat with wands. Because just as the road brought us to a stop sign at the town square, and just as I caught my breath at the county courthouse rising in front of us like a Disney castle, my son smacked his sister once again on the head with his wand, and when she shrieked, I hit the brakes and turned full around to face them.

"Quit it!" I said, giving them my sternest look. "The next time I have to say it, I'm throwing the wands out the window."

They bowed their heads a little and held still.

"Got it?" I asked, and they both nodded.

Just as I was turning back around, I heard a man on the sidewalk shout, "Hey! Watch out!"

I looked up, but it wasn't me he was calling to. It was someone in the crosswalk in front of us—and at the same moment I realized that, I also realized my car was not exactly stopped. Turning all the way around in my seat had eased my foot off the brake, and we were rolling forward.

I stamped my foot back down in time to see a girl standing in the crosswalk, directly in front of my car. She had turned her head at the shout, too, and thrown her hands out toward the hood as if they could protect her, just as we lurched to a stop, tires squeaking, less than two inches from her knees. She looked straight through my windshield, and we locked eyes for longer than I'd ever held a gaze before.

I threw the transmission into park, but before I was even out of the car, the man who had shouted at us appeared in the crosswalk and grabbed the girl by the shoulders. And that's all I saw as I leapt from the driver's seat and arrived beside them: her dazed face and a white-haired guy with a mermaid tattoo on his forearm.

The tattooed guy was shouting, "Jesus, Sunshine! Watch where you're going!"

She waved him away. "I'm okay," she said. "I'm fine."

Then he turned to me. "You almost killed her!"

I was out of breath. "I'm sorry! I thought my brakes were on! My kids were fighting! I've been up since five!"

"Killed by a minivan," this girl, Sunshine, said, as if she were reading a headline. "That's not how I'd prefer to go."

"No," I said. "Of course not."

"Killed by an ice cream truck, maybe." She shrugged, as if that suggestion were less bad. "Or killed by a Jet Ski." She looked down at the stripes on the pavement. "Maybe a paragliding accident."

My kids were back at it in the car as if nothing had happened. I could sense the wands in motion and hear squeals. Cars were lining up behind me. I was just about to excuse myself when she snapped her fingers, met my eyes, and pointed right at me.

"Shark attack!" she said.

It felt odd to brainstorm the best headline for this girl's death. But it also seemed rude to deny her anything she wanted. So I faked it: "Yes!" Then I nodded. "So much better than a minivan."

She could tell I was faking, though. She let her hand drop and stuffed it in her pocket.

"I'm so sorry," I said again.

"Don't worry about it," she said.

That's when I realized the tattooed guy was studying me. "Are you who I think you are?" he asked.

"Um," I said. "Who do you think I am?"

"Are you Jeannie's niece?"

It was so odd for him to know that. And I had never in my life heard my aunt called "Jeannie," much less with such affection. But he had me. "Yes," I said. "That's me."

And then he did the strangest thing. He stepped over and hugged me. Tight. A big hey-howdy Texas hug. "Welcome to Atwater," he said when he finally let go.

I wasn't quite sure what to say. Sunshine was turning to leave. We'd been in the road too long.

Just at that moment the driver of the truck behind us got tired of waiting. He leaned on the horn. The sound startled us all, and something about it woke Sunshine up. She turned back and seemed to see me for the first time—seemed almost to recognize me, even. She stepped back in my direction, took my hand for a second, and ran her eyes over my face.

"That husband you lost?" she said, out of nowhere. "I can find him for you."

That husband I lost.

The day I lost him, we'd had a fight.

I had dreamed he was cheating on me with—and I'm not kidding here—a trapeze artist from the circus. In the dream, I caught them having coffee at Starbucks, him in my very favorite ice-blue tie, her in a sequined leotard with a plunging, faux-flesh neckline. Needless to say, she was more beautiful than me. No doubt more limber. And far sparklier.

Danny didn't understand my point. "It was a dream," he kept saying. "It wasn't real."

"It was real to me," I said back.

He was getting ready for work—towel around his waist, shaving at the sink. My daughter, Abby, then four, was still sleeping, as was her little brother, Theodore, a.k.a. Tank. I could hear their separate breathing sounds on their separate monitors.

At first Danny thought the dream was funny. "How do you know we were even having an affair?" he said. "Maybe I just wanted a trapeze lesson."

Under my bathrobe, I was still wearing the little lacy thing I'd put on the night before in hopes of sparking a night of romance. The same one I'd fallen asleep in before he even made it home, actually. Though, in his defense, I was down for the count by eight-thirty.

"Trust me," I said. "You wanted much more than trapeze lessons."

"You don't know that," he said.

"I do know it," I said. "Because I was there."

Danny met my eyes in the mirror. "That's a critical point," he said. "Because I wasn't."

He was right. I shrugged. "It just tore me up to see you, okay?"

Danny took a breath. "Please tell me you're not truly angry at me for something you imagined in your own head while I was fast asleep next to you."

"I know it sounds crazy—" I started.

"It doesn't just sound crazy." His voice was tightening. "It actually *is* crazy."

I looked down.

"What if I had some insane dream about you?" he went on, pushing his advantage. "What if I woke up one morning steaming mad because you'd burned the house down? Or totaled the car? Or bought a tiger as a pet? And then I walked around all day resenting you for it?"

"Point taken," I said.

This was not the first time I'd had a dream like this about Danny. In fact, we'd worked out a fully developed theory about how my neglectful mother, who had once driven off with the moving van before realizing she'd left me behind, had given me a fear of abandonment. But it didn't seem to change much in practice. I still kept expecting him to leave me. And nothing he could do—including repeatedly *not* leaving me every day for eight years—could convince me otherwise.

This bugged him. After a while, it really bugged him. Because he was a good guy, and he got tired of being treated like a scoundrel.

The problem, in some ways—and we'd discussed this, too— was that he *was* such a good guy. He was exactly the guy I'd always hoped for. He was fun, he was affectionate, he helped with the dishes. But the trouble with getting what you've always wanted is that once you have it, you have to worry that you'll lose it. And the more you tamp down that fear, the more it comes out in funny ways. Fear of burglars, for example. Or natural disasters. Or trapeze artists.

My life before Danny—or maybe it was just my mother—had taught me to expect the worst. And yet the worst never seemed to happen. So, about four times a year, I'd get mad at Danny for something I made up.

In my defense, dreams can be very real in their own way.

"But," I started again—and here we got to the crux of the matter—"you're still in love. With me, I mean. Right?"

It was a stupid, vulnerable question—one I felt ridiculous even asking. One that had a razor's-width range of possible right responses. And as he squeezed his eyes shut in irritation, I knew for certain that he'd get it wrong.

He turned around. "Where the hell does that come from?"

I couldn't have answered him even if I'd tried. Maybe the fact that he'd been working twelve-hour days for over a year. Or the fact that he always seemed like he was in a rush to get somewhere else. Or the fact that his life was 90 percent grown-up stuff, and my life was 90 percent kid stuff, and I wasn't sure anymore where we overlapped.

I did not seriously think that he was having an affair. Still, I'd have taken a little reassurance. I wouldn't have said no to that.

But that's when Abby woke up, and we heard her shout, amplified on the monitor: "Is it morning yet? Hello? Is it morning?" And that woke her brother in turn, which started the wheels cranking on our morning routines—the kids and me heading downstairs for banana coins and oatmeal, and Danny sweeping past us later in his suit, pausing just long enough to kiss all three foreheads on his way out to the car. I wasn't sure if we were still fighting or not, honestly, by the time he was gone. And by noon that day, I'd left several voice mails apologizing and asking if we were okay.

"Just checking in," I said, substituting singsongy for actual cheer.

I'd been to Gymboree, made fruit salad and mac 'n' cheese for lunch, dropped Abby at art camp, and put Tank down for his afternoon nap before I heard anything back.

In the late afternoon, a text from Danny finally arrived. "We R OK. C U @ dinner."

But I did not see him at dinner.

That evening, as Danny entered a busy access road after picking up Abby, a pickup truck crashed into his Jeep. The impact was so strong, it crumpled Danny's side of the car before he had his seatbelt on. And it crushed Abby's femur into enough pieces that she still walked with the tiniest limp. Danny lost consciousness on the way to the hospital, and that text message turned out to be our final conversation. One that I'd decided—in a moment I would regret forever—not to even answer.

Now it was three years later. Three impossible years later. And I was doing okay. I had, in fact, somehow managed to carry on, like they say you're supposed to.

But that's not quite right. I hadn't so much carried on as been carried. All I'd really done was remain in the current of the living world—something that was less of a choice than a lack of choice— and let it pull me along.

Three years is a long time. In three years, our kids had gone from two and four to five and seven. Tank had gone from being a dumpling-cheeked toddler to a long, skinny *boy*. Abby had lost four of the baby teeth she'd worked so hard to grow, started reading chapter books, and grown her brown hair down to her waist—not to mention all the work she'd done to heal her injured leg. The accident and its aftermath had become the past, and neither of them remembered their dad as more than a photograph, or maybe a feeling. And, in truth, I didn't remember him as well as I once had, either.

The sharpness of grief had given way to a dull ache, one that for a long time I had assumed was a response to loss. Though in recent months I'd begun to suspect that the ache came not so much from loss anymore as from location. My location in particular, and its proximity to my mother. Who had her good qualities, but who was also, as they say, a real piece of work.

Moving in with her had seemed reasonable after we'd lost our house. In fact, it had seemed like the only option at the time. It turned out Danny had made some bad investments without telling me, and then—also without telling me—he had used our savings and his life insurance to get square. Which would have worked out fine if he'd lived, because he was good at making money, and he had a plan, from the looks of his papers, to put it all right again. Instead, he died. And I was left with a house I couldn't pay for, full of things I couldn't keep.

And so, within a year, I'd sold it all off, bit by bit, and taken a job as a bank teller, which was the best position my B.A. in math qualified me for after years as a stay-at-home mom. I'd also moved the kids out of their fancy schools and resigned myself to the sofa bed in my mom's condo so they could have the guest room.

I got through the day focusing on minutia: lunch boxes, permission slips, grocery lists, bills to pay. I had no interest in seeing the big picture. I kept my head down and my eyes on just what lay before me. Anything else made me dizzy. I was alive, though I wouldn't exactly call it "living."

The night my aunt Jean's letter arrived at my mother's place, my mom was trying to convince me to get highlights in my hair. It was four days after Christmas, but she'd already taken down the fake tree and packed away the wreath.

"Just a little brightness around the face," she said. "A girl shouldn't look middle-aged at thirty-three."

I didn't respond.

"Or you could go whole hog and become a blonde again, like when you were little." She squinched up her face in sympathy. "I hate seeing you all mousy."

I was still in my blouse and skirt, doing dishes after standing for a full day at work and making dinner and putting the kids to bed. I filled the sink with soapy water.

Next she started insisting I needed a man. That was her plan the whole time—to get me out of her condo via the New Husband Express. "We need to snag you a provider," she liked to say.

I said, "I'm not the type of woman a provider is looking for, Mom."

"Not anymore," she agreed. "But we could fix you up! You used to be quite pretty."

"Mom," I said, "I don't want to talk about this."

"Why not? I'll pay."

I closed my eyes. "And then what? I'll hit the bars and go trolling for a husband?"

"If you have to. Yes."

"And what am I supposed to do with the kids?"

"Sweetheart, that's why they invented television."

"Really?" I said. I had such a headache. "*That's* why they invented television?"

She didn't care about the details. "Libby, I'm trying to help," she said. "I just don't want you making the same mistakes I did."

It was too mean, but I said it anyway: "Mom, if I spend my entire adult life chasing after men and ignoring my children, I *will* be making the same mistakes that you did."

True. But so what? So she had forfeited friendships, meaningful work, and even her relationship with her only child, just to be disappointed by three different husbands. What was she going to do now? See the light? Change the past? Get to work weaving a rich tapestry of varied and satisfying human relationships? Hell, no. She was going golfing with her boyfriend, Jerry. And stopping for a squirt of Botox on the way.

My mother blinked. "I just want to see you happy again."

At this, I rinsed my soapy hands—one of which still wore my wedding ring—under the faucet, walked over to her, stood inches away, and said in a quiet voice meant to end the conversation, "I will *never* be happy again."

My mother gave a sigh. "I know it's been hard."

For a moment I couldn't help but hope that I'd gotten through.

Then she went right on with the talking. "But that's a bad attitude. You'll never find a man that way. I know lots of widows—*tons of them!*—and the trick is getting back in the saddle. Do you think I wanted to go to that fat farm after my last divorce? I did not! But I reinvented my relationship with food and lost twenty-five pounds! Do you think I'd be with Jerry now if I hadn't?"

Jerry wore polo shirts with sprigs of chest hair at the V, and his standard greeting was to squeeze your upper-arm fat. Then he'd use your name over and over in conversation: *Libby, great to see you! Your mom doesn't agree, Libby, but I think you're looking wonderful. Tell me, Libby—when are you going to quit that awful bank job and start modeling?* Squeeze, squeeze.

"I don't need a fat farm, Mom," I said.

"Well," she said, "you couldn't afford it, even if you did."

"Mom?"

"What?" Her feelings were hurt now.

"We're done here."

I went back to the dishes, my head now throbbing, and she

picked up a stack of mail and began to sort noisily—and with narration: "Bill. Bill. Catalog. Junk mail. Bill."

I was just about to start banging my face against the fridge when she said, "And a letter for you from Aunt Jean. That crazy cow."

I went over to look, and I had to wrestle the thing out of my mother's grip. I ripped it open as she tried to read over my shoulder.

"What does it say?" she asked.

I moved to the other side of the island and read to myself:

> *Dear Libby,*
>
> *It occurs to me that you and your two children have been living with your mother for—dear Lord!—two whole years, and I'm writing to see if you'd like to be rescued.*
>
> *I run a little farm in Atwater, and as I get older, I find it's harder to get my chores done. Do you need a place to stay? If you'd be willing to help on the farm, I can pay you a little and offer room and board.*
>
> *I was very sorry to hear about your husband. He must have been quite a guy. I have never seen so many people at a funeral.*
>
> *Let me know what you think!*
>
> *Warmly,*
> *Your horrible aunt Jean*

My mother was leaning across the island, trying to read upside down. "What does she say?"

"She's offering me a job on her farm."

"On her farm? That bitch."

"I hate that word, Mom," I said.

"It's the only word that fits."

I'd been hearing about horrible Aunt Jean forever. She was a "hippie," a "weirdo," and a "freak." According to my mother, she did not wear antiperspirant or use soap. She washed her dishes with dirt. She shot squirrels with a rifle and ground them into burgers. She was our standing reference for the lowest form of human existence. Whenever my mother saw a wild-looking homeless person, she'd say, "There's your aunt Jean." And as much as the adult part of me thought my mother had to be exaggerating, the childhood part of me that had Aunt Jean in the boogeyman category kind of expected to see smears of dirt—or possibly even squirrel blood—on the letter itself.

I'd met Aunt Jean once. She'd showed up at my high school graduation in overalls and gave me a tight hug that stuck in my memory. She hadn't looked weird or particularly filthy. Just no-nonsense, with salt-and-pepper hair, and—okay, maybe a little eccentric—a crumpled straw hat. She also remembered my birthday every year, which is more than I could say for my mother. And now, apparently, she'd come to Danny's funeral, too. If I'd seen her there, I didn't remember—but I didn't remember much from that day.

"She came to the funeral?" I asked.

My mother nodded. "She was the fat lady in the balcony."

"I don't remember a fat lady in the balcony."

"Don't you?" my mother asked. "You don't remember a fat lady and the stench of goats? I could smell her from the front row."

Atwater was the town where my mother and her sister had grown up. I'd never been there, or even seen pictures, but Aunt Jean had moved back home with her hippie boyfriend in the seventies. A lifestyle choice my non-hippie, non-goat-farming, non-fat mother did not condone.

"She must have extra space in her house," I said.

"Extra space!" my mom burst out so loud I thought she might wake the kids. "She sure does. And it's not a house. It's a mansion."

"It's a mansion?"

"Didn't you know that?"

I shook my head.

My grandmother, in her will, had left the hundred-year-old family homestead and four-hundred-acre farm to Jean—and Jean only. It had happened when I was maybe four or five. Now, all these years later, whenever the topic came up, my mother still got so mad I thought she might pass out.

"Well," I said, "I think I'm going to take her up on it." The words, even to my own ears, sounded like a plan to go live at the city dump. A lifetime's worth of anti-Jean propaganda flashed through my memory.

"What?" My mother put her hand out for the letter. "You can't be serious."

But I pulled the letter in toward my chest. I couldn't explain it, and I knew I might be making the wrong call. But something about that word *rescued* was shining a light on my heart. Would I like to be rescued? Hell, yes. I sure would.

"There's not enough room for us here, Mom," I said. "We've been here two years."

"And this is how you thank me?"

"Mom!" I said. "We're driving each other nuts."

"Untrue," my mother said.

I smacked myself on the forehead. "Oh! My! God!" Did I have to remind her that, not two days before, she had announced to all of us that she "could not take it anymore"?

Yes. Apparently I did.

But my mother wasn't having it. "You can't leave me for Jean."

I tilted my head at her. "I'm not leaving you for Jean. I'm leaving you for—"

I stopped. I didn't know what to say. Because no one whose life was even tolerable would read a one-page letter from a near-stranger/eater-of-rodents and decide to move in with her. There was no way to argue it. I wasn't leaving her for Jean. I was leaving her for anyone. Anyone at all.

At last I said, "You should be delighted!"

But she wasn't. No matter that Jean's offer solved most—if not all—of our problems. No matter that my mom had wanted to get us out since the day we moved in. It was clear she'd rather keep us all miserable forever than let Jean get hold of her daughter and grandkids.

She turned her eyes toward the window, even though the blinds were closed, and let out a loud, dramatic sigh.

"What is your problem with her?" I demanded.

"She got everything," my mother said, "and now she gets you."

"She doesn't *get* me, Mom," I said. "I just need a place to stay."

But she wasn't listening. She was busy gearing up for this pronouncement: "If you go there," she said then, "you are no longer my daughter."

I waited for some gesture of self-awareness, some acknowledgment of the craziness. But it didn't come. I said, "Do you hear yourself talking?"

"I'm dead serious."

And in that moment, my decision was made. Rodent burgers or no, my only choice was to move in with Jean. If for no other reason than to avoid any more conversations exactly like this one.

"I'm going to call her in the morning," I said.

"I guess that's it, then," my mom said, turning toward her bedroom. She was leaving in the morning for a New Year's week in Cabo with Jerry. She had packing to do, she told me, and she wasn't going to stand around and argue. "Just be out of the house before I get back."

The next morning, I let my kids watch cartoons while I called Jean to get the scoop.

"Aunt Jean?" I asked when she answered on the seventh ring.

"This has to be Libby."

"It is. Hello."

"Sweetheart, I can't believe you've been living with Marsha this whole time."

"Well," I said, "I lived with her my whole childhood, so I've had some practice."

"I lived with her *my* whole childhood," Jean said, "and I never got the hang of it."

"It's not for the faint of heart," I said.

"I bet you're tough as nails," Jean said.

"Not really."

"Here's my idea," she went on. "Unlike your mother, I'm getting old. I've got arthritis in my hands, and I can't milk my goats like I used to. And there are a million other farm chores I just can't get done. I need a helper, if you're interested. I can offer you room and board and a small salary, and I'd be happy to look after your kids."

I knew there were many questions I should ask her about the farm, what exactly I'd be doing, what our living quarters would be like, and what that "small salary" would be. As the only remaining parent for my little family, I ought to be making slow and circumspect decisions. But I just couldn't think of how any situation could be worse than the one we had now—me standing full days at a bank window with my toes crushed into the points of my brown pumps, the kids in aftercare until six every day, my mother harping on me to get my eyelashes dyed.

"Yes," I said. "Yes to all of it." I felt a tiny sting of anxiety. It was without a doubt the rashest decision I'd ever made.

"Terrific!" she said. "Why don't you come out on Saturday?"

It was Friday. "Do you mean tomorrow?" I said. "New Year's Eve?"

"Is the year over already?"

"It is."

"Tomorrow, then!" Jean practically sang into the phone. "Just don't bring your mother."

My mother, in fact, had just marched out with all her suitcases, slamming the door behind her. "I don't think you have to worry," I said.

Looking back, Jean might have meant she wanted us to come out Saturday for a *visit*. But that's not what I heard. Within an hour of hanging up, I had quit my job, had notified the kids' schools that they wouldn't be back after vacation, and was fighting an urge to hop in the car right that minute.

It took less than a day to load up everything we needed. Most of our furniture was still in storage, anyway, even after all this time. And the ease of our getaway forced me to wonder if I'd been half expecting this all along: that a moment would come when I would not just want, but absolutely *need*, to take flight.

Chapter 2

Just minutes after almost killing that girl Sunshine, I was back in the minivan, creeping at ten miles an hour around the town square and swearing up and down to be more careful. It was New Year's Eve, for Pete's sake. I was starting over. At the very least, I could manage to *not* kick off the year with vehicular manslaughter.

The square was so cute, it was almost cutesy—but I kept my eyes strictly on the road. Until we passed a sign that read, WEL-COME TO ATWATER, TEX.! POP. 12,001! WE'RE GLAD YOU'RE HERE!

"We made it," I told the kids, wondering who the "1" out of 12,001 might be. "What do you think of our new town?"

"Fancy," Abby said.

"Do you know how many people live here?" I asked.

"How many?" Tank asked.

"Twelve thousand and one," I said.

"I wonder who that 'one' is," Abby said, and I felt that bittersweet flash of seeing yourself in your children.

"And they're glad we're here," I added, just to make sure we all felt welcome.

"All of them?" Tank asked.

"All of them," I confirmed.

"Except maybe for that lady we almost just killed," Abby added.

I didn't want to think about "that lady"—or what she'd said. I pushed her out of my mind with an ease that should have been alarming, even to me.

We fell silent for a minute as we turned onto Broken Tree Road. We were almost there, and we could all feel it.

"Where am I supposed to turn again, Tank?" I asked, already knowing the answer, as we neared the spot.

"At the red barn!" he shouted, kicking the back of my seat.

Jean's directions were perfect. Next came the rusty windmill, then the rusty water tank, then the famous broken tree—which really was broken: an oak split in half by lightning but still going strong. And right after that, the gate. I'd barely even met the woman, and I knew right away it was hers. Starting with the purple wisteria growing on the entry posts—somehow magically in bloom in the middle of winter.

Abby knew, too. "This is it!" she shouted. "This is definitely it!"

We pulled over a cattle guard and up a gravel drive.

Tank yelled out, "I see the goats!"

Before I had even set the parking brake, the kids jumped out of the car. I felt an urge to say something ridiculous, like *"Don't let them kick you with their pointy hooves!"* But then I changed my mind. How often do you get to run toward a new life with such abandon? As I watched them both tear across the yard, my gaze fell on Abby and the tiny limp left in her gait from the accident. Was it noticeable? Would I see it if I didn't know to look for it? I couldn't tell. Like with anything you've studied too hard for too long, I couldn't see it clearly anymore.

Of course, I didn't really care about a tiny, almost imperceptible limp. I was just using Abby's body as a measure of her heart. What I really wanted to know, and checked over and over impatiently, almost compulsively, was this: Had we put our sorrows behind us yet? Or would we carry them with us forever?

I heard a screen door slam and looked up to see Aunt Jean coming out of the side of one of the barns.

I knew her right away. She did not look filthy. She was not missing teeth. And she certainly wasn't *"fat."* Not the way my mother had said it, at least. She was more like *"plump."* Or *"womanly."* Or some other, kinder word. Her hair was white, cut in a short bob and tucked behind her ears. She had a round, cheery face with crinkles at the eyes, and if she'd had a poofy red dress, she could have passed easily for Mrs. Claus. She wore overalls and possibly the same straw hat I remembered from fifteen years before.

As soon as I saw her, walking across the farmyard in her muddy farm boots, I wanted to march up and give her a hug. But she beat me to it.

"You made it," she said, squeezing me tight. She smelled like oranges.

"Thank you for rescuing us," I said.

"It's a bit overdue," she said, explaining that a childhood friend of theirs had bumped into my mother over the holidays and gotten the scoop. "I'd have invited you here ages ago if I'd known."

"Well," I said with a shrug, "we're here now."

She gave me another hug. "At last."

We walked toward the barns, where the kids were now wading through a mosh pit of goats.

"I see they've found the ladies," Aunt Jean said.

"They're not penned in?"

"The girls? Lord, no!"

"They just roam free? Don't they escape?"

"No," Jean said. "They like it here."

I looked at the goats' long, solemn faces, smooth and brown with enormous eyes. I'd been expecting the Billy Goats Gruff— little beards and conical horns. But these were smooth-haired and hornless, with long ears that flapped down past their chins, almost like overgrown bunnies. Except for the hooves, of course. And the enormous, exaggerated udders bouncing between their hind legs.

"Nubians," Jean said, watching me watch them. "Creamiest milk in the world."

"Abby warned her brother not to expect them to be wearing little human clothes like in Richard Scarry," I said to Jean. We both let our eyes fall on Abby as three goats nuzzled her at once. "Which makes me think she was kind of hoping they would be."

"No human clothes," Jean confirmed. "But that's not a bad idea."

The farm had a whole collection of barns, ranging from tumbledown and rusty to brand-new and powder-coated. A wooded hill rose behind the farmyard, but the yard itself was a big clearing with a pond, a pigpen, and more enormous pecan trees than I could count. And, of course, farm machinery and animals everywhere.

From where I stood, I could see piglets, at least ten dogs of all different sizes, five or six cats, chickens galore, ducks, turkeys, some other birds I couldn't identify, peacocks, and, of course, the goats.

"You sure have a lot of pets," Tank called to Jean.

Jean smiled. "On a farm," she called to him, "we just call them animals."

She turned to me. "Everybody has a job here," she explained, gesturing around. "The cats keep the mice away. The hens lay eggs. The dogs protect the chickens from the coyotes. The goats make milk."

"What about the turkeys?" I asked. "What's their job?"

"Their job is to be eaten," she answered.

"What about those cute piglets?" I asked.

"Their job is to eat the whey that's left over from making cheese."

"Oh," I said, a little relieved.

"And then to be eaten."

"Oh," I said again, making a mental note to keep the kids away from *Charlotte's Web*.

"They won't be nearly as cute by then," she added.

"When will that be?" I asked.

"About two hundred pounds from now."

Jean kept going, pointing at one group of birds and then another. "The peacocks' job is to look pretty, and the guinea hens' job is to drive me crazy."

Tank started chasing a rooster that was almost as tall as he was.

"Tank!" I shouted. "Leave the bird alone!"

But Jean said, "That's Dubbie. He can take care of himself."

Now waist-deep in goats ourselves, we started making our way toward the kids. The rooster took off with a scrabble of wings, leaving Tank in the dust.

"What's Dubbie's job?" I asked.

Jean frowned at me for a second, then said, "His job is to make the sun come up every morning."

Once we reached the children, we made formal introductions. Abby waved shyly at Aunt Jean, and Tank held out his hand to shake, the way he'd been taught in preschool. As we headed toward the vegetable garden, I explained to the kids that Aunt Jean had bought quilts for each of them when they were born.

"Bought?" Jean turned to me. "I made those quilts!"

"You made them?"

Jean nodded.

They'd been full-sized and patchwork. It had never occurred to me that Jean might have made them. Who makes something like that?

"All hand-stitched, too," Jean added. "No machine."

"How long did they take you?" I asked.

"Maybe about a year," she said. "Each."

"A year!" I couldn't imagine why this almost-total stranger would spend a year of her life making quilts for children she'd likely never even see.

She sensed what I was thinking. "It was time well spent," she said. "Y'all are my only family. Except for your mother. And she hardly counts."

"I'm thinking back, trying to remember if I sent you a thank-you note," I said, now cringing a little. "I hope I did."

"I have no idea," Jean said. Across the yard the dogs started howling, and she hushed them. "Do you use the quilts?"

Here I had to lie. My mother had insisted we put them away. She had wanted to *throw* them away, but I'd convinced her we might someday sell them on eBay. Even she had to admit they were adorable.

"We did use them," I lied. "All the time."

Jean looked happy. "Then that's thanks enough for me."

At the garden, some of the dogs followed us in. Abby closed the gate after everyone, but when she turned around, she was face-to-face with the biggest dog either of us had ever seen—like a golden retriever crossed with a polar bear. She skittered over to hide behind me.

"He's friendly," Jean said.

"He's taller than Abby," I said.

"Yes," she agreed, "but he thinks he's a Chihuahua. He defers to anything beagle-sized or larger."

Sure enough, his legs were surrounded by little dogs: a shih tzu, a rat terrier, and a dachshund.

"We've got two packs here," Jean explained. "The big guys"—she pointed to a group of knee-height mutts by the barn—"and the little guys." Her eyes fell on the enormous dog and his tiny friends. "But," she added, "they'll all play together in a pinch."

"Kind of like people," Abby volunteered from behind my leg.

Jean tilted her head as though she were seeing Abby for the first time. "Yes!" she said. "Kind of exactly like people."

Jean kneeled down beside her and said, "Let's go make a proper introduction." She took Abby's hand and led her over to the big dog. He stood very still, and when Abby got close enough, he licked the tips of her fingers. Before long she was letting him slather his enormous tongue all over her face.

"What's his name?" I asked as Jean walked back toward me.

"Bob Dylan," she said.

"Can he play the harmonica?"

She shook her head. "He refuses to practice."

We hadn't been in the garden long before Jean put the kids to work. She showed them where she kept a rain barrel "to collect the runoff from barn gutters," demonstrated how to turn the spigot, and then asked them to fill her watering cans for the plants. As they got to work she said to me, "Let me show you the house."

"Are they safe there?" I asked, hesitating. It was not very often—like, never—that I left them unsupervised.

"Who?" Jean asked.

"The children." I knew I sounded nuts. It was a garden, for Pete's sake, not a snake pit.

"Of course! Yes! They'll call us if they need us."

I glanced back at the kids again. "Are there ever snakes in the garden?" I asked, trying to seem casual.

"Oh, no," Jean said as she opened the door. "You just stomp around nice and loud when you first get there in the morning, and that scares 'em off."

It's uncommon to move into a place sight unseen. Usually, even if you're going to a hotel on vacation, you've at least seen the website. As we walked over, it hit me that I had probably never been less prepared for what I was about to see. Though after all these years of living with my mother's fierce jealousy and bitterness over the house, I couldn't help but expect something big. Big enough to sustain a thirty-year feud.

Of course, nothing in life is ever what you're expecting.

It was not a mansion, as my mother had claimed. I stopped in my tracks and gaped. It looked like a plump little English cottage—like something from a magical forest. It had exposed crossbeams, rounded dormer windows, planter boxes with flowers, and plants all around it in full bloom. The whole thing was lopsided, almost like a life-sized gingerbread house.

"Whoa," I said. "Is that roof made of license plates?"

"Yep," Jean said. "Frank collected them."

"Who's Frank?"

Jean turned to study my face and frowned a little, as if she thought I should have known. Then she turned back to the house again. "I guess Frank was like my husband. Except we were never married."

I nodded. Frank was the hippie boyfriend.

"He's been dead ten years now."

Something about the emotion in her voice made my eyes fill with tears.

Without looking up, she seemed to know it. She grabbed my hand and squeezed it. "It gets easier, sweetheart. It really does."

I glanced back to check on the kids, who did not appear to be in grave danger, and then turned my attention back to the house.

"Frank was a recycler," Jean explained. "Almost everything here came from the junkyard." He had pressed decorations into the wet cob—broken glass, smooth stones, animal bones—as he built each wall. The front door was rounded at the top, and the front porch, which ran the width of the house, had posts of cedar and an awning made out of enormous antique metal gas station signs welded together side by side: HUMBLE OIL, MOBIL, SINCLAIR, and TEXACO.

It was pure whimsy. It was folk art you could live in. And each thing you noticed seemed like the best—until you noticed the next thing.

"Frank was amazing!" I said, and Jean nodded.

We went inside.

We stood face-to-face with an enormous river-rock fireplace.

"Is that part of a car?" I asked, staring at the red mantel.

"A tailgate," Jean answered. "From the junkyard."

Furniture-wise, the house was spare, with a mixture of hand-made pieces Frank had created in his workshop and heirloom family pieces. A red-painted drop-leaf table in the kitchen, some iron beds in the bedrooms, and a rocker in the den had all belonged to Jean's great-aunt Cortie.

"Which makes her your great-great-aunt Cortie," Jean said.

"And the kids' great-great-great-aunt Cortie."

At the mention of the kids, I realized I'd done something completely inconceivable: I'd forgotten about them.

And then, as if in response to that fact, I heard Abby scream.

I was out the door in less than a second, and Jean was right behind me. I crossed the yard full tilt, knowing for certain it would be a snakebite. Knowing for certain Abby would die in my arms from venom as we sped toward the nearest hospital.

When I made it to the garden, Abby was standing with fists on hips, looking less mortally wounded than mad.

"What? What happened?" I asked, out of breath.

"Tank!" Abby shouted. "He bit me!"

A bite. I was half-right.

Tank copied Abby's stance, affecting his own outrage. "She took my watering can!"

"Oh, God," I said, and leaned over to put my hands on my face. "You scared me to death! Please do not scream unless you really have something to scream about."

"Like what?" she asked.

I could have answered: *A killer bee! A brown recluse! A wasp! A wolf!*

A bear! A rattlesnake! A fire! An earthquake! A serial killer! Instead I just said, "A real emergency, Abby. Use your good judgment."

"But he *bit* me," she insisted, pulling up the sleeve on her T-shirt to show a red mark on her arm.

Aunt Jean had caught up and was now kneeling next to Tank, talking in a voice that sounded familiar. It took me a second to realize it was my own parenting voice when I was at my best —a perfect balance of firm and friendly at the same time. "People aren't allowed to bite other people out here in the country," she was saying. "There are too many other things that really do bite."

She stated it like it was just a rule. Nothing personal. And I could see in Tank's eyes that he was making a note of it.

Next Aunt Jean dusted off the knees of her overalls and said, all business, "Who wants to see the house?"

Jean looked so much like my mother—the unpainted version— that it was mind-boggling to watch her step in with the kids and handle them that way. I tried to think what my mother would have done if she'd been here. But there was nothing to compare it to, because she would've been at the nail salon.

The kids jumped up and down when they saw the house. Jean showed them the weather vane, the porch bell they could ring at dinnertime, and the spot under the steps with a litter of orange kittens still lapping up a fresh bowl of goat's milk.

We walked around back to the screened porch, which was almost the size of the house itself.

"I like the way everything's at an angle," I said.

Jean smiled. "Frank was a big fan of imperfection."

"I haven't been here before, have I?" I asked then. "This place feels familiar."

There was a pause. "No," Jean said, "you haven't."

I knew why, of course. Because my mother hated Jean. Which suddenly made me wonder if Jean hated my mother, too. I wanted to ask, but I didn't know Jean well enough to know how to phrase it.

Standing there, it hit me that in all those years of Jean sending me birthday cards and money, I had never once written to her. Or thanked her. Or invited her to my wedding. It was almost like she hadn't even been a real person. She was some fictional lady living a crazy hippie life far away. I would no more have written to her to ask how she was than I would have checked in on Santa. How strange to just now figure out she was real.

"My mom said you lived in a mansion," I said. "Was this the—"

"The family home?"

I nodded.

"No," she said. "I don't live there. And I wouldn't call it a mansion, either."

"You might want to mention that to Marsha sometime," I told her. "She imagines you living in obscene luxury."

"She grew up in that house," Jean said. "She knows exactly what it is. But she never did let reality get in the way of resentment."

The kids had climbed onto the porch swing. Jean studied them, then said, "Is she pretty mad at you for coming here?"

I nodded. "You have no idea."

"Oh," Jean said, wrinkling her nose, "I think I do."

I couldn't help making air quotes with my fingers as I said, "She's 'never speaking to me again.'"

Jean arched an eyebrow. "That'll last."

"My money's on two months."

"My money's on two weeks."

I let out a breath that was part laugh. It was so strange to not know each other at all, yet have this one burden in common—the burden of dealing with my mother. Before I could think better of it, I heard myself say, "But it lasted with you. For almost thirty years."

Jean dropped her smile. "I suppose that's true," she said. "Except I'm actually the one who's not speaking to her."

Chapter 3

~~~~~~~

There was no question that Jean was eccentric. In the next few weeks I'd discover that she never used paper towels, composted the leftovers of every fruit or vegetable that came through the house, and saved all her old shower, rain, and cooking water to pour onto her garden. She had solar panels on her roof. She went to "the church of nature," only ate meat that came in trade from friends, and did yoga at sunrise every morning to greet the day.

She was about as different from my mother as you could get. My mom had certainly been right about that. But she hadn't been right about what Jean's life actually looked like. The grizzled old survivalist's hovel I'd always pictured did not exist.

I looked around that first day and saw charm and more charm: the candles everywhere, the cabinet full of board games, the laundry line out back with white sheets blowing in the wind. I was so charmed, in fact, that I did not notice the things that were missing. Things like a clothes dryer. A dishwasher. A cordless phone. A microwave. Things I was so used to—that were such a *given*—that long after I knew for certain they weren't there, I'd still continue to look for them.

It was hard not to feel giddy about this place as our new home, though the sleeping arrangements made me a little nervous. Jean's room was upstairs, and so was the guest room, where the kids would sleep.

"They're going to sleep together in the same bed?" I asked. "Won't they keep each other awake?"

"Nah," Jean said. "They'll sleep better that way."

"But where will I be?"

"You're downstairs," Jean said, leading the way back down a hallway to a small room with its own bath and a door that led out to a patio facing the woods.

"This used to be Frank's office," Jean said, and pointed out that her own office was next to it. "I figured that after two years of living with my sister, you could probably use a room of your own."

"The thing is," I said as politely as possible, "it's kind of far away from the kids."

"I can keep an eye on them," Jean said.

I wasn't used to anyone but me doing anything for the kids. My mother had never offered to babysit, or take them to the park, or handle bedtime, and I would have refused even if she had. In three years of doing it all myself, I had come to believe that I was the only person who could possibly get it done, anyway.

"They're not great sleepers," I said. "Tank still gets up almost every night."

"Probably time he stopped doing that," Jean said.

I nodded and tried not to look irritated. Yes, of course it was time he stopped doing that. "Nothing works," I said. "I've tried everything."

Jean patted me on the shoulder. "You haven't tried sleeping downstairs in Frank's old office."

"True," I said.

I wanted her to offer me her room, right next to the kids. It seemed like the only sensible arrangement. But she did not.

I could already see the disaster ahead. After five years, I had the system down with Tank. Getting him back to sleep when he woke up meant getting him quickly, before he woke up fully. If you waited or messed around at all, he could be up for hours.

Abdicating my nighttime duties seemed both impossible and irresponsible. Still, who was I to tell Jean what to do in her own house?

She walked me next door to a similar room. "And this is where I see my clients," Jean said.

"Your clients?"

It turned out Jean was not just a goat farmer but a certified therapist—something my mother had never once mentioned, and I wondered if she even knew. Jean saw clients in the afternoons out of this office—just two or three people a day, she pointed out, but she pretty much had the whole town covered.

"Everybody needs a little help sometimes," she said.

"Tell me about it," I said, as if I knew exactly what she meant.

But she would, actually, have to tell me about it—because I didn't know what she meant. I certainly knew what it was like to need help. I just wasn't clear on what it was like to ask for it. I had learned at my mother's knee that help was for the weak—and how vitally important it was to stay strong at all times, even when the earth was crumbling beneath your feet. At your husband's funeral, for example. With your two-year-old in your arms.

Even my mother had marveled at the way I held that stoic smile on my face as friend after friend of Danny's dissolved into tears.

"He was a good guy, Libby," one after another said, their faces collapsing. Then we'd hug, and somehow I found myself patting their shoulders instead of the other way around. Only later—kids asleep, dishes done, laundry folded—did I lose it. Only when there was absolutely no one around to offer any comfort. A fact that might have made a good topic for therapy, if I believed in that sort of thing.

I smiled at Jean. My aunt: therapist and goat lady. How was it possible she and the woman who raised me shared any genes at all?

"You must be good at keeping secrets," I said at last.

"Honey," she said, putting her arm around my shoulders for a quick squeeze, "I'm a vault."

Before bedtime that night, Jean bathed the kids in the claw-foot tub.

As Abby started to undress, I realized that I hadn't warned Jean about the scar down the side of Abby's leg from the accident. It was about ten inches long and still pink, and I worried that Jean might gasp at the sight. But I underestimated her.

"Cool scar," Jean said as Abby wriggled out of her leggings.

"Thanks," Abby said.

"I've got a scar, too," Tank said then, pointing to the spot on his chin where he'd once hit the sidewalk.

"I've got one myself," Jean said as the kids stepped into the bathwater. "Though it's not as impressive." She pulled up her sleeve to show them the dot from her smallpox vaccination.

"It looks like the moon when it's full," Tank said.

"Mine looks like a river on a map," Abby said.

Jean nodded. "It sure does. Like the mighty Mississippi."

Eavesdropping a little, I bustled in the kids' room, unpacking their PJs, their favorite books, and framed family photos. Every single time my mother and I had moved when I was growing up—once a year, at least—my first order of business was to make things homey. Just the way hiding under the bed on moving day was always my last.

Jean's place didn't need much work to feel homey, but I needed to go through the motions. I set out stuffed animals. I fluffed pillows. I inspected the room for deadly spiders. I sized up the width between the iron bars on the headboard to decide if I needed to worry about broken necks. And then, at last, I borrowed a piece of wire to fasten shut the dormer window in case one of my kids might suddenly take up sleepwalking, climb out the window, and plunge to his or her death.

Jean obliged me without comment, but I couldn't help but defend myself in my head. These things happened all the time. Mothers heard these stories constantly: normal, likable, unsuspecting parents who just went to answer the telephone and came back to find their children killed in unimaginable ways.

I knew the kids had been safer in my mother's beige condo in the middle of the city, from which dangers like rattlesnakes had long been purged. If I dragged my children out to the country and one of them got, say, eaten by a bear, I'd have no one to blame but myself.

Did they even have bears in central Texas? I'd have to Google that later.

By the end of the kids' bath, it was already an hour past bedtime. We skipped toothbrushing, and even skipped the vitamin E that we always rubbed on Abby's scar at tuck-in time. I was ready for the day to be over. The kids had forgotten it was New Year's Eve, and I had no intention of reminding them. Last year I'd reset the microwave clock and let the kids count down to "midnight" at about seven-thirty. But this year they were so tired I didn't even have to pretend.

Before I turned off the light, I reminded them where I'd be sleeping, and described in detail how to get there. I had this crazy feeling that I was abandoning them.

When I'd finished tucking them in at last, Jean showed up at the door and said, "If you go straight to sleep, tomorrow I'll show you where the pirate treasure is buried."

Usually bedtime in our lives was a lengthy ordeal. I can't even describe all the hours I'd spent begging them to go to sleep as they came out over and over, asking for water and cheese sticks and back rubs. Tank often asked for one more kiss and then, when I bent over, clamped his arms around my neck in a "love lockdown" until I physically wrestled myself free.

That night, though, as Jean and I headed downstairs, there was only quiet in our wake.

I waited for the sound of feet on the stairs while Jean made us tea.

I waited as we got situated in the comfy chairs in the living room.

And I continued to wait as Jean asked me all about my life. What were my interests? My hobbies? My passions? What had I majored in? What was my favorite time of year? Favorite holiday? Favorite animal? At first I was just polite: I liked to water-ski, though it had been years. I'd gone through a knitting period that produced several scarves I never wore. I liked to work crossword puzzles. I liked to read biographies. I liked black-and-white movies of every genre.

Jean leaned on her hands and soaked it all in as though I were the most fascinating person in the world. Before I knew it, an hour had gone by—and I had forgotten about the kids entirely for the second time in a day.

"I think they're asleep," Jean said when I finally took a breather.

"Not possible," I said. "They don't just fall asleep."

"Never underestimate pirate treasure," she said.

"Sometimes when it's really bad, I just let them watch TV until they conk out."

Jean shrugged. "No TV."

My eyes snapped open. "No TV?"

She shook her head.

"None? Not even one?"

"Nope."

I looked around her living room in disbelief. No TV. After all the crazy things I'd seen that day—the stool in the bathroom made from a turtle shell, the picnic table with old truck tires for legs, the eight deer that had sauntered through the yard that evening single file—*this*, this one thing, was blowing my mind.

"Not even a tiny one in the kitchen?"

Jean shook her head. "Nope."

"No Internet, either," she added with a note of pride.

I gaped.

"You'll have to hit the library," she added. "That's where I update the farm's Facebook page."

"The farm has a Facebook page?"

"Of course," she said.

Several moments passed as I tried to absorb it. Finally I said, "What on earth do you do for fun?"

"Oh, lots of things. Take walks. Look for stones. Read in the hammock." She studied my face and then offered, "I do have a radio in the kitchen."

"A radio?"

"A loud one."

And what good, exactly, was a radio? Who curled up in front of a radio at the end of a long day?

"We have our own public radio station here in town. It's got a great bluegrass show."

I couldn't even fake it for her. She wanted me to replace *Project Runway* with bluegrass? This whole move suddenly felt like a mistake. I wasn't a goat farmer. I wasn't even a small-town person.

"I have a record player, too," she said.

I felt queasy. I didn't belong here. What had I been thinking? Not only was I going to have to crawl back to Houston and beg for my old job, I was going to have months, possibly years, of I-told-you-so faces from an extra-self-satisfied version of my mother.

But I'd been up since five, and it was close to eleven. I'd left every familiar thing behind. I'd gambled on a new life that had turned out to be too much. I felt that thickness in my chest that you get before you start crying, and, as if to make a literal escape from it, I stood up.

Jean blinked at me.

"I should probably hit the sack," I said, faking a stretch.

"Sure," Jean said, plainly reading every feeling I was trying to hide. "Of course."

I turned to go, but she called for me to wait one second.

She popped out of the room and then reappeared with a pair

of faded overalls over her arm. One knee had a heart-shaped patch. "For you," she said, holding them out. "You will absolutely live in them."

I stared at them. "I will?"

Jean nodded happily. "Go on to bed."

I was mid-escape when I stopped at the door on a matter of business. "Jean?" I asked, turning back.

She had picked up our teacups. "Yes?"

"If every night of the last five years of my life is any kind of pattern, Tank will wake up between two and three in the morning, calling for me."

"Okay," she said.

"When that happens," I went on, "will you come and get me?"

"Of course."

"And Jean?" I added, anticipating that sometime after breakfast the next day I'd be packing the car up to head back to Houston.

"Yes?"

"Thank you so much for all those birthday cards."

I took a shower in the tiny white bathroom, and then dug around until I found my nightgown. There didn't seem to be any point in unpacking, so I just flipped off the light and crawled on top of the bedspread. It was old-timey cotton chenille, and I ran my palms over the nubs of fabric as I stared at the ceiling.

How had life taken me here? How had I ever become so dependent on the kindness of strangers? Not that long ago I'd been a bona fide, functioning adult at the helm of a tidy, sensible household with a sweet bear of a husband at my side. A mom like any other, with a grocery list, a full calendar of play dates, personalized notepads with my name in script, and evidence all around me that I had made the right choices. Now it was all gone. I was off the grid. I had no model for a life like this. I had no sense of where I was headed. Or any idea how it would turn out.

Off in the distance, I could hear the crackle and pop of fireworks. The people of Atwater were ringing in the New Year, making the choice to celebrate whatever was to come. But I couldn't do the same.

When I'd moved in with my mother two years before, after twelve months of trying to manage the wreckage of my life, I'd been too shell-shocked to even contemplate looking back. Now, though—with my little ones at the far end of the house and nothing to do but stare at the ceiling—my mind drifted back for the first time in ages to linger over what I'd lost.

The last New Year's Eve I'd spent with Danny, we'd both conked out by nine-thirty at night. When the fireworks started at midnight, they woke us up, and we lay side by side, eyes open in the dark, holding hands and making resolutions.

"I'm going to go to the gym this year," I'd said. "At least once."

"I'm going to clean out the garage," he said.

"I'm going to learn how to make crepes."

"I'm going to teach myself how to juggle."

I turned to study his profile. "I don't see you as a juggler," I said.

"My dad couldn't do anything cool," he said. "I want to be the kind of dad who's sort of a badass."

"You could learn to do magic tricks, too," I said.

"Next year," he said, tugging on my hand to pull me closer. "One awesome thing at a time."

It had been a miracle, really, to have had a real home for the first time in my life. Even if I didn't always trust it, and even if I worried too much about it, it had been a real thing. A real thing I'd planned, deep down, to keep forever.

Now, limp against the bed, I let myself ache for the past. My old bed, my old house, my old life. And then, maybe because I was so tired, or maybe even because it was long past time, I let that ache surround me, and swallow me, and pull me down into a lightless, airless, dreamless sleep.

Chapter 4

I n the morning I found the kids at the kitchen table, dunking whole-wheat pancakes in the shapes of their initials into warm plum jam. Jean was frying bacon at the stove. The kids informed me it was a New Year's feast. And everybody was acting as if they'd all done this a million times before.

"Bacon?" Jean asked, tilting the pan at me. "It's homegrown."

"Maybe just coffee," I said. I was happy to notice a delightfully modern and high-tech coffeemaker. "Nice coffeemaker."

"I don't mess around with coffee," Jean said.

"Mom," Abby said, "come eat this jam."

"Aunt Jean made it herself," Tank added. He had a clown mouth of it.

I sat across from them at the table with my coffee and rested my hands around the warm mug. "You want to hear something amazing?"

"What?" they asked in unison.

"There are two children at this table, but zero children woke me up last night."

Tank started to cackle.

"How is that possible?" I asked.

"Mom," Abby said in her most informative voice, "Tank slept all the way through the night last night."

Tank was proud. "Yup."

I gave him a high five. "How on earth did you manage it?"

Tank stuffed a whole pancake into his mouth. "Well," he said, all muffled, "I just really wanted to see the pirate treasure. So I pretended I was sleeping until I accidentally was."

Jean set down a plate of bacon. "It's a busy day today," she said. "The children and I will dig for—and hopefully find—massive amounts of pirate treasure. And you'll stay here and learn about the goats."

"If you're digging for treasure," I said, "how do I learn about the goats?"

Jean smiled. "O'Connor."

"Who's O'Connor?"

"He's kind of like my farm manager." She stepped over to the kitchen window and pointed out. I followed her gaze to see the shaggiest man I'd ever laid eyes on. He was Muppet shaggy. Caveman shaggy. Bigfoot shaggy. His furry head seemed to overpower his entire body, and even his jeans and his work boots seemed shaggy. When he turned and I saw his face, it was all shag, too. Except for a pair of blue eyes and a vertical strip of nose, his beard had taken over his entire face.

"That's not a farm manager," I said. "That's Chewbacca."

"The beard is a shame," Jean agreed. "And the lack of—"

"Hygiene?"

"Grooming," she finished. "But he's handsome underneath, I promise."

I didn't care if he was handsome or not. As long as he didn't have fleas.

"He's very handy," Jean went on. "If there were an Olympics for handiness, he'd have a gold medal."

"There *should* be an Olympics for handiness," I said, still watching out the window. And I knew, in the way that sometimes you just know things, that I'd pleased her by saying so.

Jean went back to work, picking up breakfast dishes and submersing them in soapy water, but I continued to watch him for a minute as he filled the dogs' water bowls. Then, as if he could feel my eyes on him, he turned, glanced at the window, and—to my horror, since I was wearing only a very thin cotton nightgown—started making his way up to the house.

I sent the kids to get dressed, but before I could scurry off myself, he was standing on the back porch by the open door, looking in at us in the kitchen. I could see up close that he had mud from his boots to his knees.

At that moment, I remembered something. I was wearing underpants with little strawberries on them. I knew for a fact—as Danny had pointed out many times—that a person could easily see, and even count, every single strawberry through this particular nightgown. I held absolutely still in the hopes of disappearing into the background.

"Gate's fixed," he said to Jean, as if nobody else were in the room.

"Thank you," she said, moving toward the door and waving me over to join her. I crossed my arms over my chest and stepped forward. She opened the screen door so we could all see one another better. "James O'Connor," she said, "meet Libby Moran."

"Happy New Year," I said.

O'Connor seemed a little surprised that it was New Year's Day and frowned a second before getting back to introductions.

O'Connor looked at Jean. "The long-lost niece," he said, like I was part of some famous story. He held out his hand to shake.

"Yes," I said, taking it. "Lost, but now, you know, found again."

"At last," O'Connor said, just as the kids clomped down the stairs and froze in their tracks at the sight of him.

Abby stepped in front of Tank.

"You protecting your brother?" O'Connor asked.

"Yes," Abby said.

"Why?" O'Connor asked.

"In case you are a beast."

O'Connor tilted his head and looked at Abby with appreciation. Then he said, "You're very brave, big sister."

"She's also very strong," Tank piped up. "You do *not* want to make her angry."

"Good tip," O'Connor said, his eyes still squinted.

"Don't worry," Jean said to the kids. "He's human under all that fur."

Everyone was ready for the day but me, so I sent the kids out to the yard and promised to meet O'Connor by the milking barn in fifteen minutes. But first I had to stop by the kitchen sink and wash—with very hot water and dish detergent—the hand that had shaken O'Connor's. And not just once, but a second time for good measure. Just in case he did have fleas after all.

———

Touring the farm, I got the feeling Jean had told O'Connor to start with the most basic of basics about farm life. When we walked past the barn, he said, "This is the barn." When the goats gathered around us, he said, "These are the goats."

"I know what goats are," I said. Then, more politely, "Do they have names?"

"Depends on who you ask," O'Connor said. "If you ask Aunt Jean, she'll rattle off twenty names in twenty seconds."

"And what if I ask you?"

"I'll tell you they're all named Goat."

I paused for a second, then said, "Why do you call her Aunt Jean?"

O'Connor had bent down to inspect one of the goats' ears.

"I mean, she's not your aunt," I went on. Then I frowned. "Is she?"

"No," O'Connor said. "She's not my aunt. But I've known her since I was a baby. She was friends with my mother."

I noted the "was" but didn't say anything.

"Plus," he went on, "she's my therapist."

"You have a therapist?"

"Everybody in this town has a therapist," he said, starting to walk me toward the back field. "And it's Aunt Jean."

"All twelve thousand and one people in this town are clients of Aunt Jean's?"

"Well," O'Connor said, "not all at the same time."

"Somehow," I said, following, "when I think 'tiny Texas town,' I don't think 'therapy.'"

"This town's half hippies," O'Connor said over his shoulder.

"It is?" I asked.

"Sure," he said. "They came for the hot spring."

I'd heard of the hot spring, but I'd never been there. It had billboards on the interstate and everything. Some people believed it had healing waters, and Jean was one of them. She went for a soak every morning between yoga and breakfast.

"The hippies came in the seventies," he added, stopping to tie his shoe, "and started cross-breeding with the farmers." When he looked up, there was a wry arch to his eyebrow—one of the only parts of his face I could see.

"Making farmer-hippie hybrids?" I asked.

"Yep," he said, turning his attention to a chained gate. "Here's the rule about gates on a farm," he went on, suddenly all business. "Always leave them the way you find them. If they're open, leave them open. If they're closed, close them behind you."

"Okay," I said.

"Some of the latches are rusty," he said, pointing one out for me to try. It was a simple metal clasp. But when I pressed on it, it didn't give. He said, "Push on it before you slide it back."

I pushed on it, but no luck.

"Push," O'Connor said again, as if I needed clarification.

"I am," I said.

"Harder," he said.

"I am!" I said.

Finally his hands couldn't stand it. He put one on top of mine and pressed down on my thumb with his thumb—so hard that the clasp slid right away.

"Ow!" I said.

He let go, and I shook out my hand.

"Sorry," he said. "Maybe I'll just replace that one."

"No," I said, following him through the gate and watching as he latched it again one-handed. "I'll just do some" —I hesitated—

"some thumb exercises." The words sounded even stupider out loud than they had in my head.

From the pond in the back field, we could see the whole farm—the heavy woods on the hill behind us, the pastures Jean leased to cattle ranchers down below, and the farmyard. It was lovely. Just green against green as far as I could see.

Something about the houses and fences and buildings in the city must kill off the wind. Because that was the thing I noticed most about being out in the country—the constant sweep of wind against your skin. It rustled tree leaves and clanked windmills. It swept over the long grass. It was a force, something alive, something more than just air.

I closed my eyes, but when I opened them, O'Connor was halfway back to the farmyard, on the other side of the relatched gate. I trotted after him, but rather than try to work the latch again, I just climbed over.

Back at the barn, the goats nudged their heads up under our hands until we petted them like dogs while O'Connor showed me what I needed to know. The old barn with the rusty tin roof had been a speakeasy in the 1920s. Now it housed hay and chicken roosts and barn cats. The new barn was sharp and clean, powder-coated a rain-cloud gray. One side was surrounded by a pen, and as we walked, O'Connor said, "That's where the goats wait to be milked."

"Do they like being milked?" I asked.

"They don't *dislike* being milked," he said.

Inside, he showed me the platform the goats stood on, the metal bars that closed around their necks to hold them in place, the buckets of treats they got, and the milking machine.

I was a little disappointed to see the machine. It wasn't quite as Heidi-esque as I'd been expecting. "We don't milk them by hand?"

"Hell, no," O'Connor said. "That would take all day."

The milking machine had long plastic tubes with suction cups and a motor like a vacuum cleaner. O'Connor had already done the milking that morning, so he didn't demonstrate, but he did show me what things were for. When we got to the suction cups, I said, "And this part goes on their. . ." but then I faltered. "Their, um. . . nipples?"

O'Connor put his hands over his eyes. "Animals don't have nipples," he said. "They have teats."

"Same idea, though," I said. "Right?"

"Same idea," he conceded. "Wrong word."

I noticed a little radio on a shelf, but then I wondered how anyone could possibly hear it over the noise of the milking machine.

O'Connor saw me looking. "It's broken," he said. "We just make our own music."

I looked over. "How?"

He tilted his head at me. "By singing."

"You sing?" I asked. He seemed too cranky to sing.

"Sure," he said. "The goats love it. Sometimes they join in."

Our next stop was the cheese kitchen, the room next door in the milking barn. We had to change shoes on the way in—into the Crocs that were piled up just inside the doorway—because this room, unlike the milking side, was scrubbed down and squeaky-clean, with stainless counters and restaurant-grade cooking equipment: big sinks and sprayers, a work island, tubs and pots hanging from a rack on the ceiling, and, over in the corner, a walk-in fridge.

"Be careful of this thing," O'Connor said, gesturing at the fridge. "Something's wrong with the door latch, and it gets stuck sometimes. Don't ever go in without propping it open." Then, sizing me up, he changed his mind. "Actually, just don't ever go in, period. Call me if you need something."

I looked around the fridge. It seemed to do double duty as a storage closet, housing tubs of cheese as well as boxes of supplies and even a couple of folded wool blankets.

"Seems like a lot of fridge for not very much cheese," I said.

"We're low right now, but it's never full," O'Connor said. "Frank installed it when they thought they were going to expand. But then he got sick, and they never did."

"What did he get sick with?"

"Parkinson's," O'Connor said.

"Oh," I said. "And now Jean's got arthritis."

He nodded. "So you'll do her jobs now—mostly milking and making cheese."

"What do you do?" I asked.

"Everything else," O'Connor said. "And I help with the milking. It's faster with two."

"And then what do we do with the cheese?"

"We sell it."

I smiled at him instead of rolling my eyes. "Where do we sell it?"

"At the farmers' markets in Houston and Austin." He gave me an evaluative look. "But you're not ready for that yet. We need to get the basics down first."

Back outside, we crossed the farmyard toward the house.

"So, that's pretty much the day," O'Connor said, a few steps ahead of me. "Milk in the morning, do farm chores, make cheese in the afternoon, milk again in the evening."

"Sounds like a pretty good life," I said.

"It's a great life," he said.

He slowed under an oak tree near the house, and that's where he told me I needed to make a run to the feed store for him. He handed me a list of supplies, along with an envelope of cash to use.

"Save the change and the receipt," he said.

"Am I like your assistant, then?" I asked.

"Kind of," he said. "Though you can call yourself an 'apprentice' if you like." He tossed over the keys, which I didn't manage to catch, and told me I could take the farm truck.

"Is it open today?" I asked. "I mean, do people work on New Year's?"

"People work every day in the country."

I got the feeling he was teasing me. "So the store is open?"

"Nah," he said. "Not on New Year's Day. But Tom's left a bag of feed for us by the back door. Just drop a twenty through the mail slot."

Drop a twenty through the mail slot. Of course. "How do I get the receipt?"

"Write one up."

I wanted to take the minivan—if for no other reason than to be back in my own space for a little while. But I got the feeling I was supposed to do things the way they were done. So I found the truck—powder blue, parked by the old barn—and, after pausing to read the bumper sticker that said EVERYTHING IS CONNECTED, I got in. The truck had a bench seat and no shoulder belts, and the windows, which rolled with a crank, were already down.

I pulled out onto the road and hung my arm out. I tried to remember the last time I'd driven anywhere by myself, sailed along an open road with my hair blowing, or spent a morning with so many furry animals—farm manager included.

I'd needed to change my life for a while. And even though this wasn't what I had imagined or wanted, there was no denying that this was different. I wasn't sure if I'd made things better or worse, but there was no question I had made a real change at long, long last.

Or maybe, in truth, Jean had done it for me.

Chapter 5

nd so we stayed. Though I didn't make a decision to stay as much as I made one not to leave.

It wasn't exactly a seamless transition. The kids, for example, did not like Aunt Jean's food. She didn't dine on squirrel burgers, which was a relief, but there was no sugar in the entire house. With the exception of her world-famous pancakes, she ate only homegrown meat, vegetables, and fruit because, she said, "carbs will kill you."

So no bread and no pasta, but lots of butter. Which tasted good—I'd forgotten *how* good. At my mother's house, there had only been margarine. And Olestra.

Anything different from life at my mother's had to be beneficial, I told myself, by definition. I told myself the same thing about the sudden disappearance of TV, which was also a shock to my children's systems.

TV had been our go-to transition activity in the city, as well as our go-to time killer. Not to mention babysitter, cheerer-upper, and put-to-bedder. Suddenly, here we were doing all those things on our own, wobbling through our daily activities like someone had stolen our training wheels. Because keeping busy is a learned skill. As are: exploring, playing pretend, and running around outside. Jean just expected my kids to know how to do all that stuff. That first week, she'd say, "Go outside and play," and they would dutifully troop outside. But then I'd watch them stand around in the yard, not quite sure what to do next. I'd give them a few minutes, the way you do with a fussy baby, and when I couldn't stand it anymore, I'd go out and give them a suggestion.

"Why don't you water the garden?" I asked over and over in those early days. Before long the rain barrel was empty. "Why don't you feed the chickens?" I suggested next.

"Mom," Abby said, "Jean says only one cup of pellets per day. We don't want them to become obese."

Our third night there, which we called our three-night-aversary, Jean let the kids set off firecrackers in the farmyard, since we'd missed New Year's Eve. We bundled up tight in our parkas and knitted hats and stayed out until we got too cold.

Abby worried about the goats. "Won't we scare them?"

"Nah," Jean said. "They know humans are crazy."

Afterward we went inside to warm up and roast marshmallows for s'mores in the fireplace.

The same week, I got the kids enrolled at the giant public elementary school that served three counties at the point where they all intersected. I had been imagining a little one-room country schoolhouse for the kids à la *Little House on the Prairie*, and so the sight of the prisonlike 1960s structure of concrete bricks was disheartening. Also disheartening: the student-teacher ratio of thirty-seven to one and the budget cuts that had eliminated all teacher assistants, art classes, and music.

I fretted in bed until three o'clock the night before the kids started their first day. Tank would be okay, but I worried about Abby. Her leg was officially healed. We'd finished physical therapy a year before. She had a scar that ran down the side, but that was easy to cover up with pants. But she still limped just the tiniest bit when she walked. Sometimes I thought it was noticeable, and sometimes I didn't. It wasn't bad enough to keep her from doing anything, but it was bad enough to keep her from doing many things well. The issue surfaced more and more as the kids got older and stronger, and I heard Abby criticizing herself for being slow.

I didn't know what to say to her about it. How do you tell a kid that she's always going to have to work twice as hard as the other kids to be half as good? I didn't have the words for that. All I knew was that watching your children survive their childhoods was so much worse than surviving your own.

Thrashing in bed, I beat myself up for pulling them out of a city school that wasn't perfect but where, at least, they were settled. Now they'd have to go through it all again—meeting new people, finding new friends, figuring out who to talk to on the playground and what to play. And I didn't know what kids wore here or what toys were cool, or have any other insights that might help them fit in. And how would a teacher give them any help or attention with thirty-seven kids to manage? It felt like I was just turning them loose in an empty pasture to fend for themselves.

The day-to-day plan was for Jean to pick them up after school and watch them in the afternoons until I was done with the evening milking. On that first day, though, I just had to race out and check on them as soon as I heard the minivan pull up.

The animals and I all surrounded them like paparazzi as they got out, and I expected to see them stressed and shaken from a whole day's worth of everything new.

"How was it?" I asked, peering most closely at Abby.

Abby's reply was a generic "Great." Then, to Jean, she asked, "Can we play with the kittens?"

At Jean's nod, both kids took off, leaving me behind, shouting, "Was it great for you, too, Tank?"

No reply.

"I'll assume it was great," I said to Jean.

"They seem good," she confirmed.

Of course, seeming good and actually being good are not the same thing. Unlike grown-ups, who register and process struggles as they happen, kids often don't seem to notice until much later.

"They seem good for now," I said to Jean, quietly refusing to unclamp my heart. Maybe I'd relax in February, when we were settled. Or maybe I'd wait until summer, when we knew our way around. Or maybe I'd just wait until we were really in the clear. Like after they'd graduated from college.

Until then, I'd just try to remind myself that I could only control what I could control. Like my goat-milking efforts. Which maybe were not A-level just yet (I'd gotten one caught in the metal milking harness that week) but were improving steadily under O'Connor's tutelage.

"You really need to relax," he told me somewhere around week three as we both sat down at our milking stations.

"I am relaxed," I said.

"The girls can feel that tension," he said. "And it makes them nervous."

"I'm making the goats nervous?" I said. "How can you even tell?"

O'Connor shrugged. "Body language."

"Mine?" I asked. "Or theirs?"

"Both, actually," he said.

"I haven't really spent a lot of time around animals," I said. "Other than a box turtle I had as a kid. Briefly. Before my mother ran over him in the driveway."

O'Connor nodded as I tried to coax one of the goats up onto the milking platform. The more I pulled, the more she pulled back, until we created a full-fledged standoff.

"Hey there," O'Connor said. "Take it easy."

"She's the one being stubborn."

O'Connor studied the pair of us, then came around and gently led the goat up onto the platform, latching her into the milking harness in one graceful motion. Easy.

"Show-off," I said.

A few minutes later O'Connor glanced up again. "Here's what you do," he said. "Sing to them."

"Sing what to them?"

"Anything. Whatever you like. The Beatles. Show tunes."

"Sing show tunes to the goats?"

"I sing them love songs," he said. "Since they're all in love with me."

I tried to decide if he was kidding or not. It was hard to tell with his face hidden under all that hair. "Well," I said at last, "I can't sing."

"Can't or won't?"

"Can't *and* won't." I looked over at him. "I never sing."

"You don't even sing in the car? Or the shower?"

"Nope."

"What about when it's someone's birthday? Do you sing 'Happy Birthday' to them?"

"I mouth it."

"Why?"

"Because I stink at singing."

"But, I mean, who cares?"

"I care," I said. "And you would care if you had to hear it. Plus the goats would take off running to the far pasture."

O'Connor regarded me for a moment. "Now I just really want to hear you sing."

I shook my head. "Not going to happen."

Over the next few weeks, I decided that he was, generally, much more agreeable than he'd seemed at first. He did whatever Jean asked, quickly and precisely—and she wasn't kidding about how handy he was. From painting signs to working a bulldozer to repairing broken tractor engines, he could do absolutely anything.

He frequently caught us fish from the pond to cook for dinner, which both delighted and disgusted Abby and Tank as they watched him do the gutting. He seemed to have a natural ease with kids, too, and it wasn't long before he was calling Tank by a whole host of nicknames, including "T-bird," "Tornado," and, somehow, "DJ Raptor." Abby got just plain "Mamacita," which made her beam right away every time she heard it.

So there it was: instant intimacy with the first adult male to even skirt the sidelines of our lives in three solid years. I, of course, was still hanging back like a pro. If my kids couldn't reserve their judgment, then I'd just be reserved enough for all three of us.

We'd been there about a month when O'Connor showed up at the back porch one evening during dinner.

"There's something strange out in the yard," he said to Jean.

She frowned before she read his face. "Something strange?"

"Two strange things, actually," he said with exaggerated concern. "Maybe the kids could help me figure it out."

At the words, Tank was up and out the door. Abby, though, turned to me and said, "Can we go?"

I nodded and got up to follow, too.

I was not even outside before I saw what it was. Out on the biggest oak tree in the yard, two old tractor tires hung from the tree's fattest branch.

In seconds, the kids were swinging and twisting on them, and O'Connor was pushing them, too. Jean showed up beside me in the yard.

"That was thoughtful," I said.

"Yes," Jean said. "He's thoughtful."

"And handy," I said.

"Very handy," Jean agreed.

"And you've known him since he was little?"

"Oh, yes!" Jean said. "The two of you—" but then she stopped herself.

I looked over.

"The two of you are exactly the same age," she went on.

"You were friends with his mother?"

"Yes," Jean said.

"But not anymore?"

"Well," Jean said, "she moved away."

"Oh," I said. "Did his dad move away, too?"

Jean turned to face me. "It's tricky for me to talk about these things because I know so much about people's business from their visits to my office."

"Oh," I said.

"Maybe you should ask O'Connor," she suggested.

"Okay," I said, though of course I wouldn't.

We watched quietly for a minute. Then Jean said, "That boy sure needs a haircut."

"Who? Tank?" I asked.

"No," Jean answered. "The other one."

And before I really thought about what I was doing, I said, in a voice that sounded like an offer, "I've got clippers."

"You do?"

"For Tank," I explained.

I could feel her about to suggest that I use them on O'Connor, and it's safe to say that I had no desire to cut—or even stand anywhere near—his hair.

And yet I'd brought it up.

I tried to backtrack. "You're welcome to borrow them if you like."

"Me?" Jean wrinkled her nose. "Oh, Lord. I'd turn him into a topiary." I gave a courtesy laugh just as she turned to me with intention. "What could I bribe you with to get you to cut it?"

I let out a whistle. "Pirate treasure?"

"I'll get digging," Jean said.

"So," I said, "you're not asking me, then?"

"No," Jean answered. "I'm not asking you. Yet."

I was grateful she wasn't. Because if I knew one thing for certain, it was that I wouldn't be able to refuse Jean anything.

It wasn't too many days later that Jean came up with a way to get the kids to eat her food. She started putting it on skewers. Everything became a kebab. Fruit kebabs, meat kebabs, pickle kebabs. Anything on a stick was fun, and once she'd stumbled on that principle, we were good to go.

We fell into a routine pretty quickly. I got the kids ready in the mornings and drove them to school. Then Jean picked them up at the end of the day in the minivan while I finished my chores, and I met them in the yard at around five-thirty before we went in for dinner. It wasn't that different from our city schedule, really, when I'd picked them up from aftercare after work. But something about the fact that they were so nearby—that I could look out the little window and see them—made it harder.

Still, I had to admit that they seemed happy. Jean was phenomenally great with children. Even-handed, calm, fully engaged. She never got fussed by them, and she had unlimited imagination. I'd look out the window and watch them make her crowns out of leaves. Or she'd stir a stick in a bucket as the kids gathered rocks, mud, and feathers for magical concoctions. Sometimes they'd all sit on the porch swing, reading. I never heard a cross word from her. Her patience far outlasted my own, not to mention that of my mother.

By the end of January, I was convinced that the move to Atwater had been a no-brainer. Who wouldn't want to live in this beautiful, magical, pastoral place? Who wouldn't love small-town life? Especially a small town like this one—such a great mix of old-school rural and New Age goofy. Plus I was learning things. I'd forgotten how satisfying it was to work hard at something. I'd had weeks of uninterrupted sleep at night. I was working my way through all the different recipes for chevre—with O'Connor's help—and starting to turn my eye toward conquering feta. I was getting to know the goats, all named after famous women in history and literature: Harriet Tubman, Pocahontas, Jane Austen, and Lois Lane were my favorites so far. And there was nothing funnier than hearing the kids talking about the goats once they knew their names, too.

"I think Helen Keller looks pregnant," Abby had said the day before.

"Does she?" I asked. "I don't know."

"She's way fatter than Toni Morrison or Lady Bird Johnson," Abby went on.

"But not nearly as fat as Helen of Troy," I pointed out, "who isn't pregnant at all."

Jean and Abby were also making little decorations for the goats' collars, cutting shapes out of felt to glue onto the backs, and Abby very seriously referred to their work as the "spring fashions." As she had explained to me, "Just because they're goats doesn't mean they can't look pretty."

Moving to the country had opened things up in every possible way. It was like I had braced myself against the onslaught of my life, but now in little unexpected moments, like when a breeze swept over the farmyard, I felt twinges of something I could only describe as happiness.

And then I ran into Sunshine again.

Chapter 6

Trips into town were always a little frantic. Everybody I saw wanted to stop and meet me and hug me and tell me about how much they loved Jean. Being her niece made me a minor celebrity in Atwater, and everybody seemed to know somebody she'd sat with in the hospital, or said just the right thing to when nobody else could find the words, or jumped off the trestle bridge with to go skinny-dipping.

All I could really do was nod and say, "She seems very wonderful."

On the particular day that I saw Sunshine again at the feed store, I had just received a free pair of bird feather earrings from a lady named Selma. When I turned to the register, and saw Sunshine standing right behind it, I almost dropped my bag of goat treats. I'd forgotten all about her.

I hauled the bag up onto the counter, trying to covertly double-check her name tag at the same time.

"Hello, Sunshine," I said.

She just gave a little wave.

"I'm sorry again," I said, "about almost killing you that day."

The people behind me started listening.

"Don't worry about it," Sunshine said. "It was fate." She had colored her fingernails black with a Sharpie.

"I think it was just bad driving," I said, handing over some twenties from my envelope.

"No," she said with a shrug, "it was destiny." She took the bills, but instead of making change, she just held them in her hand, leaned in, and said, "I wasn't kidding about your husband." She blinked. "I can find him."

I looked at the name tag again, just to have a place for my eyes.

"I'm not looking for my husband," I said. I knew I had to explain, but my throat seemed to close up and I had trouble saying the words. They felt like the most private words I could possibly speak, and this total stranger was going to force me to say them—now in front of every single person in the long line behind me.

"My husband is not lost," I said. "He died."

Now she had it. The whole room did. I felt a collective sigh of sympathy like a little breeze. I looked down at the counter. Whenever I had to tell anyone about Danny, I always got the exact same look of sympathy. Every time. Different people, different times of day, exact same face.

Not that day, though. Not with Sunshine. In fact, her face went the other way.

"I know!" she said, her eyes bright with excitement. "That's what I do." And then she glanced over at our audience, both in the line and peeking out from the aisles, and waved me to lean in closer. I tilted across the counter, near enough for her to cup her hand over my ear and say, in words that seemed to blow straight into my head and swirl around like smoke, "I call up the dead."

"Okay!" I said, too loud, straightening back up. "Thanks!"

I grabbed the bag and didn't even wait for change. I walked straight out of that store, countless puzzled faces behind me, and before I knew what I was doing or where I was going, I found myself not back at the farmyard but driving too fast down the highway in the wrong direction, pedal to the floor, in hopes of getting as far away as possible.

By the time I slowed down, I was passing the sign for the Atwater Spring. And so I followed it, turning right and then left, passing a picnic area, then cruising to a stop in a parking lot. The sky had been darkening all afternoon. I got out and felt a heavy breeze brush my arms and face. Without thinking, I followed the trailhead through mesquite trees down toward the spring.

I did not, of course, believe that Sunshine could really talk to the dead. I did not believe in ghosts, séances, or even—if I'm being really honest here—an afterlife. Even though I'd painted some pretty vivid pictures for the kids of their daddy up in heaven with a cloud of marshmallows for a bed, I didn't actually believe it was a real place.

So I wasn't sure, stepping along the path, what had spooked me so much. But I could still feel that girl's breath in my ear. All I knew was this: I was finally moving on. Houston had been drenched in memories of Danny, but now I was in a new place with no reminders of the past. I didn't want to talk about Danny, think about Danny, or chat in the feed store with people who thought they could have conversations with Danny.

He didn't belong here, and that was that.

And so I knew what I had to do. I had to tell O'Connor that I couldn't make any more trips to the feed store. I had to convince him to do them himself. Then I could stay away from that girl. I could stay on the farm, where no one would ever bring Danny into the conversation without my permission again.

When I came to a ravine, there in the crease was the famous spring, which was disappointingly small and looked a little like a hot tub.

I stepped to the edge of the water, and then I kneeled down. Here, in this quiet place, surrounded by gusts of storm winds, I felt something rise around me that I couldn't quite articulate. Suddenly, under that heavy and darkened sky, everything really did seem connected. It's one thing to see those words on a bumper sticker, and it's a hell of another thing to actually feel them.

Then the rain hit, and I took the path back up to the truck at a run. By the time I had the key in the ignition, I was out of breath and wet down to my underpants.

I drove back going ten miles an hour, and that felt fast under the downpour. The truck's wipers did their best, but they weren't much use. The water was so thick I could barely see out, and I wondered if I should just pull over to the shoulder and wait for a break in the sky.

But it was time to get back. And so I crawled the truck back to town, around the square, and onto Broken Tree Road, where the rain began to ease a bit and I could see a little better.

Past town, the road slanted down to a creek before rising back up a long hill toward Jean's house. Climbing that hill, I noticed a bicyclist pumping up the road toward the crest, and I wondered about how crazy he'd have to be to ride the hill in this weather. He'd barely been in my sights for a second when I saw his front wheel go sideways and the bike flip forward over the handlebars all in one surreal moment, tossing its rider up and over into a skid along the shoulder. I slammed the brakes and pulled over. By the time I'd climbed out and run up to help him, he was already up on his feet. When I got close enough to peer through the rain, I realized that it wasn't a *him*. It was Sunshine.

"I'm good," she said, but her face was scraped and bloody, and so were her hands.

"Sunshine," I said, "I saw it happen!"

She pushed strands of wet hair off her face with the back of her wrist. "Probably looked worse than it was."

"It looked horrific," I said.

"I'm fine," she insisted. She held out her hands to let the rain wash them off, palms up. I could see bits of gravel embedded where she'd hit.

"I'll get the bike," I said, turning.

"I'm not far from home."

"You can't ride," I told her, gesturing at her palms.

She didn't fight me. I picked up the bike and set it in the bed of the truck while Sunshine stood by the passenger door, unable to open it. After I popped it open for her, she edged in, keeping her hands cradled in her lap, palms up, trying not to bleed on anything. I buckled her seatbelt for her, the way I sometimes did for the kids.

When I got in on my side, she said, "Now it's starting to hurt."

"Okay," I said. "Where is the hospital?"

"Oh, no. Home's fine," she said. "I'm just scraped up."

I stared.

"Really," she said. And then, stronger, "Really."

So we pulled back onto the road.

She took a breath. "I'm sorry about before—"

"I don't want to talk about that."

"I still have your change, by the way," she said.

"Keep it."

"I didn't mean to freak you out."

Hadn't I just said I didn't want to talk about it? "Where to?"

"My grandpa's house," she said, gesturing ahead with a palm-up hand.

There was a little silence as we crossed the creek bridge, and then Sunshine said, "You know, he's friends with your aunt."

"Everybody's friends with my aunt," I said.

"No. I mean, he's *friends* with her."

"What?" I looked over.

Sunshine wiggled her eyebrows.

"No way," I said.

"Totally. It's totally true."

"That can't be right!" I said, kind of delighted. "How do you know?"

"Everybody knows," she said. "They're an official couple. Except she's ignoring him now that you're here."

"Oh," I said, feeling bad for him on principle.

"It's okay," Sunshine said. "He says it's good for him. Keeps him in his place. He says he can get kind of uppity, being so handsome."

The gravel road that led up to Sunshine's house was a sharp turn off the highway. We followed it deep into a pasture before stopping at the farmhouse. I parked in front and went around to unbuckle Sunshine and help her out. Then I lifted the bike out and set it up against the steps.

On the porch, I asked if she needed help with bandages, but she assured me that her grandpa was home and he'd get her fixed up.

"I'm sorry again about before," she said as I turned the doorknob for her.

"It's okay," I said, less spooked now that we were practically family. I gave a little wave as I jogged down the porch steps into the rain. But before I made it to the truck, I heard her call my name.

"What?" I shouted back.

"I promise I will never try to contact your dead husband," she called out.

"Okay," I shouted back. "Good."

But Sunshine wasn't quite finished. "Unless, of course," she added, "you ask me to."

The next morning, as Jean scrambled some hand-gathered barn eggs for the kids and I wriggled them into their clothes for school, I said to Jean, "What do you think of Sunshine?"

"Oh, well, you know," Jean said. "Sunshine's had a long road to travel."

"What does that mean?"

"Just that she worked like heck to pull herself together."

Another evasive set of answers from Jean. If I'd been asking my mother, I'd have had Sunshine's life history by now, all the way down to her bra size. But my mom was a talker, and Jean, it appeared, was the opposite. My mom was a gossip, and Jean was a vault. I wondered if they'd been born so different, or if they'd just become that way in response to each other. Either way, I decided to tell Jean my worries about Sunshine. Because if my mother made things worse, maybe Jean could make things better.

I didn't want to speak too plainly in front of the kids, so I said, nice and loud, "Has anybody seen Bob Dylan?"

"He's behind the barn!" Tank answered.

"He's digging a hole," Abby added.

"Could y'all go get him for me?" I asked. "I need some dog kisses."

The kids scooted out the back door and took off running, and it was only then that I realized they hadn't eaten yet. I looked at the scrambled egg kebabs Jean was setting on the table for them—which were really just eggs with toothpicks sticking out like bristles. "Remind me to feed them when they get back," I said.

We ate the kids' breakfasts, and they were absolutely delicious.

"It's the worms," Jean explained.

I stopped chewing for a second to study her face.

"The worms the chickens eat," she went on. "Factory chickens just eat grains. Farm chickens, on the other hand, run around eating all kinds of good things. Seeds. Bugs. Worms. Slugs."

I winced a little at "slugs."

"What's the word for that?" Jean mused. "The pleasure that comes from eating delicious things?"

I'd never thought about it. "I don't think there is one."

"That can't be right," Jean said. "We must have at least one."

I shook my head. "I don't think so."

"All the words in the English language," Jean said, "and we left that one out."

She squinted and thought for a second. "Mouth-pleasure," she suggested, but we both wrinkled our noses and shook our heads.

"Too much," I said.

"It needs to be a German word," she suggested. "Like *fahrvergnügen*."

"Or *schadenfreude*," I added.

Jean nodded. "One of my favorites."

"We need a German dictionary."

"Nah," Jean said. "I speak German."

"You do?"

"Sure," she said. "All the old farmers around here speak German. Just not the hippies."

"I thought you were a hippie."

"Well," she said, "I started out German, but I converted." Then her eyes drifted to the table as she thought. " *'Mund'* is 'mouth,' and *'vergnügen'* is 'enjoyment.'"

"Mundvergnügen!" I said.

"Or," she went on, " *'essen'* is 'food' and *'freude'* is 'pleasure.'"

"Essenfreude," I said. "I love them both."

"Which is better?"

"I guess we'll just have to get them both started," I said, "and see which one catches on."

I checked on the kids out the window. They'd climbed on the tire swings. It was almost time to take them to school, and they hadn't even eaten. But I still wanted to ask about Sunshine.

"So," I said to Jean, turning from the window, "Sunshine told me she could talk to the dead."

"Oh, dear," Jean said.

"And now she's got me a little spooked," I said.

"Understandable," Jean said. Then, as if she'd made a decision, she said, "You know about Sunshine, right?"

"All I know about Sunshine," I said, "is that she has promised never to contact my dead husband without my express permission."

"Well," Jean said, starting a new batch of eggs in the skillet, "she had kind of a tough childhood."

"Tough how?"

Jean paused. "All this was in the tabloids, anyway," she said. "So I'm not breaking any confidence."

"The tabloids?"

"Sunshine is Amber McAllen."

"Amber McAllen the actress?"

Jean nodded.

What she was telling me was impossible, I thought. For one thing, Amber McAllen had been very famous. World-famous. For another, Sunshine had to be at least ten years younger than me—but Amber McAllen and I were the exact same age.

I'd seen her many times before, of course. I'd seen her on the covers of *People* and *Redbook* and, famously, naked in a mud bikini on the pages of *Vanity Fair*. I'd seen all her movies—even the one about the pole-dancing vampire. She'd been just about everywhere in pop culture for about five years. She'd burst onto the scene at fourteen, starting out bright and plucky, celebrated everywhere for her come-hither innocence and great skin. And then, as she got a little older, she fell prey to the party scene and became a cautionary tale. After a period of ups and downs, she got fired from a Spielberg movie, went abruptly into rehab, and hadn't been heard from again.

It's rare that a movie star actually disappears in a quick way like that. Usually they follow a slower decline—struggling, relapsing, scrabbling for attention as it becomes harder to get. But Amber McAllen just quit. She quit making movies. She quit designing handbags. She quit endorsing fragrances and charities. She bought her way out of contracts. And in turn, as if all our feelings were hurt, she was decisively forgotten.

"That doesn't make any sense," I said. "What would Amber McAllen be doing here? And wearing goth fashions? And working at the feed store?"

"She's from here," Jean said. "Or, at least, her family is."

I glanced out the window. Now the kids were just going to have to be late to school—which wouldn't bother Abby much. She'd announced recently that school wasn't "her thing" and she'd rather stay home. She'd started begging every morning to work for Jean as a goat groomer instead of going to second grade.

"Why, babe?" I'd asked, wondering if I should worry about this new development. "You love school."

Abby shrugged. "I just like animals better than people."

Of course, she had to go to school. But—this morning at least—not right away.

Jean turned off the new batch of eggs and put the skillet lid on to keep them warm.

"I almost ran over Amber McAllen?" I said again, letting the idea sink in.

I didn't know how long it had been since she'd done any acting. Five years, maybe? Long enough, though, that when I'd actually come face-to-face, or rather bumper-to-knee, with the woman who had starred in two of my favorite movies, I hadn't even recognized her.

Of course, she'd changed a bit. She was no longer blond, but had dyed her hair obsidian black. She was no longer anorexically thin, but something akin to plump. All those things that movie stars do to make themselves so much more beautiful than the rest of us—starving, waxing, exfoliating, spray-tanning, Photoshopping—she was no longer doing. And so even though I trusted that Jean was absolutely telling me the truth, I still had trouble believing her.

"She doesn't look like Amber McAllen," I said.

"Looks aren't everything," Jean said, and then filled me in on the backstory. Things I knew—that everyone knew—about Amber McAllen's mother swindling her and stealing her fortune until she had to break off all ties. After cutting her mother loose, she hit rock bottom in a very public way: vomiting all over herself at a club. Someone captured the whole thing on an iPhone and then posted it to YouTube. This was followed by the Spielberg debacle. Then rehab. And then the inside story: Before she could return to L.A., her grandfather had dragged her kicking and screaming back to Atwater, insisted she start taking care of his horses, and got her into therapy—with Jean.

He expected her to run away, but she didn't.

And so Jean and Amber had set to work. They analyzed what success was, and fame, glamour, power, and popularity. They examined her former life from every angle, studied her motivations, wrote poems, finger-painted, meditated. They defined what really mattered in life, what made a person feel loved and happy, and what made it all worth it—and decided that fame was the exact opposite of those things. They coped with the fact that all her money had been spent, lent, and stolen by her mother's boyfriend. And now, at last, after taking back her childhood nickname and swearing off Hollywood forever, Sunshine was finally doing fine.

"She doesn't look fine to me," I said.

Jean's voice was protective. "You didn't see where she started."

"And the ghosts thing?" I asked as I finally signaled the kids back in for breakfast.

Jean hesitated. It was clear she felt torn: wanting to help me, but not wanting to say too much. "Well," she said at last, "it's possible she's trying to reach out more to the living than to the dead."

I wasn't sure exactly what Jean meant, but it made me feel better. Maybe Sunshine just wanted to be friends. Or maybe she just wanted attention. Either way, after that conversation, and witnessing how much Jean liked her, I gave in to the notion that I'd probably wind up liking her, too.

Chapter 7

The next week, as I trudged up from a long afternoon in the barn, caked with goat dust, Jean met me in the yard to say she'd invited some people to dinner that night.

"People" turned out to be Sunshine, her grandpa, and O'Connor, who Jean informed me was "always hungry." The words had barely touched the air when an old Mercedes station wagon grumbled over the cattle guard and through the gate, then clattered along the dirt driveway and squeaked to a stop next to Jean and me.

Jean barely had time to shrug at me before Sunshine jumped out.

Sunshine's grandpa, it turned out, was the white-haired fellow who had saved her in the crosswalk that first day. He took off his hat to greet me, gave me a bear hug, and introduced himself as "Russ McAllen, attorney at law."

That first day his hair had floated around his head in tufts, but now it was politely combed down. In the crosswalk he'd been wearing jeans, but now he was all ironed and buttoned down in khakis and a plaid collared shirt.

He said, "How's the minivan?"

I didn't quite follow, and I replied, "Good, I think," more as a question than an answer.

"No new dents?" he asked, and I realized he was asking if I'd killed anybody with it since he'd seen me last. I would have assured him that all the townsfolk were unharmed, but before I could speak, he was poking a finger into my rib cage with a tickle so unexpected and jolly that it made me laugh.

"It's nice to see you again," he said, putting an arm around my shoulder as we headed toward the house. "I'm glad you're here."

"Isn't that the town motto?"

He gave me a squeeze. "Learn it and live it," he said. "Makes a great tattoo."

He held a bouquet of flowers, and I pointed at them. "Nice," I said.

"I don't know much," Russ said. "But I do know women."

Sunshine was dressed all in black, with a baby blue ribbon in her hair. Now that I knew who she was, I couldn't help but stare.

It seemed like a long distance from million-dollar movie sets to Jean's farmyard. If Amber McAllen had been standing next to me, I'd have felt irrationally giddy to be meeting her. But I'd already met her as Sunshine. I tried to superimpose a *People* cover on top of the girl in black lipstick standing beside me, but I just couldn't make it fit.

Sunshine didn't act like a star, either. The kids were out front, kneeling by some rosemary bushes and building a fairy city out of rocks and sticks—something Jean had suggested—and as soon as Sunshine noticed them, she walked right over.

"Whatcha doing?" I heard her ask.

"Fairy city," Abby said, as if no other words were needed.

"I love fairies!" Sunshine said, and then, not even bothering with introductions, got down in the dirt with them, crisscross applesauce, taking directions from Abby almost as well as Tank did.

Russ and I watched for a minute, and it hit me that Sunshine wasn't pretending to have fun with the fairies the way most grown-ups do with kid things. She was *actually* having fun with the fairies.

"She never really got to finish her childhood," Russ said after a minute.

"I get that," I said. And I really did.

Dinner was 100 percent kebabs. It was a chilly February night, so we ate in the kitchen because the oven made it the warmest room in the house.

O'Connor showed up just as we started eating, his face a little red from the cold. Jean handed him a bottle of beer without asking, and as he tilted his head back to take a swig, I watched him. When I caught myself staring, I turned my eyes away and kept them averted for much of the meal.

Conversation at the table was lively. Sunshine and the kids disappeared under the table after eating and played happily there for a good while, which left the remaining grown-ups time to relax and visit more than usual.

I couldn't contain my curiosity about Russ, who was totally hot in a Wilford Brimley way, and who was clearly smitten with Jean. I kept watching him watch her, and I couldn't help but note that he was a man in serious love.

"How did you two meet?" I asked.

"In high school," Jean said.

"I proposed to her in high school," Russ pointed out.

"You guys dated in high school?"

"We went on a few dates," Jean corrected. "Dating was different back then."

"Mostly I just followed her around," Russ said. "Begging her to marry me."

"You did do that, didn't you?" Jean said, regarding him.

"She always gave me butterflies," Russ went on. "Even long after she'd found Frank, and long after I was married myself. Anytime I saw her around town, I'd have to just plant my feet and take a deep breath."

Jean looked over. "Is that true?"

Russ nodded and examined his beer bottle. "I just never could quite put out that spark."

Jean put her hand on top of his.

After a moment I turned back to Russ. "Tell me about your tattoo," I said.

"Darlin'," he said, snapping to attention, "don't you recognize her? That's your aunt Jean."

I tried to decide if he was teasing.

Russ shrugged. "She dared me."

"You guys seem like a great pair," I said.

"Well," Jean said, "I'm a hippie liberal, and he's a neoconservative nut job, but we make it work."

Russ nodded. "We do our part for the unity of the country." Then, to clarify, he said, "I'm really just a Republican. Jean just likes the way 'nut job' sounds."

"It has a certain ring to it," I said.

Soon the conversation veered off to farm topics, and I relaxed into the pleasant atmosphere of food and conversation—until

Sunshine popped her head up from under the table and said, "But have y'all heard about the panther?"

We all turned and stared.

Sunshine scrabbled back up to her chair. "There's a black panther prowling the spring at night."

"Prowling the spring?" I asked.

"Prowling the whole town, actually," Sunshine said. "It's front-page news at the feed store."

"Sunny," Russ said gently, "there aren't any black panthers in Texas. It's just not possible."

"Actually," O'Connor said, "there *are* mountain lions in Texas. Mostly up near Big Bend, though." He gave Sunshine a nod. "It's possible, at least."

"I like the idea," Jean said. "Who were we to run every majestic living thing out of the state? I don't think I'd want to live in a world stripped of every wild creature but squirrels and cockroaches."

"You won't like the idea so much if he gets one of your goats," Russ said.

I sat very still. An image of my two sweet children tending the garden as an enormous black beast sprinted out toward them from the forest took over my brain. Never mind the question of why they would be gardening at night.

I stood up, pushing my chair back with a honk, and announced in a non sequitur, "Time for bed!"

The kids, who were not yet aware that their lives were in peril, emerged from under the table and asked to go swing on the tires.

"Not a chance!" I said, as if they'd just asked to go play with shotguns.

"Five more minutes?" Abby, the expert bargainer, asked.

"Nope!"

I herded them both up the stairs, ignoring their protests—cries of injustice that didn't fade until they'd submerged their little bodies in the steaming bath, where they remembered that even though the underside of the table was pretty good, a hot bathtub was even better.

Six weeks of farm life had worked at least one miracle for me: My children ran themselves so ragged during the day that they had begun, for the first time in their lives, to actually fall asleep at bedtime. Which was lucky for me, because I was tuckered out myself. Usually I tiptoed back down, helped Jean with the last of the kitchen cleanup, and staggered off to my own bed. Some nights I even fell asleep in my overalls and woke up the next day with buckle prints across my collarbone.

Even so, it was satisfying to end the day completely spent. I got up when Dubbie announced it was morning, and I, like the kids, went to sleep as soon as I was horizontal in my bed. Or possibly even, some nights, several seconds before.

Jean had promised that my body would adjust and that pretty soon I'd be staying up to play Scrabble with her. But I couldn't imagine it. It was easy now to see how she lived without a TV. She didn't need one.

The kids were asleep before I'd even closed their door, and as I shuffled back down the stairs I felt the familiar tiredness in my thighs and shoulders and back that kicked in at about this time. I figured I'd just give Jean a hug good night, but when I saw the group all still sitting around the kitchen table, twinkle lights from the porch shining through the window glass, I felt what I wanted start to shift. The scene was as appealing as a campfire, and even though my body wanted to go to bed, my soul wanted to stay right there.

I eased back into my place at the table. Sunshine was doing palm readings.

"Great news," Jean said when she saw me. "I'm headed for a long life of great wealth." After many kebabs and about the same number of beers, everybody was relaxed, and Jean's announcement brought a gust of laughter.

"My turn," Russ said, laying down his big paws.

Sunshine took his right hand and studied it.

"Well," she said after a good look, "you're never going to have much money."

"Money's for people who lack imagination," he said.

"And you'll never be famous," Sunshine went on, "or even respected by your peers." I could see her stifling a smile. "But," she went on, "the love in your life will outmatch the sorrow."

"That's just about the best fortune I could hope for," Russ said.

Then he pulled Jean over and gave her a kiss right on the lips, one that lasted a little longer than anyone expected. We all politely looked around, and that's when, for the first time since dinner started, my gaze fluttered toward O'Connor. Our eyes met and then flicked away—but in that moment I noticed something about him. He was playing with something on a chain around his neck. Something that shone a little.

I snuck another look, and then I knew what it was. A wedding ring.

I caught my breath so fast that I made myself cough. A wedding ring? On a chain? Did that mean O'Connor was married? I had just spent six weeks with him, and it had never even occurred to me that he might have—or have had—a wife. Nothing about him said "married." My eyes sidled over to the choppy beard, the scraggly hair, and the plaid shirt with the goat-chewed sleeve. He couldn't be married. Wives didn't let their husbands walk around like that.

There it was, though: a smooth gold man's band. Had it been

there, just out of sight, this whole time? Why wasn't it on his finger?

Maybe that's what goat farmers did. Maybe people who worked with their hands wore their rings in less busy places. There was no denying it was a wedding ring. And there was no denying this, either: If a man has a wedding ring, the chances that he's married just have to go up.

Right on the heels of that realization came another one: I didn't want him to be married. Somehow—despite the beard and the teasing and the endless renditions of Kenny Loggins's greatest hits—I'd managed to develop a tickle of a feeling about him that I suddenly realized was the beginning of a crush.

It felt pathetic to even admit it inside my own head. A crush on a totally disinterested, chronically unkempt, and now most likely married man. Trouble was, there was no going back now. You can't unrealize a thing. And once it was out there, even just in my mind, I felt my face flush, and I had to look down at my empty plate.

But why? Why him? Was it just loneliness? Desperation? He certainly wasn't encouraging me. And it wasn't his looks—I couldn't even imagine what he looked like under all that fur. Maybe it was that he'd been so kind to the kids, letting Tank "help" him hammer things, and teaching Abby martial arts moves: fatherly skills they would never get from me. He'd taught them how to whistle with a blade of grass between their thumbs and how to find the Big Dipper. Not to mention the afternoon I'd found them all in the barn, kids laughing like crazy with their mouths wide open as O'Connor tried to squirt them from across the room—with milk straight from the goat.

He was kind to me, too, in his way. He'd laughed it off the time I left the freezer door open. And the time I dropped a bucket and spilled a morning's worth of milk. He hummed too much, but I liked that as well—I liked the way his voice was a little sandpapery. And while he let me do most of the talking, he never made me feel self-conscious about it. Most of the time, if I looked over, I'd see his eyes crinkled up in a smile.

Was all that worthy of a crush? I couldn't help but compare him to Danny, and there he failed miserably. Danny had been articulate, well groomed, successful—even if not a great investor—and an all-around catch. This guy was none of those things. It forced me to think about how far my life had fallen: that this practically homeless-looking man was the best I had to wrap my heart around.

I took a deep breath. I needed to be alone. I was just about to stand up when two warm hands wrapped themselves around mine, and I looked down to see they were Sunshine's.

"Your turn," she said.

I was too queasy with realizations to protest. She took my left hand, which, of course, had a wedding ring of its own, and spread it palm up on the table. I had no interest in Sunshine reading my palm, and if my mind hadn't been elsewhere I might have pulled my hand politely away. But I didn't.

She was dead serious as she read the lines. "Your past and your future are about to intersect. You're about to learn firsthand how joy is impossible without sadness. You can go forward or back, but you can't do both. And everything is about to change."

"Okay," I said.

"Also?" she said.

I waited.

"Nothing is ever really lost."

She wanted those words to have an impact on me. They didn't. They were just words. Words that sounded, honestly, pretty hokey.

"True," I said at last, nodding, and I hoped I didn't sound sarcastic. This was fortune-telling? If I'd been paying for it, I'd want my money back.

Now I knew for sure that Sunshine's whole paranormal thing was just a ploy for attention. Weren't we all hanging on her every word? Weren't we all captivated? It wasn't the cover of *Maxim* or anything, but it had to be better than no attention at all.

"It's all true," I said. "Thank you."

Sunshine was already turning toward O'Connor. "Now you."

O'Connor stood straight up. "Nope," he said. "No fortunes for me."

"But it's your turn."

"You know what, Sunny? I've got to get home."

Russ was still jolly. "Don't you want to hear about how you're going to get fat and lose your hair?"

"Not tonight," O'Connor said. He gave Jean a kiss on the cheek and said, "Thanks for the kebabs," as he opened the door and glanced back. "'Night, Russ. 'Night, Sunny. 'Night . . ."

Where my name should have fallen easily into the lineup, there was nothing. His eyes met mine, and I saw a little flash of surprise in them. He'd forgotten my name. Six weeks together in the barn, and he hadn't even registered my name.

"Libby," I finished for him, in what I hoped was a tone of bored irritation.

"Libby," he repeated, softer, with a little nod.

Then, as he turned, everybody called back, "Good night!"

That is, everybody but me. Because, really, if he didn't even know my name, I could easily save my good nights for somebody else.

Chapter 8

~~~~~~~~~

That was well into February. By then I could run the milking machine and find the circuit breaker when the power got overloaded. I knew where all the clean pots and pans went, and I could find just about anything in the cheese kitchen without having to look. I even knew most of the goats' names, though I did still get Elizabeth Cady Stanton and Susan B. Anthony mixed up. I now had my own pair of Crocs inside the kitchen doorway—powder blue—and I was, as Jean had predicted, truly living in my roomy, durable, and super-comfy overalls. I'd try to think back to all those mornings at my mother's, wrestling my body into pantyhose and then wedging my feet into heels, and it seemed like another lifetime. Somebody else's other lifetime.

The kids were settled in, too. Tank had ripped every single pair of pants he had, and Jean had darned them with patches from her vintage feed-sack collection. I'd given him a buzz cut out on the front porch one not-as-chilly afternoon, and then, after he lost his first tooth, he looked exactly like a Norman Rockwell painting.

Abby, too, grew more charming by the day. Her little legs suddenly stretched out long and birdlike in her favorite purple leggings. Jean had sewn her a ruffly white pinafore so she could play *Little House on the Prairie*, and she wore it over everything— even her nightgown sometimes. Abby had never been a fan of having her hair brushed, but since moving in with Jean, she'd changed her mind, and now she let Jean braid it every morning before school.

School seemed to be going okay. Tank was happy, in that sweet way he had of being happy anywhere. I worried more about Abby, and I constantly second-guessed the decision I'd made not to tell her teacher about the car accident. On one hand, if the teacher knew about her bad leg, she might be able to help her and keep an eye out for her. On the other hand, once the teacher knew, all the teachers would know, and our sad story would travel through this school as it had through others. And then Abby would become the Girl Who'd Been Injured, and it would be official. Her title. The thing everyone knew about her before they knew anything else.

I was so torn. We'd worked so hard and been so patient to get her leg working as well as it did—though, happily, Abby only remembered the operations and physical therapy in a vague, theoretical way. Not to mention the accident that had made it all necessary. We were 90 percent there. Abby was so close to being just like the other kids. We were so close to putting it all behind us. "Ninety percent there" should have been more than enough for both of us.

But life is hard enough even when you're 100 percent there.

I've seen movies where parents level with their children about their fears. I've seen actors say to their actor children, "Daddy's trapped in a coal mine, and I don't know if he's ever coming back." Lines like that are so false they make me walk out of the theater. Parents do not lay it all out like that. In fact, they do the opposite. They see their kids slash their hands open with a pocket knife and say, "Looks like you've got a little cut there." Parents thrash with worry in their beds for endless hours and then, in the morning, deny it all.

"I keep worrying how Abby's doing at school," I told Jean one morning before the kids were up.

"What kind of worrying?" Jean asked.

"The kind that wakes you up in the dead of night."

Jean was frothing goat's milk for cappuccinos. "Why don't you ask her how she is?"

"I don't want her to know I'm worried."

Jean nodded. She got that. Because then Abby might worry, too. In exactly the way you worry when someone tells you not to.

"Can you ask her in a nonworried way?" Jean asked.

I thought about the vast number of times Abby had sniffed out the things I was trying like hell to hide. "I'm not sure that I can," I admitted.

Jean paused at the counter to size me up. "I can," she offered at last.

I felt a gust of relief. "Could you? You wouldn't mind?"

"Easy," Jean said.

"Of course," I added, "you'll likely get nothing but one-word answers."

"Well," Jean said, "that's all anyone ever gives us, really. Just tiny clues." She patted me on the shoulder. "But we figure out how to read them."

"I'm terrible at reading them," I said.

Jean squeezed my shoulder. "You're better than you think."

That night at dinner, I asked, "How was school today, babe?"

Abby said, in Spanish and without looking up, *"Excelente."*

In response, Jean took the conversational reins and said, "What do you think of your teacher, Abby?"

Abby had a mouth full of salad. She thought about it while she chewed. Then she said, "She's very fashionable. I like her scarves and her nail polish. And she tries hard. Even though the boys disobey."

I should have realized that Jean knew what she was doing—that the best way to get hidden answers is to ask hidden questions. Still, all I could think about was the fact that Jean had asked the wrong question. Why had she asked about the teacher? Who cared about the teacher? I wanted to know about Abby.

And so, on impulse, I decided to jump in—and succeeded brilliantly in shutting her right back down.

"And how was *your* day today, babe?" I asked, as if to say, *Who cares about that boring old teacher?*

Abby shrugged. "Fine."

"What did you do?"

We'd lost eye contact. "School stuff."

I regrouped. "What was the best thing you did all day?"

"Practiced karate with O'Connor."

I'd seen them out by the fence, working on slow-motion kicks and chops. But that didn't count. "I'm talking about school," I said. "Who'd you play with at recess?"

A shrug. "I don't know."

"You don't know their names? Or you don't remember?"

"Don't remember," she said. And then, "May I be excused?"

Note to self: *Shut the hell up.*

Later, without criticizing, Jean laid it out for me. "The question you're dying to know the answer to? That's the one question you can't ask."

"That seems needlessly complicated," I said.

"Sure," Jean said. "People *are* needlessly complicated. That's part of what makes us all so fun."

"I'm sorry," I said, a little embarrassed at how I hadn't trusted her to know what to do.

She waved the apology away. "Nonsense," she said.

In truth, Abby didn't seem entirely unhappy. She and her brother were now pros at goat grooming, laundry hanging, and general farmyard scampering, and they played every afternoon in the most idyllic way I could have wished for them.

But I kept worrying that something was wrong. After a while, I'd turned it over in my mind so many times that I no longer had any idea if I was on to something, as I'd originally thought— something only I, with my hypersensitive mom antenna, could pick up—or if I'd invented it all myself.

"Watch for clues," Jean suggested, "but don't watch so closely that every tiny thing starts to look like a clue."

Too late.

At bedtime that night, as we rubbed vitamin E on Abby's scar, I told her my favorite story of her life: a Disneyfied version with the brightest of endings about a young heroine who was fantastically lucky—not *despite* her hardships but *because* of them. I tried my best to dramatize the moral as I always did: *Good things always come out of bad.* With each retelling, the happy ending got happier. And why the hell not? The happy ending was the whole point.

It was getting harder and harder to sell that happy ending, though. Just as it gets harder and harder to sell the idea of the tooth fairy: Your kids start to suspect you're lying, and they start trying to catch you in the lie. It becomes more exciting to chase the truth than to hold on to the tooth fairy. That's growing up, I guess. But kids don't know that once you give up the tooth fairy, you never get her back. And the same is true of happy endings. I could feel Abby starting to resist hers, and I could feel myself doubling down to keep her convinced. Because if anybody in the entire world deserved a happy ending, it was the fairy-tale version of my sweet girl.

That night, when I hit the last line—"And she lived happily ever after" —Abby resisted again.

"Happily ever after," she said, "but with a big pink scar down her leg."

"Yes," I said, sitting up a little straighter.

"A scar forever, and a little bit of trouble walking."

"Yes," I said. "Just a tiny bit."

"Enough that people could notice, if they wanted to."

I felt my stomach drop. "Are people noticing, babe?"

Abby pulled the cover up over her legs and nestled her head into the pillow. She looked up to meet my eyes, continuing on as if she hadn't heard my question. "But she has to remember to be grateful. Right? Because things could always be worse."

Oh, she was killing me. I turned my head as I felt tears in my eyes and, hoping like hell Abby didn't see them, I announced, nice and loud, "Bedtime, folks!"

Then Tank, who'd been hopping around the room like a frog, piped up, "You know what's great about your scar?"

"What?" Abby asked.

"It kind of looks like a crocodile."

We all took a look. It did kind of look like a crocodile. And God bless Tank for noticing.

"That's awesome," Abby said.

"Wouldn't it be cool," Tank went on, "if it could crawl off your leg and be your pet?"

Abby plainly thought it would. "And bite anybody I wanted it to," she added.

"Oh," I said, adding a vague moral influence as I gestured them into bed, "let's not sic our pet crocodiles on people."

"You could name him Scar," Tank went on as they settled themselves down.

"Scar the killer crocodile," Abby agreed.

Then I tucked them both under the covers, made a sincere bedtime wish for happy endings for both of them, and flipped off the light. I made my way downstairs with the uneasy feeling that the day had brought some important clues about Abby. I just didn't know what they were or how to read them.

I said all this to Jean at the kitchen sink as we finished up the dishes. "Don't put so much pressure on yourself," she said. "You're doing fine."

"I want to be better than fine," I said. "I want to be perfect."

Jean shook her head. "You don't have to be perfect. You just have to try your best."

I lifted my eyebrows. "That's what I say to the kids."

"You say it to the kids," she said, "but it's also true."

She'd surprised me. "I guess that's a good point."

"Kids don't need perfect parents," Jean said. Then she gestured at me. "You practically raised yourself."

That was just it. "What if I'd actually had some help?" I said. "Maybe I would have turned out better."

"But you turned out great!" Jean said.

I shrugged. "I don't want my kids to be like me. I want them to be better than me."

"They're going to be different," Jean said. "They're just going

to be their own selves with their own struggles and disappoint-
ments and heartbreaks."

I put my head down on the table and let it churn with worries
and unanswered questions. "It's hard," I said. "This parenting
thing is killing me."

"Well," Jean said, patting my arm, "something has to."

We wound up staying up late. Sometimes conversations get
rolling and you just don't want to stop them. This happened to me often with Jean. Just the act of talking—no matter
what we were actually talking about—was a pleasure. In truth, I
spent much of my life feeling, if not actually *lonely*, then at least
alone. "Alone" was my neutral. Even raising kids, surrounded by
life and chaos and noise, I carried this feeling around with me
most of the time.

I never felt alone when I was talking to Jean, though. It was
something about the way she listened—like there was nothing on
earth she cared more about than gathering every detail in what I
had to say: the way I'd hammered back together that cracked
spot in the fence, or the gang of turkey vultures that kept appear-
ing over the barn, or the crazy dream I'd had that human beings
walked like chickens, their heads jutting in and out with each
step. She found a way to find it interesting. It made me want to
follow her around all day the way all the dogs did.

That night we talked until we were bleary-eyed. A topic would
burn down to its ashes, and then I'd toss in some kindling and get
it going again—until Jean happened to notice the clock. "Dear
Lord!" she said. "It's two in the morning!" She was just flipping
off the lights when she added, "And you have to be up early."

"I do?"

"Tomorrow's the farmers' market," she said.

I'd forgotten. Now that I had the hang of making cheese, the next day I would be going with O'Connor to peddle it. After milking, we'd get up early, pack up the truck, and head in to Houston together to set up shop. It was time for me to learn those ropes. The kids would stay with Jean this time, though once I had my sea legs, Jean said, I could certainly take them with me.

I'd been wanting to ask Jean a question for a while now, and here, at two in the morning, suddenly seemed like as good a time as any. "Can I ask you something about O'Connor?" I asked.

"You can ask," Jean said.

"Is he married?"

Jean looked over at me.

"He's got a wedding ring on a chain," I said. "Is that his wedding ring?"

"I don't think I'm supposed to talk about that," Jean said, looking torn.

"Did she die?" I asked, trying not to sound hopeful.

Jean looked at me like she really, really wanted to tell me something, and then she clamped her mouth shut.

"She didn't die," I said, as if Jean's face were a book I was reading aloud. "But she's out of the picture?"

Jean kept her mouth closed and shook her head.

"She's not out of the picture?" I asked. "She's still in the picture?"

Jean gave the tiniest nod, and then she burst out with, "I can't tell you!"

"You can't even give me hints?"

Jean shrugged. "Therapist-client confidentiality."

I sighed. "And you really have to abide by that?"

She nodded. "Just ask him yourself! You'll be with him all day."

"Do you think he wants to talk about it?"

"No," Jean said. "But better him than me."

I sighed. She really wasn't going to tell me. It was time to get going. "You don't want to come along?"

Jean shook her head. "You'll have your hands full," she said. "And we've got big plans, anyway."

"Big plans?"

"Goat spa," she said with a wry smile. "Hoof painting, fur styling, scented candles. That type of thing."

Chapter 9

The next morning, O'Connor and I milked the ladies before dawn, loaded up the cheese in coolers in the back of Jean's pickup, and took off for Houston. The kids ran after us down the gravel drive in their PJs and slippers, waving as we pulled away.

I waved, too, out the window, until the kids were out of sight.

When I finally sat back against my seat and rolled the window back up, the cab of the truck seemed awfully small. I was used to being with O'Connor—but not in an enclosed space.

I flipped on the radio, which was preset to an oldies station, and a Smokey Robinson song I'd never heard filled up the silence. O'Connor joined in right away, in falsetto, and I leaned my head back to watch him sing.

I liked the veins in his forearms, and the way he rolled his shirtsleeves up past his elbows, even though it was cold. I looked at the way his jeans stretched over his kneecaps, and how worn the fabric was there. I wondered how long he'd had those jeans. I guessed he'd bought them new at the feed store years before—dark blue, not prefaded—and then worn them and worn them until they were as soft as suede. I wanted to reach out to touch the fabric, but I didn't.

At the end of the song, O'Connor turned the music down.

"The farmers' market's easy," he said. "I'm not sure why Jean waited so long."

"Maybe she wanted me to settle in first."

"I'm sure she did." Then he sized me up. "Are you settled in?"

I nodded. "Yes. Very."

"She's glad to have you here."

"I'm glad to be here."

"Think you'll stay for a while?" he asked.

"Well," I said, "not forever. I'll need to get a job at some point. A real job," I added, not considering that my not-real job was his job, too. "What I mean," I went on, "is that I probably ought to make more money. To save for college, if nothing else."

"Nah," O'Connor said. "College is unnecessary."

I glanced over. "People have to go to college."

"Why?" he asked.

"So they can get jobs and live a good life."

"I take it you went to college," he said.

"Yes."

"And how much did you pay for all those years of drinking and sex?" he asked. "Fifty thousand dollars?"

"More," I admitted.

"And now here you are," he said. "Milking goats."

"Okay," I said. "But my life didn't turn out like it was supposed to."

"That's true for everybody."

"Not everybody," I said. "Some people are lucky."

He just glanced over and said, "Nobody is lucky all the time."

"But I learned things in college!" I said. "I read Shakespeare. I studied Marx. I went on an archaeological dig!"

"You can read Shakespeare for free," he said. "You can dig right here in the yard."

"So you're against school?"

"I'm against paying for it," he said, looking over. "It's a racket."

"You can't *not* send your kids to college."

"None of that stuff's going to be any use, anyway," he went on. "The world's going to fall apart pretty soon, anyhow."

Either he was messing with me or he was crazy. Or both. "Fall apart?"

"Sure," he said with a shrug. "We can't keep going like this. Financial systems will collapse. Technology will run its course. Global warming, mass extinction. The whole shebang."

"Okay," I said, turning my attention back to the road. Time to shut it down.

"What you should teach your kids," he said, "is hunting. And fishing. And how to hotwire a car. Things that will actually help them in the charred dystopian hellscape we're headed toward."

I cracked the window a little bit. "You don't really think that."

"Sure I do."

"So," I said, looking him up and down, "you're like a crazy survivalist?"

"Survival's never crazy," he said.

I eyed his profile. "And a reader of way too much science fiction."

"Is there such a thing as too much?"

"And you're definitely not an optimist."

"I'm just owning up to who we are," he said. "Can you honestly see any other future for the human race?"

"I can see lots of other futures for the human race," I said.

"Do you believe in any of them?"

"Yes! I believe in all of them!" Then I added, "Potentially."

He tilted his head a little, as if toying with seeing things differently. Then he grinned. "Nah," he said. "We're doomed. Nature will take back over. We'll scuttle like rats through the ruins of strip malls, shooting at each other and eating cockroaches to survive."

"Awesome," I said.

"But your kids'll be okay," he said. "That Tank's a crafty one. And I'm already teaching Abby self-defense."

I turned back to meet his eyes. "You're teaching Abby self-defense?"

He nodded.

"Why?"

He shrugged. "One day I was telling the kids how I could kill a person just by looking, and she asked me to show her how."

So that's what they'd been practicing in the yard. "Why would she want to learn that?" I asked.

"All kids want to know that stuff," O'Connor said. He frowned, amazed I didn't know that already. "They like to feel powerful."

It seemed like a strange new interest for Abby. Tank? Sure. He could turn a Scrabble board into a battlefield. But Abby?

"Don't worry," O'Connor went on. "We're not at a lethal level yet. We're still working on maiming."

"Maiming, huh?"

He nodded. "She's really into it."

"That's so weird," I said, wondering how it was possible for O'Connor to know something about Abby that I didn't. "I had no idea."

"She's a hard worker," he said. Then he added, "They're good kids, Libby."

I nodded and gave him a smile. "That's true," I said. Though I was surprised by how good it felt to hear someone say it. "They really are."

Chapter 10

W e made it to the market just after nine, and I was surprised to find us parking in my old neighborhood—just a few blocks away from the house I'd lived in with Danny. The market had started up since I'd moved away.

The white tents of the vendor booths were already there. O'Connor backed up to one of them and hopped out to let the truck bed down. We sold the cheese in half-pint containers with stickers on the lids that featured a black-and-white photograph of the goat that Jean insisted was the most photogenic (Eleanor Roosevelt) and Jean's brand name, Lucky Lady Farm. We kept the tubs in coolers, stuffed down among refreezable ice packs. When we arrived, I pulled out one tub of each flavor—jalapeño, garlic, and cilantro—along with a red-and-white checked table-cloth and a box of crackers.

I set out our sign, too, which featured Rosie the Riveter—the goat, not the girl—wearing a red-and-white polka-dot kerchief.

Jean would never admit it, but Rosie was her favorite—and also the mascot for Jean's super-secret-recipe chevre, We Can Do It.

O'Connor also set up a boom box that played old-time western swing. When he saw me watching him, he said, "Jean says it lulls the customers into buying more."

Then he sat on the truck bed and swung his feet to the music as we waited for customers. The music caught me by surprise, and I found myself resisting the urge to sway back and forth.

"Good, right?" O'Connor asked, seeming to notice me not dancing.

"What?"

"The music," he said.

"It's very catchy."

"You can dance around a little if you like."

"No, thanks," I said.

O'Connor assessed me. "But you want to."

"Not as much as I don't want to look like a goofball."

"It's our band, you know."

"Whose band?"

"Ours. Mine and Jean's. And some other people."

"You have a band?"

"That's me, playing the bones. Hear that smacking sound?"

"The bones?"

"The chicken bones."

"I didn't know you guys had a band."

"It's kind of an Ernest Tubb tribute band," he said. "We're on hiatus right now."

I regarded him for a minute. "What does Jean play?" I asked.

"The jug."

"The jug?"

He pointed at the boom box. "Hear the *oomp-oomp*? That's Jean, blowing into a jug."

I listened as people started to filter into the market. It was a chilly day. My legs were cold inside my jeans, but I had three layers on top and a scarf. The breeze had turned O'Connor's nose a little pink, but he wasn't fidgeting the way I was, and I wondered if the fur on his face functioned as an extra layer. He offered to get me some hot cider from two booths down, but I said no—even though, in fact, I really would have loved some.

We kept our eyes on the people strolling in and got quiet for a minute before starting up the conversation again.

"Did you and Jean always come here together?" I asked.

"Never," he said. "She does Austin and I do Houston."

"Who's doing Austin today?"

"Nobody," O'Connor said. "We're taking a break from Austin until you're trained."

"And then I'll do Austin?" I asked.

"No, then I'll switch to Austin."

"Why switch?" I asked.

"She figures it might be nice for you to come home." He shrugged. "She wants to make sure you have fun."

"I'm not sure it matters if I have fun," I said.

"It matters to Jean."

Before long, customers started collecting in lines, wandering past booths, stopping to chat in clumps. I saw a few dogs go by, and some strollers. It was just as picturesque as I would have thought, though I found myself feeling a tiny bit nervous about dealing with customers. What if they didn't like the cheese? What if I gave somebody the wrong change?

In fact, I did fine. Everybody was nice. At first. Until a former neighbor walked up to our booth that first day and tasted three different cheeses before she recognized me.

"Oh, my God," she practically shouted, throwing her arms wide and giving me an airy hug across the table. "I haven't seen you in ages! What are you doing here? Is this your cheese? Are you a cheese farmer now?" Then, shifting from what you might call "exaggerated delight" down to "memories of sad things past," she said in a kind of stage whisper, "How are you?"

Her name was Jessica Boone, and she was married to one of Danny's old college buddies, a guy who everybody called "Boone Dog." We'd been part of the same broad social circle, but even though Jessica had lived only two blocks away, we'd never really become friends. In fact, as I stood there, I could not even remember Boone Dog's first name. But I did remember this about Boone Dog: He was the nicest guy in the world. Which had always fascinated me, because his wife was the opposite.

"I'm fine," I said, nodding as an underscore. "I'm good."

"And"—she looked me over—"*making cheese?*"

Her voice made it sound ridiculous. "Yes," I said, trying to counter with a voice of my own that made it sound pastoral and awesome. "The kids and I are living in the country on a farm."

"That's adorable," she said, with so much emphasis on *"adorable"* that she changed its meaning to the opposite.

Now I remembered the trouble with retail: You're stuck with your customers. O'Connor, who had been rummaging in the glove box for his wallet, came back around and touched my arm. I turned.

"You're freezing," he said. "I'm getting you some hot cider whether you like it or not."

"I'm really fine."

"Whatever you say."

Jessica watched him walk out of the booth, and, once he was gone, she leaned into me with a twinkle.

"That guy is super hot," she said.

"You think?" I asked, following him with my eyes.

His shaggy hair was back in a ponytail this morning, and he had a light blue T-shirt with a Superman *S* on it under his work shirt and jacket. Of course, even with his hair back, every part of his face save the forehead and eyes was covered by his beard. All I saw, really, when I looked at him was a big, furry animal.

"Everybody hates the beard," she admitted. "But he's famous around here."

"Famous?"

"We all call him the Hot Farmer."

"You do?"

"Sometimes he's the only reason I come here. Just to get an ogle."

I wondered what Boone Dog would think about this confession. But Jessica had a way, I was starting to remember, of sharing pseudo-intimate information about herself in hopes of getting you to do the same thing back. Then, once she had your secrets, she told them to every single person she saw until she lost interest.

I reminded myself not to share.

Jessica sized me up. "And the two of you," she said then, "are *making cheese* together?"

She made it sound X-rated.

I wasn't sure exactly what we were talking about now. A little warning light flashed somewhere in my brain. *Caution!* But some other, feistier part of me wanted to be way past worrying or caring about people like Jessica Boone. Who cared? Women like that didn't scare me! And then, in a moment I'd wind up regretting, I met her eyes.

"Yes," I said, my voice just a hint X-rated itself. "We are making a *lot* of cheese."

At her next expression, it all came back to me—the way Jessica saw all conversation as competition. And it took her about one second to remind me why I was an amateur and she was a pro.

"That's so interesting!" she said. "I'd have thought you might still be, you know, in mourning. Wasn't Danny the sweetest guy ever?"

The mention of Danny. Of course. It had been a trap. I'd just opened a door for Jessica straight into the tenderest place in my heart. She'd won, I'd lost—and regret flooded every cell in my body. There was no upside to what I'd just said. I couldn't possibly win. If I was still devoted to Danny, then she'd make sure I felt pathetic. If I'd moved on, she'd make sure I felt disloyal. Which I suddenly did—up, down, and sideways. No matter what, there would be consequences—not the least of which would be Jessica posting to Facebook the announcement that I was dating O'Connor before she'd even left the market.

"He was," I said. "He was the sweetest guy."

Now her face was squinched up in sympathy. "It was so awful when you had to sell your house." I looked around for O'Connor then, hoping he might return and break her momentum. "And that day you had the estate sale? How did you stand it?"

"Didn't you buy something that day?" I remembered seeing her there.

She grinned, delighted with her purchase. "Your wedding china! We had the same pattern!"

Lord, she was mean.

"They weren't buying my life," I told her, feeling the need to insist. "Just my things."

Another sympathetic face.

"Well," I said, not sure what to say, "life forces you to make choices about what really matters."

She made her face bright again. "And what really matters is cheese?"

I hated every single thing about this conversation. It was as if the oxygen had been leaching out of the air while we were talking, and suddenly I realized it was all gone. Suddenly I couldn't stand there another single second. So when I saw O'Connor heading my way with a steaming cup of cider, I did not excuse myself or even glance back at Jessica. I just walked straight toward him so fast, we almost collided.

"Hey," he said.

"Can you tell me where the bathroom is? Now?"

He pointed toward a building at the back of the parking lot, and I took off without letting myself think about how Jessica would grill him about our relationship when he got back to the booth and figure out that our "cheese making" was only cheese making. I cringed a little at the idea. But none of that mattered as much as the simple act of getting myself the hell away.

When I arrived at the bathroom, though, I didn't know what to do. Hiding didn't help. And there wasn't any more air in there than anywhere else.

I felt emotions that seemed disproportionate even to me: embarrassed and guilty and naked and vulnerable and stupid and, more than anything, as though I had let Danny down. Jessica had somehow undermined any sense I might have had that I was getting better. Lately I'd been feeling just the tiniest bit like I was improving my life, but five minutes with Jessica Boone had utterly convinced me not only that I was not moving in the right direction—but that such a thing didn't even exist.

I paced a minute, and then, as I heard some people approaching, I ducked into a stall.

I closed my eyes and did a few neck stretches. I squeezed and unsqueezed my fists. I was afraid to go back out. I didn't want to see Jessica—or, at this point, even O'Connor—and so I stayed far longer in the bathroom than I'd ever intended.

At last, though, as I reached to unlatch my stall, I heard two women walk in, and realized right then that one of them was Jessica. She was in the middle of a conversation with a friend of hers named Renée, who I'd always kind of liked, and as soon as I heard them I knew just who they were talking about.

"She was in overalls," Jessica was saying. "I'm not even kidding."

A giggle from Renée.

"Seriously," Jessica went on. "She could have been chewing on a stalk of hay. It was like something from *Hee Haw*."

Another giggle—this one part snort—from Renée.

They went into stalls on either side of me.

"I never liked her," Renée said.

"Me neither," Jessica said.

"What is it about her that's so irritating?"

"I don't know!" Jessica said. "She just bugs me."

They peed at the same time, came out of their stalls at the same time, and clanked the doors behind them at the same time. Then they paused—at the mirror, I supposed. Jessica went on: "But here's the best part. She told me she's sleeping with the goat cheese guy."

There was an exaggerated pause. Then Renée said, "She did not."

"She did!"

"She just announced it to you?"

"Pretty much."

"Impossible!"

"Apparently not."

"Why would she even tell you that?" Renée asked.

"Showing off," Jessica said.

They started to move toward the exit.

"I bet she was lying," Renée said.

"You think?"

"Don't you?"

Jessica thought for a second. "You're right. She was totally lying."

They were laughing now.

"And now," Renée went on in a high squeak, "you have to *eat* her *cheese!*"

They stepped out the door, but the last thing I heard was Jessica saying, "That does it. I'm taking it back."

It was amazing how words could have such a physical effect. The memory of them ricocheted around the walls as I pressed my head against the metal stall door. I hated these women for being so petty and mean. And I hated myself for letting them bother me. And more than anything I hated Danny for leaving me alone with nobody to protect me from a world full of bullshit.

I lingered for another minute, then I stood up straight, unlatched the door, and walked myself back to the market, hoping like crazy that those women were long gone, that O'Connor had sold every last tub of cheese, and that it was time to get the hell out of Houston.

Not quite. As I neared our booth I spotted Jessica and Renée two booths over, still shopping and in no hurry to leave.

I stopped behind the truck, and O'Connor saw me. "Hey!" he said, walking in my direction. I didn't want him to see my eyes, which, I knew, were verging on tears, so I turned away. But he came right up close. "Where have you been?"

I looked up at him.

Whatever he saw on my face made him frown. "What the hell happened to you?"

"Can we leave?" I asked. "Have we sold everything yet?"

"We haven't sold everything," O'Connor said. "But we can leave."

I turned to peer through the truck window, trying to get a read on Jessica's location. They were at the next booth over.

"I just need to get out of here," I said.

"What is it?" he said again.

"Can we just go?" I checked the glass again. Jessica and Renée were headed toward our booth, and in that moment it was clear that I had to tell O'Connor everything in five seconds or less for any hope of escape.

He had followed my glance, but I put my hand on his jaw to turn him back to me. And then I said with all the urgency I could muster, and with absolutely no pauses between words, "I accidentally told that girl right there that you and I were dating and then she came into the bathroom while I was there and she and her friend said horrible things about me, and worst of all was that they thought I was lying about us dating, which is the most humiliating of all because it's true."

O'Connor blinked. "You told her we were dating?"

"Yes!"

"Why?"

"Because . . ." I didn't know how to explain it. "Because she and all her friends think you're hot, and she's always been mean to me, and she was teasing me about making cheese, and she was so damn smug, and I didn't want her to crow over her perfect husband and how she has exactly what she always wanted, like she was somehow entitled to all her blessings like nobody else in the world—" I broke off for a second, with all the other things I wanted to say still pulsing in my chest. I could feel Jessica's eyes on us now, and I dropped my voice to a whisper. "I just didn't want to let her win."

O'Connor took this all in. Then he glanced back at our booth, where Jessica and Renée were now waiting.

He seemed to find the whole thing a little funny. "They think I'm hot?" he asked.

"Yes," I said, not finding it funny at all.

His face got serious. "And that's why you're about to cry?"

Obviously. "Yes," I said.

Jessica saw him glance her way. "Excuse me!" she called, nose wrinkled. "I need to return this cheese."

O'Connor took a step closer to me as he carefully ignored her.

"Excuse me!" Jessica called again.

O'Connor was still looking at me. "I hate people like that," he said. Then he leaned in closer and whispered into my ear, "I have an idea, but it's kind of crazy."

"Okay," I said, nodding, with no sense at all of what I was agreeing to.

He looked down at my mouth with an expression like he was about to jump off the high dive, and then he leaned in and kissed me.

At first we were both too stunned at what we were doing to enjoy it very much. It was more just assembling the technical requirements of a kiss than anything else. *Lips touching? Check. Hold position.*

But then we shifted into character. Once I realized what the plan was and got on board, and once he found his pretend-kissing groove, it was like we both made the decision at the same time to make it look real. I put my hands behind his neck, and he pressed up against me—his lips warm and cidery—until we both stumbled back against the truck.

I relaxed against him and inhaled the yummy scents of soap, salt, and hot cider. All good scents. All good everything, to be honest. We weren't French-kissing, exactly, but we made it look like we were. That's when something shifted. The people around us blurred into the background, and the moment itself—the closeness, the warmth, the tickle of his beard—became the only thing in focus. The kiss transformed into something real, at least for me.

O'Connor braced one arm against the truck and curved the other around my waist, all the while steady, with no hesitation. I had to hand it to him. He went for it. He made it seem like he was starving and I was a feast. And when, for a grand finale, he ran his hand down the side of my body, it was all I could do to keep standing.

When he pulled back a little and opened his eyes, they had a question that I couldn't quite read.

I was a little breathless as I met his gaze. Still, I pulled it together enough to whisper, "Thank you."

He stepped back to let me go as I turned toward the women at the booth. I tried not to look too triumphant as I approached them.

"I'm sorry," I said, only part of my brain giving Jessica its attention, and the rest stubbornly luxuriating in the memory of what just happened. "What was it you needed?"

Both their mouths were still open. Then Jessica, clearly still a little focused on what had just happened, held up her tub of cheese. "I'm returning this."

I squinched up my nose in false sympathy. "We don't take returns."

"But I just bought it!" she said.

"You bought it half an hour ago," I said. "Who knows what you've been up to since then?"

Jessica didn't argue. "Fine," she said in a tone that made it clear she would not be patronizing our booth again.

I watched her walk away, and then I turned to look at O'Connor, who was leaning against the truck now, lost in thought. He looked up when he felt my gaze. "Do we still need to leave?" he asked.

I gave him a grateful smile and shook my head. "Nope."

"All better, then?" he asked.

I nodded. All better. Way better. Too much better. He had kissed me. Maybe it was for pretend, and maybe he was acting, and maybe he didn't really mean it. But it had been a good kiss—that much was undeniable. A really, really good kiss.

It had been a rash, unexpected, totally inappropriate thing to do. And it was perfect.

Chapter 11

On the drive home, cheese all sold, Jessica Boone behind us, I gave O'Connor the blow-by-blow of the whole debacle with her—though I left out some of the worst things she had said about me, just in case they were true.

O'Connor kept his eyes on the road, one hand solidly on the wheel. We both made sure to remain extra casual with each other.

I'd wanted to ask him about his ring on the drive down, but there had never been a good time. Now I gave up entirely. I suddenly felt afraid of the answer.

"Thanks again," I said, to fill up the pause. "You're my new hero."

He smiled and kept his eyes on the road.

"Did you know they call you the Hot Farmer?" I asked.

"No," he said. "But the housewives love me. They think I'm dangerous."

"Are you?"

He shrugged. "I don't know. As much as anyone is, I guess."

I hadn't noticed on the way down that O'Connor was the kind of guy who drove with only one hand on the wheel, but on the way home, I fixated on it. I was sure that posture said something about him. I just wasn't quite sure what it said.

O'Connor made a one-handed turn with the heel of his hand and said, "I don't think she's winning, by the way. People that mean lose by definition."

I hadn't thought about it that way. "I suppose that's true," I said, nodding. "She has to stay with her mean self all day long."

"That's right," he said. "And we get to go home."

I felt a flicker of recognition at the word. As I thought about Jean's farm, it did feel a little bit like home. This was the first time I'd been any distance from it since we'd moved there, and the miles gave me a new perspective. Even though I still thought of my real home as the house where I'd lived with Danny, it seemed, in that moment, like maybe I could claim more than one.

I'd been planning, before the disaster with Jessica Boone, to ask if we could just drive by the old house on our way back to the freeway. It wouldn't have been much of a detour, and the fact that it was so nearby fired me up to see it again. While we'd lived at my mother's, I had on occasion, after the kids were asleep, driven over in the minivan and parked across the street. I just wanted to see the place. To rest my eyes on it. To know that the house, at least, was still there.

Of course, the events of the day at the farmers' market had not taken us in a sightseeing direction. And now we were zooming back toward Atwater as fast as Jean's old truck would let us. It shimmied like it was on the spin cycle, and, as I snuck glances at O'Connor, I wondered if he was trying to put as much distance between himself and the scene of the crime as possible.

Something about his body language—the way he held his profile so still, maybe—told me he was regretting that pretend kiss. Or at least thinking about regretting it. I shifted in my seat and stole another glance at him, and just as I did, he said, "I think it was the right thing to do."

"I agree," I said, wanting to establish it as a fact.

"I don't think Erin would mind."

"Erin?" I asked. In all these weeks, no one had mentioned an Erin. But it wasn't hard to guess who she might be. "Is Erin your—" I began, and then didn't finish the question. I could tell from his face who she was. She was the person who had given him that ring on the necklace. Whatever I was asking, she was it.

"She's injured," he said. "She was in a car accident, and now she requires . . ." He paused, searching for the right words. "A lot of care."

I didn't voice the questions in my head. *What kind of accident? What kind of care?* Jean was right. The questions I really wanted answers to were exactly the ones I couldn't ask. I had to take the information he offered and let that be enough.

"Anyway," he went on, "Erin would get it."

"Good," I said.

"It was just acting," he said.

"Yes," I agreed. Very good acting. Oscar-worthy.

"And also," he said, "honestly, I just don't think of you that way."

My heart clamped down a little. "Of course not."

"And Erin would know that," he went on. "You're not my type at all."

I nodded. "Okay."

"At all," he said again.

"Well, you're certainly not my type, Grizzly Adams."

"That's right." He was building momentum now. "We're not each other's types. But you're a nice person, and you were in need of help."

I nodded. Both true.

"And Erin hates mean people," he added. "She'd have loved the expression on that woman's face."

"Her expression," I said, trying to infuse the words with the enormous gratitude I felt, "was absolutely priceless."

After a moment I said, "Are you going to tell her?"

"No!" he said. Then, a little quieter, "She wouldn't—" He cut himself off and just shook his head. "No."

"I don't think Danny would have minded, either," I said, to cover the silence.

"That was your husband? Danny?"

I nodded.

I'd assumed that O'Connor knew all about Danny, but now it occurred to me that Jean may not have told him any more about my life than she'd told me about his. "He was killed in a car accident three years ago," I said.

O'Connor nodded but didn't prompt me to say any more. Which I appreciated.

Maybe it was the fact that he didn't ask me about it—the uncharacteristic lack of pressure to reveal the heartbreaking details—but, for the first time ever, I found myself volunteering information about what had happened and how, exactly, I had lost him.

"We were in the middle of a fight at the time," I heard myself say. "And he'd gone to pick up Abby from art camp, and as they were pulling out of the parking lot onto an access road, they got broadsided by a pickup truck." Then I added, "An uninsured pickup truck." A fact that hadn't seemed very important that day but, as my financial life collapsed, turned out to be one of the most important details of all.

I ran my fingers along the window glass as I talked. "Abby was buckled in, of course, but Danny didn't have his seatbelt on yet. It was one of those things I nagged him about. He always waited, like, half a block before he buckled his seat belt. It made me crazy. Why not just buckle first and then drive? It takes two seconds! But he thought it was a waste of time."

I crossed my legs and sat up straighter in my seat. "The paramedic from the ambulance said the truck must have been going about twice the speed limit to do so much damage," I went on. "Danny's Jeep was totaled."

I found myself staring at my hands. It was so strange to just sum it all up in this way. "He died before they reached the hospital."

O'Connor nodded.

I took a breath. "When I got there, they told me Danny was dead. Though they never actually said the words. A doctor took me aside and told me his injuries were 'very extensive.' I asked what that meant, and he just said there was a lot of internal bleeding. It was like he wouldn't say it. Like I had to be the one to say it.

"So I pushed past the doctor and started to go looking for Danny. I still had Tank in my arms. I didn't believe it. It was like, if Danny was dead, he could damn well tell me himself. Before I got anywhere, though, a nurse in SpongeBob scrubs appeared out of nowhere and took me by the shoulders and told me what I really needed to do, more than anything, was to pray for my little girl. I don't know if she was right or wrong, but I did what she said. I let her lead Tank and me to the waiting area for the OR, and then I prayed like hell.

"And this sounds crazy, but I always think about that very short time when I didn't completely believe them about Danny being dead as a time when he wasn't entirely and completely gone yet. I keep wondering: If I'd gone to him right then, instead of turning my attention to Abby—if I'd held on to him just a little harder and flat out refused to let him go—could it have helped? Could it have changed anything?"

"No," O'Connor said.

I looked over at him, pulling myself back to my present life so fast that it was almost a surprise to see him there.

He met my eyes. "No. It would not have changed anything."

Something had changed in his expression.

"Of course not," I said. "I know."

"I used to be a firefighter," O'Connor went on. "I've seen a lot of car accidents. If they told you he was dead, there was no changing anything."

The way he talked, it was like he knew more about what happened that day than I did. Which he probably did, in a way. I'd certainly never been to the scene of a car accident. I'd never witnessed something like that for real. Just a thousand times in my imagination. Which isn't the same thing.

It was weird to think that O'Connor could see the story I was telling better than I could myself. It was as though he'd crowded himself into my memory of that hallway in that hospital. Yet if I'm honest, part of me liked having him there—and liked not always having to live the memory the way I had that day, so completely alone.

"I didn't know you were a firefighter," I said after a bit.

"Used to be," he said.

We drove on a little longer, and it was a few minutes before I noticed how quiet he was. My thoughts drifted back to Danny, his memory now refreshed in my mind. "He really was a good man," I said in a small voice.

O'Connor seemed to intuit that I was ready to talk about something else. "And what is that?" he asked. "A 'good man'?"

"Well," I said, leaning back a little and letting out a breath. "A good man buys you tampons when you run out. He does the dishes. He makes you coffee before you're awake in the morning. He listens to you when you're talking, even if it's about home décor. He goes out of his way to touch you, even if it's just your hand. He doesn't call it 'babysitting' when he looks after his own children. He calls you from work just to hear your voice. And he always thinks you're beautiful, even—no, *especially*—when you don't."

"That's a tall order," O'Connor said, letting out a whistle.

I turned my head toward his and studied his profile. "What's your definition?" He lifted one hand off the wheel and reached back to rub his neck. I kept expecting him to start talking, but he didn't.

"Well?" I said.

"I'm thinking."

I waited a little longer, trying to picture what his face would look like without his beard, until at last he said, "A good man does the right thing, even when it just about kills him."

I let my gaze skim up from his beard along his profile. When nothing more came, I said, "So? Are you a good man?"

"I try like hell," he said. "I'll say that for myself."

We both smiled at that, and then O'Connor said, "I haven't kissed anyone other than Erin in ten years."

"I haven't kissed anyone other than Danny in fifteen."

"No?" He glanced over. "Not even—lately?"

"I know I'm not married," I said. "But I don't exactly feel single, either." I looked over. "You know how when you commit to somebody, you, like, take down your antenna for other people?"

O'Connor nodded.

"I haven't been able to put mine back up."

He nodded some more, like he really got that. "And even if you could," he added, "you wouldn't want to."

"Exactly," I said, though I wasn't being completely truthful. My antenna might not have been entirely up and running, but it wasn't quite broken, either. The pretend kiss had cleared that right up.

I said, "Was it weird for you?"

He knew what I meant. "Yes," he said.

"The facial hair was a new twist for me."

"For me, too."

"And you taste like cider," I added.

He shrugged. "I drank your cup."

"Thanks for saving me, by the way."

"No problem," he said. "But I don't think we should mention it to anybody."

"Of course," I said, though I hadn't thought about it.

Jessica Boone was probably on speakerphone telling everyone she knew right that minute. There was no changing that. All I could do was respond to the moment at hand, and to the person who had stood up for me when I really, really needed it.

If O'Connor wanted it forgotten, it was forgotten. As much as something that good ever could be.

Chapter 12

~~~~~~~

After that, O'Connor and I were officially pals. I had needed to be rescued that day, and he had needed someone to rescue, and the symmetry of it—not to mention our common enemy, Jessica Boone—paved the way for a harmonious cheese-centered friendship.

For about a week.

Until the following Friday, the first of March, when I got a call from Abby's teacher at school, saying Abby had been fighting on the playground. And by "fighting," she meant the real thing: *fisticuffs* fighting. Abby apparently had used a serious self-defense move on a boy in her class named Jimmy Gaveski and had punched him in the stomach so hard that he peed in his pants.

"It was quite crippling," the teacher said. "I've never seen anything like it."

"Are you sure it was Abby?" I asked. "She doesn't even hit her brother."

"It was Abby," the teacher confirmed, "and she is suspended from school today. Please come pick her up."

On my way out to the minivan, I ran into O'Connor.

"Did you teach Abby how to fistfight when you were doing self-defense?" I asked.

"You betcha," he said. "How to make a proper fist. Where to aim. Yep."

"She just punched a kid at school," I said, in a *how-could-you* tone of voice. "And now she's suspended for the day."

O'Connor nodded with appreciation. "Suspended for fighting."

"She really hurt this kid, O'Connor," I said. "He wet himself."

He shrugged. "The girl's got moxie."

"Are you insane?" I said. "She's eight years old!"

"She said she was getting picked on," O'Connor told me. "And I didn't think she should just have to sit there and take it."

I stared at him. "She was getting picked on?"

He nodded.

My mind spun back through the past several months, looking for clues I should have noticed sooner. I thought about how often she'd asked to stay home from school this year. Why hadn't it raised a red flag? "Who?" I demanded. "Who is picking on her?"

"The boy she just beat the crap out of, I imagine."

"Why didn't you tell me?" I asked, my voice shocked into a kind of whisper.

"She asked me not to."

"That's not a reason!" I said. "You don't keep information like that from a child's mother."

"I was helping her handle it," he said.

"It's not your place to help her do anything!"

"Hey," he said. "She came to me."

"What's that supposed to mean?"

"She probably knew you'd freak out," he said. "Like you're doing right now."

It was time to go. Abby was waiting in the principal's office. "Yeah!" I said, getting in the car. "I'm freaking out. She's in second grade!"

"She can handle herself," O'Connor called after me.

"Stay out of it, O'Connor!" I shouted out the window as the minivan spat gravel down the driveway.

I expected to find Abby at the principal's office with her head down in shame. When I saw her, though, she was on a wooden bench by the nurse's office reading a book about mermaids. Someone had given her a lollipop.

I guess I was expecting her to suddenly look like a tough kid. But she was just her sweet, usual self.

She raised her hand when she saw me. "Hi, Mom."

I squinted at her. I couldn't read her feelings. Was she guilty and sorry? Was she triumphant? I couldn't tell. I said, "You punched a kid?"

She shrugged and looked up to meet my gaze. "He deserved it."

And right there, I believed her.

She stood up, and I put my arm around her shoulders. "Come on, ladybug," I said. "Let's go home."

In the car on the ride back, I knew that we were waist-deep in a teachable moment. Except I wasn't sure what I was supposed to be teaching.

"Abby, you can't just hit people when they're rude to you," I said. "That's not how we treat people. Hitting is never okay."

Abby didn't say anything. She was still working on her lollipop.

"Who is this kid, anyway?" I asked.

"His name is Jackie Chan. He was held back last year."

I paused. "His name is *Jackie Chan*?"

Abby shrugged. "That's what he says."

"What do the teachers call him?"

"Jimmy Gaveski."

"And he's teasing you?"

Abby shrugged.

"What is he teasing you about?"

Abby just gave me a look. We both knew what he was teasing her about.

"Did you talk to your teacher?" I asked.

"She said that if she didn't see him do it, she couldn't discipline him."

"And?"

"And she never saw him do it because he's very sneaky."

"What does he do?"

"He calls me 'Limper.'"

Oh, God. "How would he even notice that?" I demanded, more to the universe than to Abby.

"I think he's paying close attention," Abby said.

I took a breath. "What do you say?"

"I say, 'Incorrect! I am not limping! I just have a little trouble walking.'"

My knuckles were white on the wheel, but I kept my voice level. "Why didn't you tell me about this?"

"Because you'd freak out."

"No! I wouldn't!"

"Like you're doing right now."

"I am not freaking out right now," I said. "If you want to see freaking out, I will show you freaking out!"

"I don't," she said. "I don't want to see it."

"I'm going to talk to your teacher tomorrow morning before school."

Abby shrugged. "Okay," she said. "But she can't really do anything."

"We'll see about that," I said, just as we pulled through Jean's gate.

O'Connor was tinkering with the tractor, and Abby rolled down the window as we slowed to a stop near him.

"O'Connor!" she shouted.

"Hey, Mamacita," he said without looking up.

"Got him in the solar plexus!"

Now he looked up. "Nice work!"

"And then he peed in his pants!"

The glee in her voice was disturbing to me, but clearly not to O'Connor.

"You know what you can call him now?" O'Connor said.

Abby shook her head.

"PeePants," O'Connor said.

Abby laughed first, then quieted. "But I'll only do that," she said, "if he calls me something mean first."

"That's fair," O'Connor said.

When Abby opened the car door to step out, the goats surrounded her. I wasn't sure in that moment if I should punish her by sending her to her room for the afternoon or just let it all slide. I stopped her at the running board and said, "Abby?"

She turned back. "Yes?"

"You are not allowed to hit that boy again," I said. "Don't let Jimmy Gaveski's bad behavior change who you are."

Abby sighed back at me with a weariness beyond her years and said, "Okay, Mom. I'll really try not to."

"And Abby?" I said.

"Yes?"

"Way to stand up for yourself."

Abby was right about her teacher. She really couldn't do much. It was her first year of teaching, for one thing, and she looked like she was about fourteen years old, for another. She was overburdened as it was and hardly equipped to monitor every conversation the children had. I got the feeling during our emergency next-morning meeting that the teacher was on Abby's side—but she really wasn't much of an ally.

"Don't worry, Mrs. Moran," she said as she walked me toward the door. "She's not the first gawky child to be teased."

I spun toward her. "She's not *gawky*!" I said. "She has an injury." I gave that a second to sink in, then I went on, "From the same car wreck that killed her father."

The teacher's eyes went wide.

"We've done years of physical therapy, and she's worked harder to get where she is than Jimmy Gaveski will ever work in his whole life, and so the last thing on earth she deserves is some pudgy little bastard with a martial-arts complex taking out his self-esteem issues on her without even one adult stepping in."

It had come out more forcefully than I'd intended.

"I'm sorry," the teacher said, and she looked like she meant it. "Of course."

"So if you wouldn't mind keeping an eye on her," I said then, "I'd appreciate it."

"I will," the teacher said, and the true sympathy on her face made me feel, on the drive home afterward, like she might even actually do it.

S he might," Jean said that night after the kids were in bed as we discussed the matter and washed dinner dishes. "Or she might not."

"Well, it can't hurt to ask."

"No," Jean agreed.

"I have to do something," I went on. "Just because O'Connor's a brute doesn't mean Abby should be."

There was a creak on the floorboards then, and we both turned to see O'Connor standing just outside the screen door. He coughed.

I looked down.

"You're still here?" Jean asked.

"Just finishing up a few things," he said.

"Coffee?" Jean offered, glancing at me with a maybe-he-didn't-hear-you shrug. Before I knew it, he was standing beside me with a cup, making sure I knew he had heard me.

"It's not a bad thing for her to know how to defend herself," O'Connor said then, looking right at me.

"No," I said, keeping my eyes on the sink full of dishes. "On the other hand, I don't want her beating people up."

"That kid PeePants was asking for it," O'Connor said.

The way he flat out refused to consider any nuances of the situation made me glare at him. "Violence doesn't make things better," I said. "It just always makes things worse."

"You have to stand up to bullies," he said.

"I just want that kid out of the school," I said.

"Not going to happen," O'Connor said. "Where would they even send him?"

"Maybe I'll take Abby out of school," I said then. "Maybe I'll homeschool her."

"And who would milk my goats?" Jean asked.

"They're pretty smart," I said. "They could probably milk themselves."

"The point is," O'Connor said, "Abby handled it. She did fine."

"But she shouldn't have to!" I said.

"Maybe not," O'Connor said with a shrug.

"What does it do to her self-esteem to be called Limper?" I said.

O'Connor tilted his head. "What does it do to beat the crap out of the kid who said it?"

I wasn't really sure. The only thing I knew was that I didn't want to see this boy change her. He didn't have the right to do that. "I don't know," I said. "And I don't really want to find out."

"I'm betting you won't find out," O'Connor said. "It'll be months before that kid even teases his own shadow."

"I hope you're right," I said as the screen door slapped closed behind him. "I really do."

And he *was* right. For about three weeks.

Abby confirmed, every day after school under intense questioning, that PeePants Gaveski was no longer teasing her, or even speaking to her.

"Promise me," I said.

"I promise," she said. "He just sits under the bleachers."

"You'd tell me if he bothered you, right?"

"Yes," she promised.

Even after he stopped hiding under the bleachers, he didn't talk to her.

"He glares at me a lot," she said. "But he doesn't tease me."

After a while I backed off. I figured she'd let me know if something happened. I was tired of hovering over the topic so obsessively. I was tired of this kid PeePants's constant presence in our minds. I didn't want to go looking for trouble. I just let the idea of him float away.

And then Abby got sent home for using the *f*-word.

On the drive home, catching her eyes in the rearview mirror, I said, "I didn't even know you knew the *f*-word."

"O'Connor taught it to me," Abby said.

"Did he?" I said. "Did he tell you what it means?"

"No," Abby said. "He just said it's the worst of the worst."

"It's a bad one," I said.

"He said I wasn't allowed to hit PeePants Gaveski with my fists anymore, but that I could hit him with my words."

"Did he?"

Abby nodded. "Words are powerful," she explained.

"I agree," I said. "What was it exactly that you said to Pee-Pants?"

Abby sat up a little straighter. Her voice was plain. "I said, 'Back the fuck off.'"

I shook my head. "What?"

She shrugged. "Except I said it very menacingly."

"Did O'Connor teach you the word *'menacingly,'* too?"

"Mm-hmm."

"And what did PeePants do when you said these words to him?"

"Well," Abby said, "he backed the fuck off. Or at least he started to. Then the teacher swooped in and took me to the office."

"And you said this because he was teasing you?"

She nodded, with one small correction: "Taunting."

"What was he doing?"

"He kept saying, over and over, 'Limper, Limper! Now you are a blimper.'"

"That's the stupidest taunt I've ever heard," I said. "What does that even mean?"

"I don't know," Abby said.

"Did he get in trouble, too?"

"No. Just me."

"Why just you?"

Abby was gazing out the window. "I guess because *'fuck'* is a bad word, but *'blimper'* isn't."

Where had the teacher been? Why was *Abby* getting sent to the principal's office? Is bad language worse than picking on a kid with an almost imperceptible limp? Was this the kind of world we had to live in?

Abby had been thinking about it, too. "Also," she said, "I think he might be kind of mad because Limper has not caught on as a nickname for me the way PeePants has caught on for him. Lots of people are calling him PeePants now."

"And what are they calling you?"

She shrugged. "Just Abby."

After a bit she said, "Are you mad at me?"

"No, babe," I said. "I'm mad at O'Connor for teaching you that word. And I'm mad at your teacher for not protecting you. And I'm mad at that little asshole Jimmy Gaveski. But I'm not mad at you."

"Mom?" Abby said.

"What?" I said.

"I think *'asshole'* might be a bad word, too."

Chapter 13

Abby getting picked on was not something I knew how to handle. It had never happened before. I'd always worried about it happening, and dreaded the idea, and fretted over what I would do, but I'd never actually had to do anything.

Now that the moment was here, there didn't appear to be much I *could* do. Even if I'd figured out a solution, there would have been no way to put it into practice. We were at the mercy of the teachers and administrators, not to mention budget cuts and limitations. Despite several meetings with the principal and the teacher and the PE coaches, it just didn't seem to be physically possible to monitor this kid's behavior toward Abby at all times—which was exactly what I wanted to do. She was under strict instructions to report any further teasing to the teachers, but what exactly the teachers were going to do about it remained unclear.

I wasn't sure what to do, either, other than completely reverse my policy on how much people at school should know about

Abby's health. The teachers now had photocopied packets, complete with diagrams and photographs, that summed up her medical history. They'd all met with me to discuss every nuance of Abby's triumphs and challenges. I had even offered to come and explain all about it to the class—an offer that was politely rejected.

"Don't you think it would have helped?" I demanded of O'Connor one day in late March on the drive back from the farmers' market. Jean was still insisting that he come with me, even after several weeks, but I wasn't totally sure why. It wasn't rocket science. And Jessica Boone had not been back to the market, much to my relief.

"You're not ready to go it alone," Jean had said with finality. "O'Connor will keep you company."

And so here we were again, driving back from another uneventful trip. I didn't need him, it was true. But I did enjoy having him around. I never would have asked for him to be there, and maybe Jean knew that, but I was glad she made him go.

Even though, of course, he made me crazy. Like the way he thought he knew what to do about Abby. After I told him about how badly I wanted to go to school every day at recess and stand on the playground giving that kid the hairy eyeball, O'Connor said, "It's a wonder you haven't literally exploded from worry."

"You don't have kids," I said. "You can't understand."

"I don't have kids," he said, "but I have loved ones. I understand that."

"It's not the same," I said.

"Sure it is," he said. "Love is love."

"You think that," I said, "because you don't have kids."

He shook his head. "That's bullshit."

"I dare you," I said, "to live my life for one hour and not go crazy with worry."

"I'd be great at your life," O'Connor said.

"Really."

"I'd make all kinds of improvements."

"Like?"

"I'd sing more," he said. "I'd ask for help when I needed it. I'd do nice things for my coworkers, like bake them cakes and give them presents." Then he eyed me. "And I'd chill the hell out about Abby."

"You really don't know what you're talking about."

"The world is full of kids like PeePants," O'Connor said. "How is she ever going to learn to deal with them if she doesn't get any practice?"

"She shouldn't *have* to deal with them!" I said.

"She shouldn't have to, but she will."

He was so wrong, I didn't even know how to explain it. "Normal playground stuff," I said, "that's fine. I get it. But a kid calling her Limper? That's unacceptable."

O'Connor shrugged. "She punched him in the solar plexus," he said, as if no other solution were needed.

"Violence," I said, as I told the kids just about every day, "is not the answer."

"What *is* the answer?" O'Connor challenged.

"I don't know," I said. "But I'm going to figure it out if it kills me."

When we got back to the farm, Jean and the kids were out in the yard with tinfoil hats on their heads. "Mama!" the kids shouted when they saw the truck pull into the yard. They ran to meet us, the dogs and goats trotting behind. I had to work my way through the herd to get to the kids, and while we were hugging, I heard Jean speak to O'Connor in a grave voice.

"I've been trying to get you on your phone," she said.

O'Connor swung the truck door shut. "I forgot to charge it."

"There's a problem with Erin," Jean said, and then they both looked over and waited for the kids and me to make ourselves scarce.

I herded the children over to the tire swings and satisfied myself with occasional glances over toward Jean and O'Connor, huddled in intense discussion. I strained my ears to listen, but I couldn't catch anything more than the hum of voices.

It was a long wait to get the scoop. It wasn't until after bedtime that Jean gave me the basics—the parts, at least, that affected me. The neighbor who'd been looking after Erin while O'Connor was at work had had a stroke that morning. She was in the hospital and doing well, but she would not be coming back to help him, even after her recovery period. That neighbor had been helping out for close to free, and O'Connor could not afford another caretaker.

"What does that mean?" I asked.

"That means he's going to have to do it himself," Jean said.

And so, I realized with a little drop in my stomach, we'd be seeing a lot less of him here at Jean's place.

"What's wrong with her?" I asked.

Jean frowned at me. "You know she was in a car accident?"

I nodded.

"Well," Jean said, "she's paralyzed now. Even worse, she's just kind of gone. She can hear sounds but not process language. She can see things but not read faces. She's awake, but she's in her own world."

I sighed. "With no hope of returning?"

Jean shook her head. "There was some hope early on. Not anymore, though." She poured hot water for tea. "She can't be left alone at all."

I studied Jean's face to see if things were as bad as they seemed.

"But O'Connor can still help with the milking, right?" I asked.

Jean shook her head. "Not unless he finds someone to help him—someone he can afford."

"He's not going to be here at all anymore?" I asked.

"Not until he figures something out."

"What's he going to live on? How's he going to make it?" I asked, fully expecting that Jean would know.

"Honestly," she said, frowning, "I really have no idea."

And so that evening I did the milking by myself—which took twice as long and felt twice as lonesome. I missed O'Connor's help, and I also missed his noise. The milking barn was awfully quiet with only the sound of that terrible machine filling it up. Where were O'Connor's a cappella renditions of "Stairway to Heaven," or "Hound Dog," or "More Than a Woman" in Bee Gees falsetto?

The barn felt darker and the work took longer, and out of desperation I even tried a little singing myself: Patsy Cline, in my best tribute voice. Which really just made things worse. The goats looked at me as though I'd gone mad. If they'd been able to place their hooves over their ears, they would have. After a while I asked Eleanor Roosevelt to convey my formal apology to the other girls, and we finished the rest of our work in silence.

———

Over the next week or so, Jean started many projects with the kids, including helping Tank write his own comic book series, sewing Abby-designed collars for the goats, and building, of all things, a treehouse.

Given the arthritis that was making it impossible for Jean to do the farm chores, it seemed like a fairly impossible undertaking when she first mentioned it one night at dinner.

"But how are you going to build it?" I asked.

Jean shrugged. "I'll delegate."

"Who are you going to delegate to?" I asked. "I'm working 24/7, O'Connor's gone. Who's left?"

"The children," Jean said, as if my kids built play structures in trees all the time. "And Russ can help. He's always looking for an excuse to come over."

It sounded vastly overambitious to me.

"It's going to be great," Jean said, in that convincing way she had. They'd already been collecting sticks and rocks and old coffee cans for a totem pole. Jean had some construction-grade timber stored in one of the barns. "And if it's a disaster," she said, reading my mind, "that'll be okay, too. We'll have had fun trying."

Truth be told, I worried less that they wouldn't get it done than that they would. The tree they'd picked was enormous. What if one of the kids fell out? What if the thing collapsed? Why on earth did people always have to go looking for trouble?

I didn't ask that question, though. I already knew how Jean would have answered it: *"Don't let worrying get in your way."* She'd said it to me countless times since we'd arrived—her own folksy take on carpe diem.

In fact, for everyone's own good, Jean and the kids had started doing dangerous things I never allowed—but doing them behind

my back. Like swimming, for example. Since Danny died, I had
only allowed the children to swim during lessons with a qualified
instructor. I never took them myself, because there was no way I
could watch both of them at the exact same time. I'd once read in
a child-safety article the words "drowning is silent"—meaning
don't expect your kids to splash and call for help if they start to
drown, because they won't. You'll just turn to ask a friend about
her vacation in Italy and your child will slip into a liquid grave.
That's what I thought of when I thought of "swimming." Not
splashing in the water, or tossing a beach ball, or the lovely
weightlessness you feel in water. I thought of death. People who
suggested I take the kids swimming might as well have suggested
I take them *drowning.*

Jean didn't understand it. "When you were a little kid, you ran
completely free," Jean said. "And you're fine."

"I'm not fine!" I said. "And you know I didn't run completely
free—not with a mother like Marsha."

Jean almost said something, but then she closed her mouth.

"Look," I said, "I don't care about me thirty years ago. I care
about these guys now. And if I have to give up some fun to keep
them alive, I will."

Anger sparked in Jean's face. "You don't get to raise them in
straitjackets, Marsha." Then she turned and marched up the hill
toward the house.

I followed. "Hey!" I shouted. "Hey! You just called me 'Marsha.'"

Jean paused and turned back. "Did I?" she said, as if she
hadn't noticed. Then she put her hands on her hips. "Well, you're
acting just like her!"

And there was the trump card. Calling me Marsha. In that
moment, without even speaking a word, we enacted a don't-ask-

don't-tell policy on what Jean did with the kids. When she was in charge, she got to be in charge. And if they did anything other than sit quietly in the library and read, I didn't want to know about it.

"I know what you're thinking," Jean said about the tree house at dinner that night. "And I'm very proud of you for not saying anything."

"I'm fighting with myself something fierce," I said.

"Good girl," she said. "Keep up the fight."

The sun was setting. We were at the red kitchen table with a spring breeze blowing through the screen door. Jean had barbecued ribs for dinner and convinced the kids to pretend they were lions devouring the meat of their prey. She had taught them the words *"devour"* and *"prey,"* too—along with *"carnivore"*—which sounded so funny coming out of their mouths.

"Has anyone noticed me *devouring* my *prey*?" Tank kept asking, his face covered in barbecue sauce.

And Abby piped up with statements like, "I am *devouring* my corn on the cob, too, even though I am a *carnivore*."

The kids had so much sauce on their hands they looked like they'd been finger-painting with it. After an entire day of working in Jean's garden and building mud forts and tumbling around the farmyard, they were filthy—covered in grass stains and dirt smudges. But they looked wonderful. Taller and leaner than when we'd arrived. And happier.

I was admiring them when we heard a car pull up outside, tires popping the gravel on the driveway. My eyes met Jean's. It might have been Russ, scavenging for dinner. It might have been Sunshine, doing the same. Or—and I found myself involuntarily snapping to attention at this idea—it might have been O'Connor.

It was too dark now to see out the window. We kept eating as the car door slammed, footsteps crossed the gravel and knocked up the steps, and someone appeared under the porch light at the back door. We turned to look, and there, in high heels and pantyhose, with the exact expression she might have worn if she were standing on the steps of a crack house, was my mother.

Jean froze, and so did the kids. Something about the way she appeared out of the blackness—and the shadows the light from above cast on her face—made her seem far more terrifying than any visiting grandmother ever ought to be.

After a pause, Jean seemed to make a choice to go back to eating. "Screen's unlatched," she said, not as an invitation, but to make sure my mother knew that she wasn't going to interrupt her own dinner to open the door.

I stood up as my mom stepped in. "Hi, Mom."

She edged carefully into the room, as if she might get ambushed at any minute. The kids tried to move in for a hug, but my mom backed away when she saw their sauce-covered hands and faces. I intercepted quickly, as I was always doing, to cover. "Let's save those sweet hugs for Grandma," I said, "until after you've had your bath."

I wiped them down a little with my own napkin and herded them outside to sit on the porch swing for "one minute only."

A good thing, too, because the screen door had barely smacked closed when Jean said to my mother, "I don't know what you think you're doing here, Marsha. But you are not welcome."

"I'm here to see my *daughter*," my mother said. "And my *grandchildren*."

"She may be your daughter," Jean said, "but this is my house. And you've got five minutes before I drag you out of it by the pantyhose."

Jean followed the kids to the porch. I had never seen her talk to anybody like that. I had never heard her voice so low and threatening. There was really only one word for it: *hatred*. It wasn't air that was moving through her vocal cords right then. It was hatred.

My mother shrugged it off. As soon as Jean was out, she turned right to me, all snappy and businesslike.

"I'm here to bring you home," she said.

"I thought you had disowned me," I said.

"That's ridiculous."

"You told me that if I came here, then I was no longer your daughter."

"I never said that."

I knew she'd deny it. Denying things was her signature move.

She waved her hands, as if to fast-forward the conversation. "You can come home now," she said again, as if spelling out the obvious.

"Mom," I said, "I don't *want* to come home."

She wasn't listening. "Let's move quick, before she gets her shotgun. Or sets the goats on us."

I sighed. "We're not leaving. We're fine here."

She wasn't about to believe it. "I don't know what I've done to make you so rebellious and angry—"

"I am not rebellious! Or angry!"

"Look at you," she went on. "In those overalls! You're filthy. Your children are filthy! You're living in a—" She looked around. "In a hovel! You must hate me so bitterly to keep yourself here."

"This is not about you!" I said. But it was useless. As far as my mother was concerned, everything was about her. If I was five minutes late, I didn't love her enough to be on time. If a TV show got canceled, the network didn't want her to be happy. If a traffic light turned red, the universe was slowing her down. I knew that. She'd never been any different. She just couldn't conceive of a world that didn't make its choices based on how those choices made her feel.

"That's fine," my mother said, taking a new tack. "I drove all the way out here, but that's fine."

"I didn't ask you to drive out here."

"No!" she agreed. "Because you aren't speaking to me!"

"Hey!" I said, stupidly trying to set the record straight. "*You* are not speaking to *me*."

"I go on my vacation," she went on, a tone of amazement in her voice, "and when I come back, the house is cleaned out. No note. No phone call."

She'd been doing this my whole life: taking perfectly true facts and reshuffling them until they weren't true anymore. "You *told* me to go! You *told* me to be out before you came back!"

"It's like I don't even have a daughter."

I was shouting now. "You *told* me you didn't have a daughter!"

Now she had me where she wanted me. "That's fine. You needed me, and I was there. You were widowed and alone, and I was there. Who opened her home to you when you had nowhere else to go?"

Then, right there in the kitchen, my fingers still covered in barbecue sauce, looking at the face of the woman I'd fought with so many times, I realized I didn't have to fight. I didn't have to answer her questions, justify my behavior, or follow her rules. And then I knew, out of nowhere, how to shut her down. So I summoned up my parent voice—one that sounded remarkably like Jean's—and I used it on my mom.

"I have to put the kids to bed now," I said, "and it's time for you to go. You're welcome to say good night to them. You're also welcome to visit us whenever you can do so in a pleasant way. We're happy to see you whenever you can behave appropriately."

And then I walked out the screen door and let it slap shut behind me.

Jean and the kids were at the tire swings by now. "Bedtime!" I called out.

My mother followed me to the yard. "I don't know what you—" she started, but I held up my hands.

"Stop!" I said. Then, to the kids, I said, "Say good night to Grandma."

The kids made their way toward us, Abby stopping to let Tank climb up onto her back for a precarious-looking piggyback ride. "Good night, Grandma," they said in unison.

My mother sighed. "Good night, children," she said. "I hope your mother will let me see you again someday."

"And we're done!" I practically shouted, pushing the children up toward the house and leaving my mother and Jean facing each other in the yard.

"Why does Grandma *hope* that she'll see us again?" Abby asked, old enough now to pick up on subtleties.

"She's kidding," I said as we stepped inside, trying for the millionth time in my life to make it seem like she wasn't so bad.

Once the kids were down, I returned to the kitchen to start on the dishes, planning to recount the conversation to Jean. But when I got there, the room was empty. I looked around. Barbecue sauce was everywhere—every wall, surface, pot, and plate. We had similarly devastated a pot roast of Jean's a few nights before, and as we'd joined forces to start cleaning, she'd looked around with a satisfied nod and said, "We really know how to live."

That night, though, I found myself looking at the kitchen with my mother's eyes—thinking about all the work it was going to take to scrub those pots and how I really hadn't managed to teach my kids any manners. Same kitchen, different view. I kept trying to shift my perspective back to Jean's, but it wouldn't budge.

As I stood at the sink, running hot water for the dishes, I heard my mother's voice through the window screen, and then I heard Jean's. I scanned the dark lawn for their shadows, and when I found them, I couldn't help but listen in.

They'd been at it for a while, judging from the strain in their voices.

"I don't care," my mother was saying. "And you wouldn't care about me if the situation were reversed."

"I don't know how I would feel if the situation were reversed," Jean said. "But it's not reversed, Marsha. It is how it is."

"Maybe I'll just tell Libby," my mother said. "Maybe she deserves to know."

"There are a lot of things Libby deserves to know that I haven't told her," Jean said. "And if you tell her my secrets, I'll be more than happy to tell her yours."

"I'm surprised you haven't told her already," my mother said.

"You're the one who should have told her," Jean said. "Years ago."

"You just want her to hate me."

"I don't care what Libby thinks of you," Jean said. "I only care about what she thinks of me."

Then a pause. I could see their silhouettes out on the lawn, staring each other down.

"When you tell her," my mother said, "she'll leave. She'll be gone so fast she'll leave tire skids on the road."

"Maybe," Jean said.

"And she'll come back home to me, and you'll be forgotten."

"Just like old times," Jean said. The bitterness in her voice cut the air.

A few minutes later I heard my mother's car start up and, just after, Jean creaking open the screen door. She paused at the sight of me.

"Hello," I said, all innocent.

"Hello."

"What did my mom have to say?" I asked, scrubbing the skillet with steel wool.

"Oh," Jean said, "same old same old." She rubbed her eyes and then asked, "Could you hear us talking?"

"Some," I said with a shrug.

Jean started clearing plates off the table and bringing them to the sink. "How much?"

"Well, you both have secrets you don't want me to know," I said. "But I didn't catch what they were."

"Oh," Jean said, her brow still in a tense frown.

I could have taken this moment to ask her what they were talking about, and I'm sure she would have told me. For some reason, though, I just didn't.

Looking back, it's hard to imagine that I could have made such a decision. I think, more than anything, I wanted to keep things the way they were. I didn't want anything about our life on the farm to change. Especially not just because my mother had decided to pay a surprise visit. It was a kind of protecting what was mine. My new life. My new job. My new beloved aunt Jean.

We stood side by side at the sink for a bit after that, me washing and her drying. Bob Dylan barked now and again and got the

little dogs yipping, and I felt like Jean and I were making a mu-
tual silent decision to drop it.

A little later, though, as Jean went to wipe down the table, she
said, "I need to tell you something."

I felt a sting of anxiety. I wanted to beg her not to tell me.
Whatever it was.

"That woman really isn't welcome here," she went on. "You
don't have to take on—" She paused. "My *sorrows* just because
you're here. I understand if you want to see your mother or visit
with her. That's your right, and I don't think it's a bad thing." She
took a breath. "But just not here. I don't ever want to see her in
my house again."

"Of course," I said, relieved. "I understand."

After Jean had gone upstairs, I stepped out the back door and
sat on the porch swing. Yes, my mother was a narcissistic pain in
the ass. Yes, she never let anyone else be right, even for a minute.
Yes, she was exhausting, and crazy, and infuriating. But I had to
admit she had some good qualities, too. She was wickedly funny
sometimes. She had great taste in jewelry. And she was a great
cook when she was in the mood. We were fighting now, and she
was always at her craziest during a fight—but I couldn't help
thinking that some other time, when we weren't so mad, she
might have enjoyed a visit here. From a distance—sometimes a
great distance—she wasn't so bad.

The thought made me miss her just the tiniest bit, and the feeling took me by surprise. But there was nothing to be done. Instead I just sat there, circling around all that had just happened,
guessing at the secrets, and trying to fathom what on earth could
have happened between two sisters to leave them so intractably
full of hate for so long.

Chapter 14

With O'Connor gone, possibly never to return, Jean wound up hiring Sunshine to help out in the mornings. Jean wouldn't say that O'Connor had quit, exactly, only that he had "other priorities" at the moment.

I was ecstatic to see Sunshine arrive—on April Fool's Day, in fact, which was perfect because she was absolutely terrible at everything I asked her to do. She was the Amelia Bedelia of farm help, but by then I had been doing everything by myself long enough that even that was better than nothing.

She was pleasant to talk to, if a little odd-looking in her black combat boots and black lipstick. It was a wonder she didn't frighten the goats. The only thing that wasn't black on Sunshine, actually, was the roots of her hair. The ends were still dark as obsidian, but the longer she went without dyeing it again, the clearer it was that the roots were a perky, cheerful blond.

"Are you growing out your hair?" I asked one day in the barn.

"Nah," she said. "I'm just going two-tone."

"But those blond roots," I said. "Is that your real color?"

Sunshine raised an eyebrow. "No blonde jokes," she said.

I wanted to ask her why on earth she would cover up that golden hair with dye, but I never did. She had her reasons. I wanted very much to ask her about her former famous life, but I just couldn't. If she wanted to avoid the life itself, she probably wanted to avoid the topic, too. Instead we just talked about little local happenings, as if neither of our lives had ever been any different. The weather. The vintage Ford Fairlane that Russ was rebuilding out in their garage. The progress Jean and the kids were making on the tree house—which now had a rope net for climbing, a roof made out of flattened tin cans, and, down low, a pirate's plank.

Also, of course, we talked about the goats. Whose lives turned out to be almost as compelling as our own—to Sunshine, at least. Laura Ingalls Wilder, for example, had eaten Jean's favorite rose bush, and Mother Teresa was pregnant again. Helen Keller had gotten stuck in the mud down at the pond and had to be rescued, a process that took an hour. And Ella Fitzgerald, Ethel Merman, and Oprah Winfrey had formed a little clique of late and would not give the other goats the time of day.

Sunshine couldn't get over the way those three isolated themselves under the bois d'arc tree. "What do you think they're talking about?" she kept asking as she glanced over.

"They're not talking, Sunshine," I said. "They're goats."

"They've got some kind of secret," Sunshine insisted. "Look at how they're huddled."

"You do know they can't talk, right?"

"I know they can't talk in a way you and I can understand," Sunshine said, taking all my condescension and lobbing it right back.

I ceded the point.

But I did like it when she was there. The rest of the day, it was mostly just me doing chores alone. Jean worked in the garden some, and she cooked all the meals, but she was also gone quite a bit while the kids were at school. She was always visiting the sick, or helping people with projects, or sewing things for auctions. She shelved books at the library and sang with the church choir, even though she didn't actually go to church. She belonged to a quilting club, a book club, and also the Ladies' BBC Period Love 'n' Romance Club, which TiVoed *Masterpiece Theater* and watched the episodes together while eating chocolate and drinking champagne.

My mom had always portrayed Jean as a lonely hillbilly out in an isolated cabin—kind of a lady Unabomber with only goats for friends. But she was the opposite of alone. She had a gravitational force that pulled people toward her. Wherever she happened to be always turned into the center of it all.

I was not the center of anything, out in the barn by myself. And so even though Sunshine and I were not exactly soul mates, we became better friends—faster—out in the barn together than we might have otherwise. At the end of our second week, when she showed up at work with her face all puffy from crying, I asked her right away what was wrong—and I felt genuinely anxious to know.

"You know about me, right?" she asked. "Jean told you who I am?"

I didn't want to get Jean in trouble. "She just told me your real name. Then I knew the rest."

Sunshine pursed her lips and blew out a big sigh. Then she grabbed a milking stool and got to work.

"What's going on?"

She sat up a little straighter, and rubbed her eyes with her sleeve. "I broke up with my boyfriend," she said.

"I didn't know you had a boyfriend," I said.

"I usually don't," she said. "I decided a while back that romance upset my equilibrium."

I walked Jane Goodall up onto the milking platform and got to work next to Sunshine. If she wanted to keep busy, we'd keep busy.

"Dating is tricky for me," Sunshine went on, "because I have a history with every boy in this town. Even ones I've never met."

"Because of that *Playboy* you did?"

She closed her eyes and nodded. "He had it under his bed for two years. Until his grandmother found it and threw it away."

"That's a long time," I said.

She nodded. "Two long, formative, hormone-driven years."

"This is why you broke up with him?"

"He wants me to grow my hair out blond. And go on a diet. He said, 'You used to be so hot.'"

I winced for her. "What did you say?"

"I said, 'I don't want to be hot anymore, you stupid gorilla.'"

"And what did he say?"

"I tried to explain to him how exhausting and crazy-making being hot is, but he refused to hear it. We went around and around. And then it hit me: He wants the centerfold. He *prefers* the centerfold."

I shook my head in sympathy.

"So I dumped him," Sunshine said.

"Good!" I said, making sure my voice sounded triumphant.

Hers sounded far less so. "I really liked him."

"Maybe he'll come around."

"Maybe," she said. "But now I know he likes the old me better.

It's like I'm competing against my old self—and losing. And that wasn't even really me! Even when I looked like that, I didn't look like that."

"Maybe you could move away," I suggested, thinking that starting over was a possibility.

"Where could I go?" she said, then added, "Besides, I can't leave Russ."

Then I had to ask. "What was it like? Being famous?"

Sunshine shrugged. "Lonesome, mostly."

I waited.

"You have a lot of things," she said. "And you have a lot of people you don't know being overly nice to you for no reason. But real friends are hard to come by. And without real friends, you can't talk about real things."

I hadn't thought of it like that. I wondered what it must have been like to downgrade from a mansion in Pacific Palisades to one room in Russ's old farmhouse.

Sunshine gave me a smile and went on. "Real friends are no walk in the park, either. But they're sure better than nothing. Which is what I had before."

That night I had a terrible nightmare. It was about Danny, and it felt so real, I woke up with no idea where I was. In the dream, I was at the farmers' market, and I looked up to see Danny talking to Jessica Boone. She was looking at him in the same lascivious way she'd looked at O'Connor, and then she took Danny's arm and wrapped it around her shoulders as she led him away.

I woke to my alarm—Dubbie the rooster letting loose on the morning—out of breath and with real tears on my face. I was still shaken by the time I'd made it to the milking barn. Sunshine was already there, and the minute she saw my blotchy eyes, she said, "What?"

"Nothing," I said, turning away.

"Horseshit," she said. "Tell me."

I met her eyes. It felt like a tipping point. Then I just said, "I dreamed about my husband last night. And it was awful."

Sunshine stood up. "You dreamed about your husband?"

"It's like he was *just* here," I said. "It's like I *just* saw him."

"Well," Sunshine said, "you know what I'm going to say."

"Actually, I don't."

"He wants to talk to you."

"No," I said. "He doesn't. That's the point! He was walking away."

Sunshine smiled and shook her head. "He walked away," she said, "because he wants you to follow him."

It seemed to me that the dream was much more about the ways that Danny and O'Connor were starting to overlap in my heart than about anything supernatural. But of course Sunshine wouldn't know about what was going on in my heart. Because of all the things I found myself discussing with her, my funny little crush on O'Connor was not one of them.

"So," I said, to steer the conversation nice and far away from my thoughts, "you think it's a sign?"

"Yes," Sunshine said.

"And you think you can talk to him?"

"I can't," she said. "But you can. And I can bring him to you."

"I don't think I want you to."

"Wouldn't you like to see him?" Sunshine asked. "Wouldn't that make you feel better?"

"No," I said, "I think it would make me feel worse."

"You need this! You deserve this!" Sunshine said. "And I can do this for you. Please let me. It's the only thing I'm good at."

I don't know exactly what it was in Sunshine's voice that made me give in. In the same way you do things for your kids that you really don't want to do, at last I found myself agreeing to do a séance with Sunshine. Not because I wanted to. Not because anything about it seemed like a good idea. I gave into Sunshine just from the sheer force of her wanting me to.

"Okay," I said, totally defeated.

"It'll be the most romantic thing in the history of humanity," she said.

I was futzing with the milking machine and didn't answer.

"Won't it?" she demanded.

"Yes," I answered. "I'm sure it will."

"We'll have to do some séances," she went on. "At least ten or so. And then, presto—there he'll be."

"Ten séances seems like a lot," I said.

"A lot?" Sunshine demanded. "For bringing back the dead?"

"Okay," I said, shrugging at her point.

"You're going to love this," she promised, eyes bright with anticipation. "And you're going to love me for making it happen." Then she came over and gave me a suffocating hug. "Lady," she said, letting go and just burbling over with delight at the whole idea, "I am so totally about to become your very best friend."

Chapter 15

Sunshine wanted to do our first séance at the stroke of midnight, but I was way too tired for that. I countered with 9:00 P.M., and even though she drove a hard bargain, we finally settled on 10:00.

"Ten it is," she said, all business. "And don't tell Jean. She'll talk you out of it."

That's how I wound up, at 9:56 on a Saturday night, sneaking out the back door of my bedroom like a naughty teenager, rolling my minivan down the gravel drive in neutral with the lights off, and hoping like hell that Jean and Russ, who were in the kitchen playing Scrabble, didn't come out to ask what on earth I was up to.

Next thing, I was stopping for Sunshine and her backpack of séance supplies—which, incidentally, included a Magic 8 Ball—at Russ's gate.

"I didn't think you'd really come," Sunshine said as she popped open the door.

"Hop in," I said, and I was pulling away before she had even closed it.

Back home, I never would have left my children in the middle of the night without telling anyone. I never would have gone anywhere at all—and if I had, I'd have left pages of typed instructions for the babysitter on how to handle any conceivable emergency.

But things had shifted. I knew my kids weren't going to wake up and look for me, because they never woke up anymore. I also knew that even if for some reason they did, Jean would handle it just fine.

We drove to the top of the hill and then took a left on a dark road that led into the woods. We had to make three U-turns before we found the entrance Sunshine wanted. Finally she spotted a fence post with neon green ribbon tied to it. "Here," she said, and I pulled into what had once been a gravel driveway. Now it was so overgrown it was almost invisible. I pulled up and stopped with the nose of the minivan almost touching a closed gate.

Sunshine hopped out of the passenger seat and opened the gate.

"Is this it?" I asked.

She nodded. "Pull forward and turn on your brights."

I did. And after we pushed through a small grove of trees, branches scraping the windows, we came to a clearing with an enormous—and, from the looks of things—abandoned house. It was perfect for a séance, with its faded grandeur and peeling paint.

Sunshine gestured with her arm as if she were introducing us. "The haunted house," she announced. "If you want to speak to the dead in this town, or lose your virginity, this is the spot."

We got out of the car and walked toward the house. Under the trees, shaded from the moonlight, it was so black I could barely see my feet, but in its clearing, the house was lit by the moon. The glow made it ethereal, and for a minute it did feel a little bit like anything was possible in its presence.

But then I walked into a picnic table—clonked my shin right into the wooden seat—and shouted, "Oh, shit!" as I hopped around and clutched at it.

"Shh!" Sunshine said.

"Who's going to hear me?" I asked. "The netherworld?"

"It's disrespectful," Sunshine said. "You kiss your children with that mouth?"

This from a girl who had flashed her thong at an entire nation on late-night TV.

Sunshine pulled a flashlight out of her bag and flipped it on.

"That's helpful," I said.

"Take it," she said, and so I did, but I found it only made the darkness darker.

I thought we must be going to the house, but we walked right past it. Sunshine was quieter and more serious than I'd ever seen her, and I noticed my own heart ticking a little faster than usual. What if I got eaten by the panther? Or chopped up by an axe murderer? Or entombed in the cellar by a vengeful ghost? I scolded myself a little for taking unnecessary risks, but I noticed something, even as I did it: Being in the woods at night, tromping along behind Sunshine with no idea where I was going, feeling a little bit scared . . . it was fun.

I felt like a wild teenager—the kind of wild teenager I had never been. Life with my mother had been wild enough, and I'd become a grown-up far too young. That was how I coped with uncertainty: balancing my checkbook, even at thirteen; doing all my homework and then some; and putting all my faith in the ideas of responsibility and attention to detail. That was my whole life—and never more so than lately, after losing Danny.

Now, however, some not-insignificant part of my psyche was begging to swirl around through life's uncertainties. Danger! Adventure! I hadn't imagined how good those things felt until I was actually feeling them.

"Let's go in the house," I suggested.

"There's not really much inside."

"You've been in?" I asked.

"Sure," she said. "Tons of times. It's empty. Except for the dead body."

It was too dark for Sunshine to see my face. "I'm rolling my eyes at you," I told her.

I was no expert, but I guessed the house was at least a hundred years old, if not more. The deep veranda, the tall windows: It had the shape of another place in time.

"What's the story on this place?" I asked, lingering.

"There are tons of stories," Sunshine said. "It's supposed to be haunted about ten different ways." Then she added, "The kids come up here before prom and play truth or dare and get each other pregnant."

I took a step closer, but Sunshine grabbed my hand and pulled me in the other direction—out to a little spot in the yard where a potpourri of discarded lawn chairs circled a campfire pit made from collected stones. Sunshine had some matches in her pocket, and there were still some half-burned logs in the ashes. A can of lighter fluid sat stashed in the crook of a tree, and she gave the logs a dousing.

The fire caught with a *fwoomph,* and then we each took a chair.

"How long has the fire pit been here?" I asked.

"As long as I can remember," she said.

"Did you grow up in Atwater?"

"No, but I came out every summer to visit Russ, so I knew everybody."

"And this is where we're doing the séance?" I asked.

"Yep," Sunshine said. She scooted her chair up close to mine until our knees were touching. Then, beside the fire, she took my two hands and told me to close my eyes. "Repeat after me," she said. "And really mean it."

"Okay."

"Danny," she said.

"Danny," I said, realizing in the moment that we were calling to him—and then feeling a sting of longing for the days when I used to do that all the time.

"Please come see me."

"Please come see me."

I waited for more, but that was it. After a minute, I opened my eyes to look at her. This was worse than the palm reading. She had relaxed back into her chair.

"That's it?" I said, disappointed despite myself.

"That's it for now," Sunshine said.

"Then what?" I asked.

"We come back here a bunch more times," Sunshine explained, as if she'd already told me.

"How many times?" I asked.

"Until it works," she said.

I tilted my head. "I'm sorry, but it doesn't seem like it's enough."

"Your love makes it enough," she said. "Trust me."

I turned toward the fire. If loving Danny was enough to bring him back, it seemed like I would have managed to do that long before now.

"Did you hear about the time I OD'd?" Sunshine asked then.

"Yes," I said. "Everybody in the whole country heard about that."

"Well," Sunshine went on, "that night? I died."

"You died?"

She nodded. "I was clinically dead for seven minutes."

I took that in.

"And while I was there, I saw my father, who was dead, too."

I nodded for her to go on.

"I wanted to stay with him worse than I've ever wanted anything in my entire life. But they pulled me back to life. Then they forced me into rehab. And in rehab I met this really cute guy named Ernesto, and we started hanging out all the time, and one night I told him about how I'd seen my dad, and do you know what he said?"

"What?"

"He said, 'I can bring him back to you.' "

"Okay," I said.

"Turned out Ernesto was stealing pharmaceuticals from the nurses' station and mixing them into concoctions with Snapples from the vending machine. The next night he mixed me up a potion, and I drank it, and when I went to sleep, I saw my dad again. We had Mexican food and margaritas."

"I can't believe a total stranger mixed up stolen pharmaceuticals with fruit juice and you just drank it."

"I'd drink anything back then."

"What if it had killed you?"

"At the time I didn't really care," she said. "Besides"—she gestured to her living self for proof—"it didn't."

All I could do was shake my head. I couldn't relate to any piece of this story. I'd always been a rule follower. Of course, even now I couldn't say that good behavior had always paid off. If trouble wants to find you badly enough, it will.

"Sunshine," I said at last, "what were you thinking?"

She shrugged. "You're missing the point. I'm telling what you what I learned."

I gave in. "What did you learn?"

"You don't need the potion. All you need is to know the truth."

"What truth?"

"That the dead can find you in dreams."

After that, we watched the fire and ate snacks. Sunshine had brought an entire bag of marshmallows, enough chocolate bars and graham crackers to feed a whole troop of Cub Scouts, and some organic beer.

"Beer?" I said.

"It's organic," she said, like that made it healthy.

Once we'd covered the basics of the paranormal, she seemed far more interested in eating than communing with the afterlife. We ate s'mores, got sleepier and sleepier, and watched the flames eat up the logs. The evening felt more cozy than spooky, and I found myself not wanting to go home.

We talked about lots of things then, with the pressure of the séance off—from raising kids to favorite books to first kisses. When the marshmallows were gone, the beers were drunk, and the fire was down to embers, we started cleaning up, and out of nowhere Sunshine said, "What do you think of O'Connor?"

"O'Connor?" I said, like I'd never thought about him before.

"Isn't he yummy?"

"Is he?" I said. "I can't tell through the beard."

"I've been crushed out on him for years," Sunshine said.

"Even though he's, like, my third cousin or something." Then a sigh. "Our babies would have two heads."

"O'Connor's your cousin?" I asked.

"Our grandmothers were cousins," she said.

"That's surprising," I said.

"Not really," Sunshine said. "In a town this small, everybody's related somehow."

We started making our way back toward the car. The night seemed much brighter now, and I didn't even turn on the flashlight. "Besides," she went on, "he's totally devoted to Erin."

"What's the story there?" I asked, as if we were still discussing the health benefits of organic beer.

"They were high school sweethearts," Sunshine said. "Though it was kind of on again, off again. Then they got married. Then the accident."

I nodded.

"It's sad for her," she said, "but it's sadder for him." We started walking back toward the car. "He can't leave her alone. He can't go anywhere, or work. He's burning through his savings. Russ thinks he'll go nuts in that house by himself all day long and he'll go running naked through the town square."

We'd made it to the car, and Sunshine kept talking as we got in and buckled up. "Erin has a sister, but she lives far away. Africa, maybe. Or Antarctica. Some continent that starts with *A*."

"So he's just trapped," I said, turning the key in the ignition and backing out onto the road.

"Pretty much," Sunshine said.

"Has he ever considered finding a place for her?"

Sunshine shook her head. "He won't even talk about it."

"He's willing to ruin his own life to take care of her," I said.

Sunshine nodded. "Yep." She was quiet for a moment, pondering O'Connor's situation and the choices he had made. "Maybe it's because that's just who he is. Or maybe it's because of the in-sickness-and-in-health part of the wedding vows. Or," she went on, leaning back against the headrest and putting a foot up on the dashboard, "maybe it's because on the night of the accident, he was driving."

Chapter 16

I figured Jean would know I had snuck out with Sunshine. I fully expected her to make a comment about it the next morning and give me a look over the edge of her glasses. The more I knew about Jean, the more I believed she was impossible to fool.

As I woke up that morning, I thought about what I would say when the moment came, and I realized I wasn't sure if Jean would applaud me for getting out and having an adventure or chide me for, of all possible adventures, choosing that particular one.

Jean knew about grief. She knew what it was like to lose the most important person in your life. She knew exactly the kind of determination it required to accept that no, you would never see that person again, and yes—you would have to go on living. To go back and toy with the idea of finding Danny—no matter how unseriously I took it—when I'd only just barely survived losing him? Now that I imagined it through Jean's eyes, it seemed like a stupid thing to do.

On the other hand, Jean also wanted me to take more risks

and to have fun. And whatever else my night out with Sunshine might have been, I couldn't deny that it had been fun. I'd come back smelling like campfire smoke and riding a s'mores-induced sugar buzz, humming with the contentment of just having a good time with a friend. When was the last time I'd goofed around like that? I couldn't even remember.

Of course, Jean was a friend, too. Many nights, after the dishes, we played Scrabble at the kitchen table, or Boggle, or cards. But Jean also had one foot in the "mother" category—or possibly the "fairy godmother" category. She was always trying to help me. In almost every conversation we had, I could find life lessons, gentle nudgings, and unspoken encouragements. I felt the pressure of her investment in me—her genuine hope that I'd figure things out and become more resilient—powering every interaction. Which was fine, and not unpleasant, but a very different thing from eating burned marshmallows by firelight with a person who's just as lost as you—or, as Tank would say, "even loster."

As it turned out, Jean never did ask me about the séance. The next morning progressed like any other. I got the kids up, and then Jean fed us all on barn eggs and homemade butter. The only thing different about that morning was me: I was quieter than usual. Because even though the séance had been about Danny and the adventure had been about Sunshine, the person it had left me thinking about was O'Connor.

How strange that we'd both lost our spouses in car accidents. What a weird connection to have with someone. Even though O'Connor's wife was still alive, if things were as bad as Sunshine said, he'd lost her just the same: the person she'd been, the marriage they'd had. And we both had guilt—mine for picking a fight with Danny, his for the fact that he'd been driving. And we both had caretaking to do in the wake of those accidents: me with two kids, one of them injured, to raise all alone (worse than alone, if you counted my mother), and him with a person who "wasn't there" to look after. Very different situations, of course. But weirdly similar. Similar enough to distract me from the kids and breakfast and getting the morning done—until I noticed Tank suddenly right in front of my face, saying, "Can we go? Can we go?"

"Go where?"

He climbed up in my lap. "To Jean's party!"

"Mom," Abby said in a very adult voice, "weren't you listening? It's Jean's birthday next week."

"It is?" I looked over at Jean, who was pouring us coffee.

"The fifteenth," she said, nodding. "The ides of April."

"She just told us that!" Tank shouted, delighted to catch me being stupid. "Earth to Mama!"

"Didn't you hear her?" Abby asked. "She said she's going to be sixty!" Abby said the word as if Jean were about to turn one thousand.

"Sixty!" I said, trying to set an age-positive example. "How wonderful!"

"Sixty is supposed to be very magical," Jean added.

Tank looked impressed. "You'll be able to do magic?"

"I can already do magic," Jean said.

"But maybe you'll be able to do extra," Abby said.

"Is Mama invited to the party, too?" Tank asked.

"Oh, yes," Jean said. "Everybody I like is invited to the party."

"So not our grandma, then," Abby said, making Jean choke on a sip of coffee. "Since you don't like her."

Tank frowned. "Jean doesn't like Grandma?"

Abby gave Tank a knowing look. "Jean *detests* Grandma," she said. Jean had just taught Abby the word *detest*.

"What makes you think that?" Jean asked.

"Oh, Aunt Jean, it's so obvious," Abby said, busting out another new word.

Tank didn't seem to care much. "I'm going to buy you Legos," he chirped to Jean.

"I love Legos," she said. "But I have a rule about my birthday. . ."

Abby had picked up on Jean's tone. "No presents?" she asked.

"Oh, no. I love presents," Jean said. "But no one is allowed to buy them."

Abby considered this a minute before deciding to clarify. "You want us to steal them?"

"Not steal," Jean said. "Find."

She was serious. She wanted gifts, but she forbade anybody to spend any money. Easy for the kids—a rock or a pinecone could suffice—but trickier for me. Jean deserved something very special from me, something that at least attempted to thank her for rescuing us in the way she had. It would have been a challenge even without this new restriction.

Jean didn't want to talk about presents, though. She wanted to talk about the party. She was inviting everyone she knew—which pretty much meant the whole town—to the dance hall for a jamboree. The guys from her old band would play, and a friend of Russ's would call the square dancing.

"The square dancing?" I asked.

Jean read my face. "You're going to love it," she promised. "It'll be the most fun you ever have."

"That's a heck of a prediction," I said.

Jean nodded in agreement. "It sure is."

"Can the fact that I'm willing to square-dance be my present to you?"

"Nope," Jean said. "You're giving me something else."

"I am?" I asked.

"Yep," Jean said. "It's all decided."

"What am I giving you?"

"A haircut," she said, holding up two fingers like scissors. "For O'Connor."

I thought about the haircut on and off all week, both eager for it and dreading its arrival.

I resolved to do a great job for Jean. She assured me that there was nothing I could give her that she'd want more.

"What's O'Connor giving you?" I asked.

"A haircut," she said. "From you."

The first time the notion had come up, months before, the idea of cutting O'Connor's hair had seemed ridiculous. And inappropriate. And unappealing. But now it felt different. I gave in to a feeling of pleasant anticipation as real and tingly as if I'd just lowered myself into a steaming hot bath. The prospect of seeing O'Connor again was good, and the fact that I'd get to run my hands all over his hair was even better.

Jean was going to help by staying with Erin so O'Connor could come over. She had also arranged for a friend from town to stay at the house a little later—during the party itself—so that O'Connor could come and join us. She said no one in the world needed a night out worse than he did.

The day of the party, while the kids were still at school and Sunshine and I were feeding the hens, O'Connor pulled into the yard in his truck for the first time in weeks. I stood up straight when I saw him, and then, without hesitation, marched right out to meet him, just to shave another forty-five seconds off the wait.

He slammed the truck door, and there he was, real as ever. The same long stride, the same jeans that bunched around the ankles of his boots. The sight of him was so delicious that I had to remind myself to keep walking—and not just stop to savor it.

When we got close, I hesitated. We should have hugged, probably. The way we'd walked toward each other certainly warranted it. Isn't that how you greet a friend you haven't seen in weeks? It would have been completely justified to put my arms around him and let him do the same. But I chickened out. We stopped short about a foot away from each other, and the moment crackled with the change of plan. After a pause, I put my hand out to shake, and we both looked at it in surprise.

Then, in a gesture of kindness that pushed all the awkwardness away, he reached out and his hand seemed to swallow mine up. We shook.

"Hey," he said.

"How are you?" I asked, hoping it felt more like a real question than a formality.

I hadn't let go of our handshake. When I realized it, I yanked back and dusted my hand on my overalls.

He put his own in his pocket. "I've consented to the haircut."

"So I see," I said.

O'Connor smiled at his boots. "Can't say no to Jean."

"Hell, no," I said.

"She said you had some clippers?"

I nodded.

"Let's fire 'em up," he said.

We turned toward the house.

"I washed it last night," he said, tousling the top of his head "Just to get all the fleas and cockroaches and old sandwiches out."

"Thoughtful," I said.

"I wasn't certain I'd really make it over here," he added, "but Jean sure has made things easy."

"Jean always makes things easy if you do what she wants."

O'Connor nodded. "Or even if you don't."

His hair did not look very washed to me, but maybe that was just the tangles. We walked toward the house together, and on the way I said, "You're sure you washed it?"

"Sure I'm sure," he said. "I used a fancy shampoo that smelled like green apples." He leaned his head toward me, in case I wanted to sniff it. Which I didn't.

Minutes later, he was straddling a dinette chair on the front porch, gazing out at the farmyard while I stood behind him with the clippers, feeling oddly hesitant. I'd cut Tank's hair a gazillion times, and before Tank, I'd cut Danny's. But those were the only two people whose hair I had ever cut. My two guys. And now, in the moment, it felt like a big deal to let O'Connor into the club.

But here we were. He was waiting. And it was just a haircut, after all.

I flipped the switch and started mowing his head, starting at the crown and working from front to back. A buzz seemed like the best solution, given our starting place, and O'Connor said he didn't care what I did. But the change was radical. It reminded me of movies about hippies who joined the army and got sheared for boot camp—the starkness of the change, the *nakedness* as the long hair fell away.

O'Connor sat perfectly still, and we did not talk. I was pleased to find once I started cutting that he'd been telling the truth about the shampoo: He did smell like green apples.

I pressed my fingers against his neck to steady him and stood just inches away—paying attention to my work, which meant, by default, paying attention to his body. I realized now, as the hair disappeared, that I'd been thinking of him more like a Muppet than a man. But now I saw many new things. The tendons that connected the back of his head to his shoulders, for example. And the lumps of the vertebrae in his neck as he bent forward. And his ears: well proportioned and flat against his head. He had a little scar at his hairline near his right temple, and I wondered how he'd gotten it.

"You're very symmetrical," I said at last, worrying I'd been quiet for too long.

"People are always telling me that," he said.

To trim above his ears, I had to fold them down. That tickled him a bit, and he wriggled. So I put my eyes in front of his the way I sometimes did with Tank and said, "Gotta be still, okay? Otherwise you'll get a zigzag."

You can't stand that close to someone for any length of time without creating a tangible relationship between bodies. I could see his chest rising and falling as he drew his breaths in and out, and that made me aware of my own. I could see his arms resting and still as he waited, and that made me aware of my own arms as they worked. I could feel him averting his gaze from my body. I, on the other hand, had to look. I had to stand close, pay attention, and run my hands all over his head and neck in a way that you never do normally.

Still, I tried to focus on the head, not the person. I had a job to do. I was radically changing his appearance, and I wanted to do it right. Or, at least, I wanted not to do it wrong.

Soon we were ready to move on to his beard. I had him tilt his head back and I started low on his neck. Before I knew it, I was edging around his jaw, then his lips. His face emerged section by section as I went. And when I was done, I stood back and beheld his face for the first time.

I clicked off the clippers and stared.

"What?" he asked.

"I've just never seen you before," I said.

"Guess not."

"I always figured there must be a face under there somewhere."

He smiled as he brushed hairs off his shirt. "Can't put anything past you."

He was ready to see for himself, and so I led him inside to my bathroom, noting, even as we walked down the hall, that I could just as easily have taken him to the half bath by the kitchen, and wondering if he was noting the same thing. I knew that he was not free—and that just because the two of us were alone in the house with no one around for miles, it didn't change anything about our situation. All the same, I enjoyed the moment.

As we passed the open door to my bedroom, an image flashed through my head of the two of us sinking onto the bed in a totally luxurious kiss. It was so vivid that I actually paused to check the bedroom and make sure that it was still empty—that we were, in fact, still out in the hallway and it hadn't actually happened. When I turned back, O'Connor was already in the bathroom, inspecting my work.

"There I am," he said, checking himself out in the mirror. The hair was gone, the beard was gone. He had a newborn quality—so much skin. Meeting my eyes, he said, "Haven't seen myself in a while."

"It's okay?" I asked.

"Jean's going to love it," he said. Then he bent his head down to scratch it with the enthusiasm of a Labrador retriever. He reminded me so much of Tank and how he hated the "hair sprinkles" that haircuts left all over him. I always put him in the bath after a haircut so he wouldn't itch.

"Let's get that shirt off," I said to O'Connor, turning the shower knobs to high. Of course, that's when I noticed the dangling black bra I'd hung to dry over the shower rod. I pulled it down and stuffed it in my pocket. And then, because everything about the time we'd spent together so far seemed loaded with unintended meaning, the bathroom seemed to shrink, and the two of us stood there, unsure of what to say next, for easily the longest three seconds in the history of time.

"It's okay," he said then. "I can just hose off outside."

"That's crazy," I said, now refusing to buckle to the idea that there was anything suggestive about instructing him to get naked in my bathroom. "Shower," I said, using my mom voice on him, "and I'll go out front. And clean up."

I handed him a towel through the door—without looking—and he handed me his hair-sprinkled shirt to pop in the washer. I didn't think about how Jean didn't have a dryer until I'd already started the load, and so he'd either have to wait for it to dry or put it back on wet.

So washing the shirt might have been a mistake. But a little later, when he emerged from my bathroom all scrubbed clean and shirtless, I did have to admit that some mistakes turn out better than others.

O'Connor lingered a good while before going home. He mended a rusted hinge and changed the oil in Jean's truck. He stacked up some bags of feed, checked on the goats, and changed a lightbulb up high on the barn. He did a good many of these activities shirtless, but even after he put the shirt back on, I still kept sneaking peeks at him. I had gotten so used to him all overgrown and hairy. For there to have been a person under all that fur all along, it had my attention, for sure.

He kept feeling me staring. "What?"

"Nothing," I said.

"You're watching me."

"You just look different," I told him. "Really, really different."

"Better or worse?"

"Human," I said. "You were more like a farm animal before."

He met my eyes, and I wondered if I'd been too mean. Here he was, all shorn and naked like a baby sheep. Maybe his feelings were, too. "I think I just made you handsome," I said, to make up for it.

He laughed. And when he did, the edges of his eyes crinkled into those fans they made when he smiled. I'd missed seeing them.

When it was time for him to go, I followed him out to the car the way you do with people you won't see again for a while.

"See you tonight," he said, starting the ignition, and it seemed like a long time away.

But Jean returned with the kids not too long after O'Connor left, and the afternoon sped up again. Tank ran across the yard when they arrived and threw himself at me using his new invention: the "cannon hug," a cross between a cannonball, like you do at the pool, and a hug. This time his knee got me in the diaphragm, and we both hit the ground as I fell.

"You've got to warn me, man," I said. "What if I didn't manage to catch you?"

"You'll always catch me," he said, wrapping his little arms around my neck. And I so loved that idea that I didn't have the heart to set him straight.

By the time the kids had played and had a snack, we had an hour to get ready.

Jean's party was at the dance hall downtown, a hundred-year-old wooden structure. I'd driven by many times but had never been in. I asked Jean what I should wear, and she said, "Oh, something pretty."

The kids picked out "party clothes" themselves. For Abby, that meant a sundress with butterflies, and, for Tank, it meant a dragon costume leftover from two Halloweens before. When they'd made their selections, I said, "Perfect."

Abby gave me a hug around the middle, took a deep breath, and said, "Mama? You smell like the goats. No offense."

Time to shower. Down in my room, Abby read to Tank on the bed, and then, when I started to dress, Tank squinted at the sight and said, "I'm sorry we don't have a dragon costume in a mama size."

"That *would* be awesome," I said.

"If I were magic," Tank said, "I'd make this one enormous so you could borrow it."

"Thanks, pal," I said.

Abby helped zip up my dress—a blue one with a flouncy hem. I put on mascara and lipstick for the first time since moving here, and I let Abby dab some perfume on me. I even blow-dried my hair.

Tank watched me looking at myself in the mirror. "Why are you getting so fancy?" he asked.

Abby answered for me. "It's a sign of respect to the birthday girl."

"Correct," I said.

Tank frowned a little, like he did with his big questions. "I didn't think old people had birthdays."

"Everyone has birthdays," I explained.

"Even Daddy?" Tank asked.

"Yes," I said. "Even Daddy."

"He just doesn't celebrate his anymore," Abby added.

"And neither do we," Tank said.

"We celebrate it in a different way now," I said, feeling all kinds of pressure to handle this moment right. "Now we celebrate by remembering Daddy and feeling so lucky that we got to have him in our lives."

Abby looked at me. "And crying."

I held her gaze. "Yes," I said. "That too."

"Mama!" Tank burst out then. "I don't have a present for Aunt Jean!"

"Yes, you do," Abby corrected. "Don't you remember how we found that dead dragonfly?"

Tank looked stricken. "But—" he started, and then didn't seem to know how to finish. Finally he said, "That dragonfly is for me to keep."

"No," Abby said. "You collected it for Jean."

"But I need to keep him!" he said, voice thick with emotion. "He's my best friend."

"A dead dragonfly can't be your best friend, Tank," Abby said with a sigh well beyond her years. "But if you don't want to give it away, we'll have to find something else for Aunt Jean."

With that, they scrambled off down the hallway as the sound of my voice calling "Do not get dirty!" went unheard.

I had one pair of shoes with heels, and as I stood up from strapping them on, I caught my reflection in the mirror. It had been a long time since I'd gotten dressed up for anything, and the sight of my lips in lipstick and my hair up on my head caught me by surprise. Maybe I looked too nice. What if Jean was wearing her overalls? What if I was the only one taking trouble over my appearance? I didn't know exactly how birthdays were done around here, and so I decided to scoot out to the kitchen and ask Jean if I was too fancy.

I had my answer as soon as I saw her. I was definitely too fancy. She was in her overalls.

She turned around at the knock of my heels on the floor, looked me up and down, and said, "Perfection!"

"I'm too dressed up," I said. "I'll go change."

"You will not," Jean said. "You're just right."

She promised that everyone else would be wearing something nice. "I just don't really have anything other than overalls," she said. "If I owned a dress, I'd be in it." In the end, I found myself under the "birthday girl's orders" not to change a thing, and so it was settled.

"Where are the kids?" Jean asked as she glanced out the window.

"Last-minute gift emergency," I said. "I'll go find them."

I stepped out onto the front porch and stood up tall to look around the yard. In that moment, I marveled at how quickly we'd adapted to life there. Before we came, I never would have let them disappear like that. Nor would they have had any idea how to do it—or any motivation to want to. But so many adventures with Jean had taught them how to work the farmyard for every variety of fun and adventure. It made me feel proud of all of us.

I didn't see them anywhere, and I was just about to ring the dinner bell when something else caught my attention.

It was O'Connor, coming out of the milking barn door and walking toward the house. He was dressed for the party in a trim western shirt and Levi's with a silver belt buckle styled like a cattle brand. He was looking down as he walked, watching his boots, and he didn't see me. The starkness of his haircut was still shocking, and I had to admit that he could really pull off a buzz, something that wasn't true for everyone. The clean-shaven version of him was mesmerizing. *The hot farmer.* I got it at last. I watched him make his way closer, and I had this crazy, almost datelike feeling. I told myself that he was just walking up to the house. Still, in some very real way, despite everything and not only because I happened to be standing there, it felt like he was walking toward me.

He was just a few feet from the steps where I stood when a gust of wind blew across the yard, and the tickle of it made him look up. When he saw me in my blue party frock and my red lipstick, his eyes caught there and he didn't look away. I felt a wash of shyness come over me—as though he knew somehow that when I was getting dressed, I'd been thinking not only of honoring the birthday girl but also, a little bit, of him: the tender skin on the back of his neck and what it had felt like under the pads of my fingers.

His pace slowed, and he stopped a few feet away. I saw his gaze slide down my body and settle on the ground.

"Hi, O'Connor," I said.

"Hi," he said to the grass. "Jean asked me to pick up some hay bales and take them over."

"Okay," I said. Then, "Do you need some help?"

"No," he said. Then, after a pause, he looked up. "That's quite a dress."

Another breeze swept across the yard, and the hem of my dress fluttered against my calves. I felt a swell of appreciation for party dresses, breezes, and womanhood in general.

"Too fancy," I said, like an apology. "Abby picked it out."

"No," O'Connor said, shaking his head. "You—"

But at that moment, the kids came around the house from behind us.

"I found a present for Jean!" Tank shouted with all his lungs. I turned to see him coming toward me at a full gallop, dangling something from his fingers. "I named him Lizardie!"

Abby was right behind him, shouting, too. "I told him Jean won't want a dead lizard," she said. "But he doesn't care."

They stopped in front of me.

"Jean loves lizards," Tank said, making his case.

"Not dead ones, Tankster," Abby said. "Not lizard corpses."

"You never know with Jean," I said, but when I turned to share the joke with O'Connor, he was already halfway back to the barn.

"Where's O'Connor going?" Tank asked.

"He's helping Jean," I said as we all watched him go. "We'll see him at the party."

Chapter 17

We didn't see O'Connor at the party.

We saw just about everyone else in town, but not O'Connor. I hate to confess that I was looking for him. But I confess. I was looking for him.

To my relief, I was not the only one in a dress. Most of the women were either in skirts, dresses, or little 1950s-style crinoline hoedown outfits. The men wore bolo ties and checked button-downs. It was clear that these folks knew how to put the dance hall to use. The lights were all on, bright and cheery, and at one end folks sat around tables eating barbecue and coleslaw. At the other end, up on a stage, a band played country music—and every single person who was not eating was already dancing.

I'd been to plenty of parties in my life, and usually the band was something people ignored—at least until they'd had enough drinks to lose their inhibitions. But these people didn't have inhibitions. Not on the dance floor, anyway.

As soon as we stepped through the doors, the kids made a run for the playground out back and Russ grabbed Jean's hand to hit the dance floor. When the crowd broke into applause for her, she did a little curtsy. Normally I would have joined the group of nondancers standing awkwardly by, but there were none. I wasn't quite sure what to do or where to go, and I was still hesitating when Sunshine showed up at my side in a black skirt and black tank top. She should have been far more out of place than I was. But she wasn't.

She leaned in close like a middle-school girl and whispered, "He's here."

"Where?" I asked, feeling a little stomach-flutter.

"He's out on the porch," Sunshine said, "and he looks completely gorgeous. He got a haircut."

"I know," I said. "I gave him that haircut."

Sunshine frowned. "You gave Tyler a haircut?"

I shook my head. "Who's Tyler?"

"My ex-boyfriend," Sunshine said. "The guy I just dumped."

"Oh," I said. "No. Sorry. I gave O'Connor a haircut."

"Thank God!" Sunshine said. "He was going feral." She glanced around. "Come and say hello to Tyler."

"Nope," I said. "Bad idea."

"You've never met him!"

"You just dumped him."

"We can still be friendly."

I shook my head. "You can't be friendly," I said, "because you are moving on. Tyler is a distant memory."

Sunshine crossed her arms in a pout, but she didn't argue. I took the opportunity to look around for O'Connor again, and Sunshine took the same opportunity to look me over.

"You're gorgeous, by the way," she said.

I wrinkled my nose at the compliment. "Thank you."

"But you seem miserable."

"I'm not a big-parties person," I said. "Or a square dancer."

"Join the club," Sunshine said.

"I'm just dreading standing around all night alone."

"You're not alone," Sunshine said. "You've got me."

"You're not going to go square-dance?"

"Hell, no," she said. "My life is sad, but not that sad."

As she spoke, a young guy in a T-shirt with an octopus on it came up to us, his eyes on Sunshine like she was the only person there.

"Hey," Sunshine said, when she noticed him.

"Hey," he said. "Thanks for the help at the feed store the other day."

"No problem," she said.

"You won't get in trouble, will you?" he asked.

"Not if you don't tell on me," she said.

He shook his head. "I won't."

Just as I was wondering if this guy was the infamous Tyler, Sunshine said, "I forgot your name."

"It's Marshall," the guy said.

"I'm Sunshine," Sunshine said.

"I remember," Marshall said.

Sunshine turned to me. "This is Russ's best friend's cousin's grandson."

"Wow," I said.

"We used to go skinny-dipping at the spring," Sunshine said.

"As kids," Marshall added. "But then I moved away."

"Now he's come back to town," Sunshine said, looking him over.

"Welcome back," I said, but he didn't seem to hear me. Sunshine had all his attention.

They ran out of things to say just as the band's song wound down, and the awkward pause that followed seemed extra awkward with ambient noise in the background. Then, as a new song started up, Marshall took a breath and said, "Dance with me?"

"Square-dance?" Sunshine said, as if there might be another choice.

Marshall nodded and held out his hand.

She gave me a what-the-hell glance, took his hand, and told him, "You talked me into it."

Before I knew it, they were gone.

With no one else to talk to, I looked around for O'Connor again. He wasn't there. I glanced at the door to the playground, where the kids were, then looked over at Jean and Russ. I watched them for a few minutes and came to admire their technique. This wasn't beginner's square dancing. This was expert level. I couldn't have joined in even if I'd wanted to. The caller gave them instruction after instruction that left things like "swing your partner" and "do-si-do" in the dust. They never missed a beat as the caller had them "cut the diamond," "spin the gears," "explode the wave," and "acey deucey." Jean and Russ were square-dancing ninjas. Who knew?

I watched for a while before starting to feel self-conscious about standing on the sidelines alone. So, just to have something to do, I headed to the far end of the room where the food was and piled myself up a plate. But then, turning toward the tables, I wasn't quite sure where to sit. I didn't know any of the few people eating well enough to join them, and so I wound up making my way to an empty table, sitting down with my plate of food, and poking at it with my plastic fork.

I kept thinking that the table would fill up, that someone would come and join me, but no one did. Maybe it was being surrounded by so many people paired off and having fun. Maybe it was the fact that I'd gone to the trouble of dressing up—and trying to look pretty for the first time in so, so long. But sitting alone at that empty table in that big room, I felt as lonely as I'd been since I came here.

Finally I took my untouched plate to the trash can and dropped it in. I decided to walk to the back door and check on the kids, but as I did, the announcer took the microphone and spoke to the crowd.

"Okay, lucky dogs," he said. "It's time to tear up the dance floor. Find a partner, pronto! I want every single person in this room dancing."

The crowd obeyed. Everybody—and I mean everybody— partnered up. People came in from the porch and left their half-eaten dinners, and the whole room settled into positions, waiting for the music to start. The whole room, that is, except for me.

And as the entire town of Atwater launched into one big hoe-down together, I felt a gaze resting on me in that inexplicable way that makes you turn your head. When I turned, there was O'Connor, up on the stage, perched on a stool with chicken bones in his hands. He'd been there all along. His eyes crinkled up, and he gave me a wink.

I raised my hand in a little wave, but the spark of happiness I felt at seeing him was promptly eclipsed by the idea not only that I was completely alone in that moment but also that O'Connor was witnessing my aloneness. That made it a thousand times worse.

I turned toward the back door and stepped out to stand by the playground. The night air was chilly, and the stars were out. The kids were digging in the sandbox with full dedication—Tank totally unself-conscious in his dragon costume. I watched them until my eyes filled up with tears, and then I had to look up to the night sky to keep them from spilling over. I took a deep breath. What was it with me? Why couldn't I ever, ever feel like I belonged anywhere?

And then I heard O'Connor's voice right behind me. "Who have you been looking for all night, anyway? Santa Claus?"

He caught me by surprise, but I held still. "Nothing," I said. "Nobody."

"You've been craning your neck around the room all night long," he said. He wasn't wrong, of course. He had me on that, and he'd probably guessed I'd been looking for him. But the fact that he'd seen me also meant that he'd been watching me, too. I wasn't sure if he'd meant to confess that or not.

"And then you ate dinner all by yourself. Or failed to eat. Why didn't you sit with somebody?"

I had no idea how to answer that question. I didn't even know the answer myself.

He was standing very close.

I didn't look at him.

"You're not crying, are you?" he asked.

"Nope," I said. "I'm looking at the stars."

" 'Cause that would be a stupid thing to cry over. Not getting picked at a dance."

"I'm not crying."

"You know why nobody picked you, right?" he asked. I could feel the cold pearl snaps of his western shirt against my elbow.

"Because everybody in this entire town has somebody but me?" I said. It sounded even worse out loud.

O'Connor shifted his weight. "It's that dress you've got on," he said. "You just look too good."

I gave a little laugh and shook my head. "I'm always having that problem."

"It's true," he said.

"It's not true," I said. "But that's nice of you." I lowered my eyes to meet his gaze. And, as predicted, the tears spilled over. I wiped them away.

"Come on," O'Connor said, hooking an arm around my waist to lead me back inside.

"Why?" I said.

"So we can square-dance," he said.

"I don't want to square-dance," I said, drying my face again with my sleeve.

"Yes, you do," he said. "It's genuinely fun."

"I don't feel like having fun," I said, glancing over at the kids.

His arm was still around me, and he moved us toward the door. "Fine, then. We won't have fun. We'll be the worst ones out there. We'll suck."

I studied his face. "I bet you're a really good square dancer."

He smiled at me as we crossed the threshold of the door and stepped into the bright room. "I am a fantastic square dancer," he said, giving my waist a little squeeze. "But I'll hide it."

Chapter 18

That night I couldn't sleep. I lay in bed in my nightgown in the dark for hours. I tried my stomach, my back, my side. I watched the fan blades spin in the night shadows. I made lists of things to do in my head. I blinked my eyes a hundred times.

On the drive home from the party, where we had stayed too late, Abby had picked a ridiculous fight with her brother—giving him a marble she'd found in the sandbox and then, meanly, taking it back a minute later. When he cried, she called him a baby. When he grabbed for it, she punched him in the chest. All the while, I was in the front seat, trying to reason with them and drive, too, saying, "Hey, we've had such a great night! Let's not spoil it!" and then, "Guys, knock it off," and finally, as the situation devolved, "No more fighting! Stop it!" None of which was heeded.

At the punch, I hit the brakes and pulled over. Abby had injured not only Tank, who was sobbing in shock over it, but also her own hand—so she was crying, too. I slid open the minivan's door and scolded and comforted them both at the same time. They unbuckled and both came in for a hug, grasping at me as they tried to push each other away.

"What were you thinking?" I demanded of Abby. "Why would you give him something he's been begging for all night just to take it right back?"

"He was being a brat," Abby insisted.

"I'm not a rat," Tank said. "You're the rat."

"Not 'rat,' you idiot! 'Brat'!"

"Enough!" I heard myself shout. Then, "No name-calling! Not another word! We are driving home and going to bed if it kills me."

Back on the road, after a few minutes of silence, I heard Abby still crying. I let out a sigh as I tried to shift from the mad person who had just yelled at her to the mother who could offer comfort.

"Babe," I said, careful with my voice, "I just can't have you calling your brother an idiot. That's not how we talk. And I can't have you punching him, either. We don't hit people. Especially not once we've had ninja training."

Then the real problem came tumbling out. Abby sobbed so loudly as she explained it to me that I could barely understand her. But I got the gist before long: Jimmy Gaveski had been picking on her again at school.

"Why didn't you tell me?" I asked.

"He said if I told anybody, he'd steal my dessert at lunchtime."

"He threatened you?"

"Well," Abby said, a little calmer now, "he threatened my dessert."

I squeezed all the details I could get from her and pieced together that he'd been taunting her in gym class for the past several days, making up chants and trying to get the other kids to join in.

"Do they?" I asked.

"Not really," Abby said. "His chants aren't very good. They don't rhyme. And when they do rhyme, they don't make any sense."

"Sounds like he's really not a very good bully," I said.

"No," Abby agreed. "But he tries hard."

"You know," I said then, in an effort to sound wise, "people who try to make others unhappy are usually pretty unhappy themselves." Something was eating at that kid. I couldn't help but wonder what it might be. Maybe he had parents who shamed him, or ignored him, or—God forbid—hurt him. I didn't know, and I couldn't fix it. I couldn't even fix things for the two children that belonged to me.

"I feel sorry for him, in a way," I said.

"Do you?" Abby asked.

"I don't!" Tank shouted. "Not at all."

Abby looked over at Tank like he was her favorite person in the world. "Thanks, T.," she said.

Back home, I rolled them into bed without even doing a bath or brushing teeth. It was too late to stay up and hash it all out. I sat beside Abby for a minute before turning out the light, and I stroked her hair. Tank had given her his lovie, a blue dog named Blue Dog, and she had tucked it between the two of them.

"You *have* to tell me if that boy teases you again, babe," I insisted, resting my gaze on her splotchy face.

"What about my dessert?" Abby said. Her nose was still stuffy, too.

"If he steals your dessert, I'll get you a better dessert," I said. "I'll take you for ice cream after school. Or doughnuts."

"Doughnuts!" Tank cheered.

"I'll tell him that," Abby said, looking pleased with the idea.

"No," I said. "Don't tell him. Okay? Just hold it in your heart and know it for yourself." I leaned in and gave her a kiss on the forehead. "Trust me on this, sweet child. There is nothing that boy can take from you—absolutely nothing—that the two of us can't replace a thousand times over."

Now here it was, midnight, and I couldn't shake the adrenaline. I did feel sorry for PeePants Gaveski, if I thought about it from his side. He was just a kid, after all. But I also felt the urge to go strangle him in his pajamas. Finally I got up and tiptoed to check on the kids and straighten their blanket. At the bed, I saw that Tank was sleeping with his arm across Abby. It made me wonder if it was what he'd needed all along. Just someone real to hold on to.

Halfway out, at the doorway, I paused to glance back. You can never appreciate your children so fully as when they are asleep, when you're just a bystander. Awake, they're looking at you—for answers, for reactions—and being looked at can make it hard to see. When they're asleep, though, it frees you to do some looking yourself.

I was fighting the urge to stand there and watch them until morning when I heard a voice from behind Jean's closed door. There was a pair of bucks sitting outside in the hall. Russ's bucks. And the voice, of course, was his, too.

"You have to tell her," Russ was saying. "She'd want to know."

And then I heard Jean. "It's too soon."

I felt the panic of having trespassed on their conversation, but I was afraid to move and risk making the stairs squeak. I froze in the hallway, eavesdropping wildly and wishing like anything I were somewhere else.

"Well," Russ said, "it's a fine line between too soon and too late."

Jean gave a soft laugh. "But I'm the one who has to walk it."

"People want you to be up front with them."

"I know that," she said. "But life is messy."

Russ's voice was extra gravelly. "I just don't want to see you wait all this time to mess things up now."

"Noted," Jean said. There was a pause, and the next time Jean spoke, she sounded impatient. "Enough lecturing. Can we please go to bed?"

I wasn't sure if "go to bed" meant "go to sleep" or "or go to *bed*," but I wasn't waiting to find out. I double-timed it down the stairs, squeaks and all, and was just about to zip back to my room when I noticed through the kitchen window that the lights were on in the milking barn. I was still awake—if anything, after catching that snippet of conversation, even more awake—and I decided to venture outside to turn it off.

I shook out a pair of Jean's Wellingtons from the collection of boots and Crocs on the front porch and popped them on my bare feet. Then I stepped out across the farmyard and felt the thrill of being out after dark. My nightgown, that same tissue-thin little billowy number, was not nearly enough protection from the night air, and I crossed my arms around myself in response.

Inside, all the lights were on, and I cursed Sunshine for being the worst farm employee in the history of agriculture. I was sure I hadn't left them on. Then again, it had been Shirtless Fence-Post-Mending Day on the farm that afternoon, and so I did allow for the possibility I might have been distracted.

I took a look around, and that's when I noticed the door to the walk-in fridge pushed in all the way back and wide open—which was, of course, a little bit impossible, since it was a self-closing door, as I'd been reminded a hundred times by O'Connor. I'd seen enough horror movies in my life to want to back out on tiptoe at that moment. Instead I took a deep breath of courage and marched through that open door to investigate.

"Hey!" I said in a big, adult voice. "What the hell's going on in here?"

It's hard to remember the exact sequence of events now. One thing hit another and then another like dominos falling, and before I knew it, everything had gone down. The best I can reconstruct is this: I walked right into the open fridge, and as I did, my shin hit something wooden—hit it hard enough to send a shock of pain shooting both up and down my leg, and I doubled over to grab it with both hands. Next, from down low, I felt a breeze, then heard a noise, something going *chunk*. I stood up to see O'Connor standing with his mouth open and a screwdriver in one hand, looking from me to the door and back again.

"Tell me you didn't just do that," he said, a little breathless.

"I didn't just do that," I said. Then I looked around. "Do what?"

He walked right past me to the door and started working the handle. Which, we both knew, was broken. Even though the handle refused to turn, he kept jiggling it anyway, the way you do when things are really hopeless. As I watched him, I was slow to realize what I'd just done. But then it became clear. I'd kicked a two-by-four across the room. The one that had been propping open the fridge door.

"You were fixing the fridge door?"

O'Connor didn't look up. "The part finally arrived."

For proof, there was the new handle, unwrapped, lying on a box right near me.

"And you were working on it in the middle of the night because . . . ?"

"Because I thought it would be safer."

"Fewer people around." I nodded. "Fewer people to—"

"Accidentally kick the door closed. Yes." He gave me a look. "Plus," he went on, "I had the night off tonight. And I felt . . ." He hesitated a half second. "Restless."

When he finally gave up on the door handle, we both looked down at the two-by-four.

"Sorry," I said.

O'Connor bent his head and rubbed his eyes.

"Well," he said at last, "there's good news as well as bad."

"Okay," I said.

"The good news," he said, looking around the room, "is that I turned off the cooling system before I started working."

"So we won't get too cold?" I said, though I was cold already.

"We'll still get cold," he said. "But it's not literally freezing in here anymore."

"No," I agreed. "More like just chilly."

"So I don't think we'll die of hypothermia."

I hadn't realized dying of hypothermia was a possibility. "That *is* good news," I said.

"The bad news," O'Connor went on, "is that it's still going to be pretty cold in here." He was looking around the room now, eyeing the possibilities. "And I'm not sure we can get out before morning."

"Before morning!" I said. I didn't voice the million-plus reasons that spending the night in the walk-in fridge was not going to work for me. Like my children. Or my terrible, ridiculous, tissue-thin cotton nightgown. I looked at the goose bumps on my arm. "Can't you get us out?"

"I'm not MacGyver," he said, his voice gruff. "It's broken."

"Can't you replace the door handle now?"

"Not with the door jammed closed, I can't."

Man, he was irritated with me. Which didn't exactly seem fair. How was I supposed to know what had been going on? Who mends a broken refrigerator at midnight? But I didn't defend myself. I just stood very still, stared at the floor, and tried to be as dignified as possible.

O'Connor wasn't noticing me, dignified or not. He was trying to pop the door off its hinges. He'd found a hammer and a chiselly-looking thing, and he banged at those rusty old hinges like crazy.

Nothing.

He tried other angles. Still nothing.

"Maybe they'll hear you?" I suggested. "Russ and Jean are still awake."

O'Connor shook his head. "Insulated," he said, gesturing around.

He tried to pick the lock with a drill bit. No luck. He tried to bust the handle off with the hammer. No luck there, either. He paced the room like a wild animal, trying useless idea after useless idea, as I just stood there and shivered.

At last I said, "O'Connor?"

He turned around as if he'd forgotten I was there.

I pointed at the shelf with the folded woolen blankets. "Can I have one of those blankets?"

He looked at the blankets, then back at me, and seemed to realize for the first time that I had next to nothing on.

"Aw, man," he said, grabbing both blankets. "You're freezing."

I was. Shivering, too. And with that, I guess, O'Connor decided I'd been punished enough, because his whole tone changed toward me. "Come here, come here," he said, all tender. I stayed still, so he stepped over to me.

He started unsnapping his western shirt—the very same snaps that had brushed my elbow back at the party.

"Now you'll be freezing," I said.

Still, I let him put the shirt on me like a jacket, and I watched his fingers as he snapped me up. Then he wrapped one of the wool blankets around me and pulled the other over my head like a hood. Next, he put both arms around me and pulled me in tight.

As cold as I was, and as embarrassed as I felt to have caused all this trouble, and as much as my shin still hurt, I admit it was nice to be held. I tried to think back to the last time anybody had enveloped me in a hug like that. It would have been Danny, of course, but I couldn't remember it. Of course, I gave hugs like this to the kids all the time. But it was a whole different thing to get one.

Without meaning to, I put my head against O'Connor's shoulder. We just fit better that way. But almost as soon as I'd settled into the moment, it was over. Next thing I knew, he sat me down on a box. Then he started pulling boxes and supplies off the shelves and stacking them up on the floor.

"What are you doing?" I asked.

"I'm making us an igloo," he said. "We need to trap our body heat."

"I thought you said we weren't going to freeze."

"No," he said. "But we're going to get pretty damn cold."

The fridge was so much larger than we needed for cheese that it also had begun serving as a storage room. The shelves held cardboard boxes with extra cooking utensils, as well as the tubs we packed the cheese in and extra buckets for collecting whey. O'Connor started pulling all the boxes down off the racks and building a little structure. One flattened box made the floor, and another became the roof. When it was about waist-high, he signaled me to step in, and I did. Then he did, too, and we wedged ourselves down among the boxes. At last he pulled the roof over our heads.

Inside, it was darker, and cramped. I sat cross-legged and faced O'Connor as he leaned back against the wall of boxes that was braced against a real wall. Conversation was sparse as we worked to accept our situation. At one point I said, "Maybe Russ will see the lights on when he leaves and come find us."

"Maybe," O'Connor said.

A little later, I said, "Maybe we should build a fire."

"Nope," O'Connor said.

I frowned. "Why not? That's a pretty good idea."

"This fridge is airtight," O'Connor explained.

"Oh," I said. "Too much smoke."

"That," O'Connor said, "and it would use up all the oxygen."

I thought about that. "Do we need to worry about using up all the oxygen?"

"Not if we don't build a fire."

A little while later O'Connor insisted we get out and move around to keep ourselves awake. We walked circles around the little room and jumped up and down some. We also picnicked on tubs of cheese, pinching off big hunks with our fingers, to keep our energy up. O'Connor had packed the tubs away in coolers before he turned the fridge off, and we went through four containers.

"This is really good," O'Connor said as we opened up another.

"Thanks," I said.

When it was time to crawl back into the igloo, I insisted he take one of the blankets, and because he'd been shivering since taking off his shirt, he agreed.

"Kinda wishing right now that you hadn't just sheared off all my hair," O'Connor said, running his palm over his jaw where the beard had been.

"You would've had your very own fur coat."

As he pulled the roof back over us, he said, without meeting my eyes, "Probably the warmest thing would be for us to squish together and then wrap ourselves in both blankets."

"Body heat," I said, wanting to support the scientific rationale. He flicked a glance my way. "If you're okay with that idea."

"Sure," I said, trying to sound super casual. "I'll try anything."

And so, in what felt like slow motion, he opened his blanket shawl, and I opened mine. I leaned forward and crawled toward him, spooning myself around the side of his hip and then pressing my chest against his side. I could hear myself breathing, and the swish of the blankets brushing the cardboard as I moved. I put my arms around him, taking in a big breath of his salty scent, and he cocooned the blankets around us.

And that's how we passed much of the rest of the night, wrapped up tight, telling stories to stay awake, him smelling my hair, which was right under his nose, and me listening to his heart, which was right under my ear. When we ran out of things to say, he'd sing— and I think he covered the entire Ernest Tubb songbook before morning came. Somewhere in there, I joined in, too.

We took periodic cheese and exercise breaks, but then we'd always climb back into the igloo and settle ourselves back together for warmth. We were cold, despite our best efforts—and uncomfortable, and overtired, and a little anxious about how we would get ourselves rescued. But here's what I remember most about those hours: I had completely forgotten what it felt like to be held, to rest against the solidness of another person. But it all came back now. And it felt really good.

"Are you asleep?" he asked.

"No," I said, lifting my head. "Just resting."

"Probably not a good idea to fall asleep."

"I'll try not to," I said.

"Keep talking," he said.

"I'm running out of things to say."

"Okay," he said, thinking. "Tell me about the most embarrassing thing that's ever happened to you."

"Hell, no."

"Come on," he said. "Humiliation is a stimulant."

"You first," I said.

He took a deep breath and thought about it. Finally he said, "In eighth grade I had a really gorgeous English teacher."

"Okay," I said.

"And she came to school one day in this silk blouse, and I literally couldn't think about anything else. We were diagramming sentences that day, and she asked me to go up to the board and do one for the class. And I was, like, really good at diagramming sentences for some reason. But I refused to go to the board." He leaned down to catch my eye to see if I understood why. "I *couldn't* go to the board."

I was too sleepy to get it. "Why not?"

"Because I was a fourteen-year-old boy in a classroom with a woman wearing a silk blouse."

I took a big breath of understanding. "I see," I said.

"Longest ten minutes of my life," he said.

"Did you ever go up to the board?"

"Nope," he said. "I went to detention instead. For a week."

"A week!"

"It was worth it."

"Well," I said, "I'm wide awake now."

"Your turn," he said.

I sighed. "Okay," I said. "In fourth grade, I had a teacher who wouldn't let me go to the bathroom. I asked and asked, and she said no over and over. I could tell I was getting myself in trouble just by asking. She was *glaring* at me. I held it as long as I could, but finally, just before the bell rang, I peed on my shoes."

O'Connor was shaking his head and wincing. "Aw, man."

"Yes," I said, nodding. "And they tried to call my mother to bring me a new pair of shoes, but she wasn't home, and so the school nurse rinsed mine out with water and made me put them back on."

"No," he said, putting his hands over his eyes.

"They squished all day."

We fell quiet for a minute.

"So you have a lot of sympathy for PeePants," O'Connor said at last.

I tilted my head at him. "No," I said. "Not really."

"But it's kind of the same thing," he said.

"It's the opposite of the same thing," I said, giving him a look that dared him to disagree.

"Children are such assholes," he said at last.

"Aren't they?"

"Grown-ups, too," he added. And I had to agree.

O'Connor wound up telling me about life in the house with Erin, and how stir-crazy he felt to be so housebound. "I've mowed the grass three times this week," he said. "Just to get outside."

"Russ thinks you're going to lose your marbles and run naked through town," I said.

"It's not a bad idea," O'Connor said.

As the night wore on, we got goofier. "If I die, you have permission to eat me as food," I said somewhere around 5:00 A.M.

"Right back atcha," he said.

"I'm sure I'll be delicious," I said.

"I've heard human flesh tastes like overcooked ham," he told me.

"You've heard that?"

"Yeah."

"How does that come up in conversation?"

"It doesn't surprise me," O'Connor said. "Humans and pigs are a lot alike."

"I think humans are more like dogs."

"But would you want to eat a dog?"

"Not really," I said.

"That's right," he said. "Dogs can do many great things. But they can't become bacon."

Despite all our efforts, by six, when Russ saw the lights on in the barn and came out in Jean's ruffled pink robe to investigate, we were fast asleep. The door opened easily from the outside, and Russ saw the empty cheese containers, discovered us inside the igloo of boxes, and pieced the whole story together.

"Looks like y'all had a fun night," he said to us as we stood up and straightened out. He put an arm around each of us to walk us back up to the house.

"You were sleeping so peaceful," he added with a wink at me, "I almost didn't wake you."

Chapter 19

~~~~~~~~~

That same morning, though, I still had to get the milking done—because you can't ever skip a milking—and so I was back in the barn after breakfast. Jean offered to take my shift, but I really was fine. Not injured or hypothermic. Just a little lovelorn. O'Connor was long gone before I came back down, and even though for the rest of the day—hell, the rest of the week—I kept expecting him to show up somehow, he didn't, and that was that.

In the barn, Sunshine was already halfway through. She had Margaret Thatcher up on the milking stand and the machine running full volume. I felt certain she was going to ask me all about O'Connor, and I really didn't know what I would say. But she didn't ask. She wanted to talk much more than she wanted to listen—and about one thing in particular: the boy she'd run into at Jean's party.

"He knows who I am," she called out over the noise. "But it doesn't seem to faze him."

"That's great," I said, lost in my own thoughts. I brought Eleanor Roosevelt in from the waiting pen and helped her up.

"And we like all the same music," Sunshine went on, "and he's really gentle and thoughtful."

"That's awesome," I said, still not listening, taking a seat on my milking stool.

"And," Sunshine added, "the sex is incredible."

"I'm sorry?" I snapped the suction cup onto my goat so fast, I made her startle.

Sunshine looked up with a shrug. "He's good in bed."

"You slept with him?" I asked, my voice all astonishment.

Sunshine lifted an eyebrow. "You slept with O'Connor."

"I didn't *sleep with* O'Connor," I said. "I *fell asleep next to* O'Connor."

Sunshine didn't argue, and instead turned back to her milking. "It just kind of happened," she said. "It was very organic."

"Sunshine," I said, "that's completely reckless! You don't know anything about him! You're still heartbroken from the other guy! Don't you think you ought to get to know him a little first?"

"Yes," Sunshine said with a nod. "I should."

"But?" I asked.

"But I just couldn't help myself," she said, shrugging

I gave her a disappointed-mom look. "You have to take better care of yourself," I said. I couldn't stop myself from lecturing. "Sex is not the same thing as water polo or mini golf!"

Sunshine wrinkled her nose in pity. "It's been a while for you, hasn't it?"

"That's not it," I insisted. "Sex connects you with something . . ." Here I searched for the words. "Something larger than yourself. The whole of human history, somehow—"

"I'm not going to get pregnant," Sunshine interrupted. "We

used birth control." She tilted her head. "Edible birth control, but still . . ."

"I'm not talking about getting pregnant," I said. "I'm telling you sex is powerful stuff."

"What am I," Sunshine said, "your little sister?"

And she had a point. Who was I to lecture her about anything?

Sunshine wrinkled her nose. "Anyway," she said, "you're so old-fashioned."

"*Sex* is old-fashioned!" I said.

She drew an air circle with her finger around the side of her head like I was loco. "Ohhh-kay."

And there it was. The chasm I came to over and over again with my own kids that separated the things I knew from the things they could understand. The vast difference between what you could learn from experience and what you could teach. "When you're my age, you'll get it," I said in my own defense.

"I *am* your age," Sunshine said.

"Right," I said. "You seem younger." And for the first time I wondered if Sunshine was young for our age—or if, in fact, I was just old. She clearly hadn't paid enough attention to life's lessons. On the other hand, maybe I'd paid too much. Either way, I wished so badly that I could just tell her everything she needed to know. That we didn't have to fail so many times to succeed. That wisdom didn't have to go so hand in hand with regret.

"Please just try to hold off a little on the jumping into bed with random people," I said.

She shrugged. "Maybe it'll work out. Maybe you'll wind up telling this story at our rehearsal dinner."

"That's exactly what I'm talking about," I told her. "You are standing at the edge of something big."

"Fine," Sunshine said. "But let's get one thing straight."

"What?" I said.

Sunshine grinned. "He is way better than mini golf."

I wanted to scold her some more but I held back, and my unspoken words bottlenecked in my throat. Something about her optimism reminded me of Abby and Tank: the sweet way they could love anybody—the assumption they made that people deserved it—and how charming, and heartbreaking, it was.

Sunshine was clearly done for the morning with being disapproved of.

"So," she said, pulling her stool over next to mine and resting her chin in her hands. "Tell me about your all-nighter with O'Connor. Russ said he found you two curled up like kittens."

I glossed over the basics of what had happened. After all the judging I'd just done, I was extra careful not to get judged myself. Instead, I maneuvered the conversation back toward a much more manageable, if far less appealing topic: PeePants Gaveski.

I confessed to Sunshine that I really had no idea how to handle it. My meetings with the teachers and the principal and the school counselor had resulted in stacks of recommended reading on my bedside table, a folder full of handouts on bullying, and assurances that the school was doing "everything" it could. Short of going to school and following Abby around with a set of nunchucks, I really didn't know what to do.

Sunshine wanted me to run PeePants over with the farm truck.

"Obviously," I said, "that's not an option."

"I'll do it," she offered. "Just give me the keys."

"Tempting," I said.

"Doesn't Jean have a solution?" Sunshine asked. "Jean always knows what to do."

"She's researching it."

"Researching what?"

"Bullying," I said.

"Well," Sunshine said, "if there's an answer, Jean will find it."

Which was true. And comforting. But only if there was, in fact, an answer.

Within a day, we were back to our completely normal routine. The door was fixed on the fridge, I had another meeting scheduled with the principal at Abby's school, O'Connor was gone again. The only thing that wasn't normal was me. That one crazy day with O'Connor—from the haircut to the square dancing to the night spent clinging together for warmth—had left me feeling anything but.

I finished my work in the cheese kitchen early the next day and went back to the house to take a shower. But from my room, as I looked out the window and started to undress, a little break in the edge of the forest caught my eye. I felt restless. My shirt was halfway off, but I pulled it back down. I walked to the spot and found a little footpath I'd never seen before. It led up the hill through the forest. On a different day I never would have noticed that spot. But on this day, there was no question: I was following that path.

And so I went walking. Sometimes you just have to do something—anything—a little different.

It was cool under the oaks and pines, and patches of sunlight cropped up here and there. Jean said the forest had never been cleared, and described it as "Texas in the wild." It felt good to walk, to breathe deeply, and to be somewhere outside my own head for a while. I kept thinking I should turn around and go back, but I didn't.

At the top of the hill, the path opened up to a clearing. I stepped into it, a little breathless from the climb. And there I discovered, of all things, the haunted house.

It didn't look nearly as haunted in the daytime. In the moonlight, it always glowed a ghostly white. In the sunlight, it was butter yellow. And it was in good shape, too. No peeling paint, after all, or rotten wood. I guess sunlight makes everything seem cheery, but bumping into this house here, so far out into the woods, felt like running into an old friend.

I climbed the steps to the porch to peer in the windows and get a good look. The rooms were all empty. Then I walked around the back and passed the fire pit, where I'd sat with Sunshine for our séances. At the back steps, I peered through the door at a kitchen with black-and-white tile and scalloped cabinet trim.

On impulse I tried the handle on the back door. It opened.

I stepped inside, amazed at my luck.

I walked all around the downstairs, my shoes knocking on the wood floors, taking in the feel of the rooms and the archways and the high ceilings. The kitchen had a little built-in hutch. It was not dusty, just empty. But it didn't feel empty. It felt expectant. Like a rental house waiting to be rented.

For some reason I didn't want to leave. I still needed that shower, and it was time to go, but instead of going, I started looking for reasons to stay. I made my way back to the kitchen and found myself nosing around, opening and closing cabinet doors. I wasn't looking for anything, really—just killing time.

I decided to find a souvenir before heading home. For some reason I'll never be able to explain, it felt crucial to do this. I went through the pantry. I looked under the sink. I even checked inside the oven. I checked every drawer in the kitchen for even a paper clip. Nothing. Nothing at all. Until I got to the last drawer. The one at the end of the counter closest to the back door. And inside it was a little pad of message paper and a couple of ballpoint pens. It felt like a major find, even though the white pad was completely anonymous and the pens were completely generic. It was something, at least. Way better than a paper clip.

I reached in to lift the pad out. I thought I might even take it home as a treasure. But when I lifted the pad, I found something vastly more interesting underneath: a vintage photograph. It was of a family—a mom, a dad, and a baby—sitting on the front porch of this very house.

I set the pad back in the drawer and pushed it shut—but held on to the photo. And then, as quickly as if I were picking the house's pocket, and without even thinking about what I was doing, I popped the photo in the pocket of my overalls and slammed the kitchen door on my way out.

Chapter 20

By the end of the day, the photo I'd found was completely forgotten. If it had been in my back pocket, I might have heard it crinkle when I sat down. If it had been in my hip pocket, I would very likely have stumbled on it with my hands when I was looking for my keys. Instead, nestled up high in that bib, it just lay against my chest and didn't make a sound. And it's embarrassing to admit how long I could wear and rewear those overalls before I got inspired to wash them, but it took me a whole week to discover it again.

Granted, the intervening week was pretty busy. Tank got a stomach virus, which he gave to Abby. Elizabeth Bishop, Cleopatra, and Edna St. Vincent Millay all went into labor in the wee hours on three different nights. Bob Dylan spent about six hours hobbling around like he'd had a stroke, but then bounced back out of nowhere and went running off to the catfish pond like a puppy. And, last but not least, Sunshine wound up in the tabloids.

Tom Hunt called Jean about it at four in the morning, when a stack of papers arrived at the feed store. Sunshine was on the front page—in a grainy, desperately unflattering paparazzi photo. The wide-angle lens made her look far plumper than she was. She was biting a Snickers bar and, Tom Hunt confessed after some prodding, something about the photo made it look like she was giving that Snickers a blow job. The three-inch headline across the paper read: "Amber McAllen Fat & Ugly!! WTF??"

Jean was at my door in seconds explaining it all. I got dressed and threw back on that same pair of overalls. "How did they even find her?" I asked. "Why were they even looking for her?"

"Who knows?" Jean said. She shotgunned her coffee and told me there was more in the pot.

I followed her down the hall toward the kitchen. "What's this going to do to Sunshine? How is she going to take it?"

"I don't know," Jean said, her jaw tight.

In the kitchen, I sipped my coffee like I was preparing for battle. We both stood at attention as we talked the situation over. Doing something had to wait until we'd figured out what to do.

"The truth is," Jean said, "people let us down and harm us and treat us like shit over and over. Part of learning to be happy is—"

"Avoiding people who do that?" I offered.

"That," Jean said, nodding, "and learning to bounce back after it happens. Because it will happen. Even people who love you will knock the hell out of you sometimes. That's just life. And the more we practice, the better we get at shaking it off."

"So suffering is good?"

"Suffering is very good," Jean said. "You come out of it stronger."

"Or it destroys you," I offered.

Jean shook her head. "It's only years later that you realize it didn't."

Outside in the yard, Dubbie the rooster woke up and started crowing. Jean went on. "They did a study a while ago that discovered old people were quite a bit happier than young people. And nobody could understand it. How could it be that people in nursing homes were happier than their sexy young counterparts? All these theories went around. Maybe it was because they'd made their big decisions already and didn't have them looming ahead. Maybe it was because they were past the intensity of dealing with children. Maybe it was some kind of age-induced brain damage." Jean set her coffee cup in the sink. "But then one researcher got it right. He said they were happier because they had already learned what life had to teach them."

Jean lifted her car keys off the peg by the door. "I think about that idea a lot when we talk about Abby and her bully—about whether his behavior is tearing her down or making her stronger. And I wonder if stepping in and protecting people from the pain of life actually makes life more painful in the end. And I'm thinking about it now with Sunshine."

"You're saying it's good for her to see this tabloid all over town?"

"It might. In the long run."

I studied Jean's face as she stood there by the door. "So you're just going to let whatever's going to happen happen?"

Jean met my eyes. "Hell, no," she said. Then her face broadened into a smile. "I'm going to gather up every last one of them and burn them all to ashes."

I smiled back. "I'm coming with you."

And that's how we wound up carrying the kids, still half asleep, to the minivan in their pajamas. We brought their school clothes and backpacks for later, and wound up feeding them doughnuts for breakfast in the car. The kids gobbled them down and sang a medley of kid songs as Jean drove us from storefront to storefront and I stole stack after stack of tabloids and tossed them in the back of the minivan. We hit the drugstore, the supermarket, the library, the feed store, the bank, the Hampton Inn, and every other place we could think of.

At one point Abby said, "Mom? Are you stealing?"

"No, sweetheart," I answered, dusting off my hands. "I'm taking out the trash."

When we'd covered the entire town, we drove the kids to school. I promised myself I'd have them in bed an hour early that night to make up their lost sleep. They dressed in the car and then brushed their teeth, rinsing with a water bottle and spitting onto the gravel road. We pulled up to the school entrance just on time, and I watched the kids unbuckle, adjust their backpacks, and make their way up the steps to face the day.

I watched the herd of kids going into the building. One of those kids was PeePants—though I had no idea which one. My eyes followed face after face, looking for malevolence. I could have stayed to eyeball every last one of them. But Jean leaned over, tapped the steering wheel, and said, "Let's move."

I turned to Jean. "What's next?"

"Next," Jean said, "we build a fire."

We made one more loop through town to make sure we hadn't missed anything, and then we drove toward Jean's south pasture, where there was a pit for burning trash. The back of the minivan was filled to the roof with newspaper stacks, and I pulled them out one by one and catapulted them in. I marched back and forth, lugging one heavy stack after another, breathing hard, my arms aching already and my shoulders sore. Jean helped some, too, and when we were done, she pulled a can of lighter fluid out of her satchel and set the thing ablaze.

As we watched the fire roar to life, we thought back through the morning to decide if we'd missed any places.

"What if she gets hold of a copy?" I said.

Jean stared at the fire. The flames cast a light on her like sun rays. "She'll handle it the best she can."

"Do you think something like this could . . ." I searched for the word. "Destabilize her?"

Jean looked at me. "Sure," she said. "She's human." We watched the flames. "As a therapist, I always tell people that it's not really what happens to you that matters as much as who you become in response to those things." She tucked her hair behind her ears. "Maybe Sunshine will handle it with grace."

"You don't really believe that," I said, "not deep down. Or we wouldn't have just burned all these tabloids," I said.

"I do believe it," Jean said, eyes on the fire. "But we burned them anyway. Because that's exactly what she'd have done for us."

Sunshine didn't see the papers that day. When I got back for milking that morning, she looked up and said, "Why do you smell like smoke?"

"I was burning trash with Jean," I said.

Sunshine didn't ask me what kind of trash, or if it had a monstrously unflattering picture of her on it. She just milked and we chatted, exactly like any other day. I kept thinking she'd figure it out, but she didn't.

Though she did keep looking over at me with curiosity. As we were finishing up, Sunshine frowned at my bib pocket and said, "What's that, anyway?"

Before I had even looked down or remembered what she might have been talking about, she'd whisked out the old photo and was studying it.

I said, "Oh, it's just something I found."

It was my first chance to really look at the photo. Here were these people again: the mother and father and baby. They were on the steps of the haunted house. The mother had the baby on her lap, and both she and the father were gazing down with that love-smacked expression parents get. It was clearly the moment before they expected the shutter to click, and they hadn't yet looked up to smile.

We studied the picture for a minute, Sunshine and I, and then she said, of all things, "That's Jean."

"It is?" I asked.

Now that she'd said it, though, it couldn't be anyone else. The hair was brown, the body was slim, but the eyes were the same. Exactly.

"Sure," Sunshine said. "That's Jean and Frank."

In the photo of Frank that Jean kept on her dresser, he was bald on top with a walrus mustache. This guy, in contrast, had a full, shaggy head of hair. And he was young, flat-stomached, and wearing a T-shirt with the American flag.

"Where did you get this?" Sunshine asked.

"In the haunted house."

"You went into the haunted house?"

I nodded. "I kind of stumbled on it. On a walk. In the day-time."

"How did you get in?" she asked. "They boarded up that window."

"The back door was open."

"That's weird."

"Yep," I agreed. And then, because Sunshine seemed to know everything, I asked her the next logical question. "Who's the baby?"

Sunshine only shrugged like she didn't know. "Why don't I just finish up here while you go ask Jean?"

In the kitchen, Jean was making tea and reading a romance novel. She waved when I walked in, and I sat across from her at the kitchen table with the photo held to my chest.

When she realized I was staying, she dog-eared her book and set it down.

"I need to ask you about something," I said then.

"Okay, shoot," Jean said.

I hesitated. I wasn't sure what her reaction would be. And I had this funny awareness that once I'd shown her the picture, I couldn't unshow it. If it was a moment from her life, and it clearly was, then I wasn't sure I had any business prying into it. I was curious about the mystery, but maybe that wasn't fair. After all, this was Jean, and her own tender life, and her memories and secrets, and her lost love—and this child I had never even heard about.

But curiosity is a powerful thing. So before long I had set the photo down on the table in front of her. "I found this last week," I said.

Jean froze with her eyes on the photo.

"This is clearly you," I said. "And this must be Frank."

"Where did you find this?" she asked.

"At the haunted house. In a drawer by the telephone."

"You went inside," she said—not a question but a statement.

"Yes," I said.

Jean stroked the edge of it with her finger. "A lifetime ago," she said. "A whole different life."

"So," I said, "it is you?"

"Yes, it's me," Jean said.

"And the man is Frank?"

"Yes," she said. "That's Frank."

"He was cute," I said with approval.

Jean smiled, but sadly.

"That was the year we convinced the town to fix up the old German dance hall. We started up a square-dancing society called the Lucky Dog Dance Club. We were the young people then," she said, lost in the photo. "People tell you it slips away, but you never believe them."

"I believe them," I said.

Jean didn't seem to hear me.

"What's a picture of you doing up at the haunted house?"

Jean looked up. "You haven't guessed?"

I hadn't, but as soon as she said the words, I did. "Because that was the family homestead?"

Jean nodded.

"The mansion my mother is so mad about?"

She nodded again. "Though not a mansion."

"And you don't live there now because . . . ?"

"Because Frank built this house for me, and I like it better."

"But you still take care of the old one."

"Yes," Jean said. "It's not good for a house to sit empty, but I never could bring myself to rent it. I keep it up and keep an eye on it. It'll be yours one day."

"Mine?"

"Who else would I leave it to?"

I hadn't thought about it. I wasn't sure what to say. "Thank you."

We both looked at the photo again.

"You and Frank seem very happy," I said.

"We were, most of the time."

I waited for her to go on, but she didn't. She seemed lost in the photo.

"And the baby?" I finally asked, since she wasn't offering. "Was she your daughter?"

Jean looked up then, like she couldn't believe I was asking the question. She studied my face as if trying to decide if I was serious or not. Then she put her hand over her mouth, and I saw her eyes fill with tears.

"Jean," I said in the gentlest voice I could muster, "did you lose a child?"

Jean shook her head and rubbed her eyes. "You really don't recognize that baby?" she asked. "Sweetheart, that baby is you."

I took the picture from Jean and peered at it closely. Me? Why would it have been me? My brain turned the idea around like a puzzle piece, trying to make it fit.

"I don't have any pictures of myself as a baby," I told Jean. "They were lost in a move."

"Lost in a move?" Jean said, her face bitter. "Is that what she told you?"

I didn't know how to answer the question, but Jean wasn't waiting for an answer. She stood up, walked out of the room, and climbed the stairs. I didn't move—couldn't move. I just sat there staring at the photograph of a baby version of me. I wanted to feel a click of recognition. Really, though, it could have been any baby at all.

When Jean came back down, she was carrying two photo albums and a shoe box. Without a word she set them on the table in front of me.

I looked at her and then back at the albums. "I don't understand."

"Open them," she said.

I took the top album off and opened it to the first page. Inside, arranged under cellophane, were more photos just like the one I'd found. Jean in a blue jean skirt with brown hair, Frank in dark glasses on a motorcycle—and, in almost every picture, a little baby. Me.

After the initial shock, I started flipping the pages faster. Me with Frank on a picnic blanket. Me in a tire swing with Jean. The three of us in front of a birthday cake. Me on a little pony. Me standing on the front porch. Me looking out the window. Me giving Frank a kiss on the nose.

There were people in the photos I didn't recognize: an old lady in a flowered housecoat, an old man with horn-rimmed glasses and coveralls. "Grandparents?" I asked Jean.

She nodded. "Mimi and Papa."

I kept flipping. And I started to notice someone absent from the photos: my mother. There were photos of me in the hammock with Papa and of Mimi giving me a bath. There were photos of me teething on a plastic ring on a picnic blanket. "Where's my mom?" I asked Jean, but she didn't answer right away.

I opened the next book. In this one, I was older, running around the same yard. I recognized the porch and the yard of the haunted house. It was yellow then, too, and had an Oldsmobile parked in the driveway.

Jean kept her hand pressed over her mouth as she watched me flip.

"Jean?" I asked as a new idea occurred to me. "Did you throw the pictures of my mom away?"

Jean couldn't seem to pull her eyes from the photos. It was almost like she didn't hear me. "Hey! Where's my mother?" I asked again, and this time her eyes met mine.

She took a deep breath. "California."

"California?" I asked.

Jean closed her eyes, then opened them again. "For the first four years of your life," she said then, "your mother lived in California. And you lived here. With us."

My mind started to spin. This was not the conversation I'd been expecting. Why would my mother have been in California? What would keep a mother from her child? Unless—and the idea made me woozy—unless she wasn't my mother after all. Maybe that's why we'd never liked each other. And then another thought, right on top of that one: Maybe Jean was my mother! Anything was possible at this point. It would explain the animosity between them, and the way Jean and I got along so beautifully. But why would Jean have given me up? What on earth would convince someone like Jean to give her child to someone like Marsha?

Jean watched my mind race, no doubt giving me a second to catch up, waiting for the onslaught of questions that were about to come as soon as I could form them.

"So," I began, "is my mother . . ." I hesitated. "Not actually my mother?"

"Oh, no," Jean said. "She's your mother."

I felt relief and disappointment at the same time. And now the beginnings of frustration, too.

"Then why was she in California?"

Jean heard the tension in my voice.

"I'm going to tell you what happened—start to finish," Jean said. "It's way past time you heard the story of your life."

She took a breath. "Your mother was always the good girl. I was sneaking out, and your mother was home, studying. I was a constant disappointment to my parents, especially after I dropped out of college and started shacking up with Frank. Your grandparents were kind people, but very traditional, and they weren't sure a girl needed an education, anyway. Once I quit school, they announced to your mother that they wouldn't be sending her to college, either. Within the month, she ran away. She was seventeen."

Jean gave me a minute.

"Our parents were frantic, and they looked everywhere for weeks. Finally they started receiving weekly postcards from her, saying she was fine and living in California and not to worry. Of course, they worried anyway. And the irony wasn't lost on them that trying to keep her with them had driven her away."

Jean stood up to pour us both fresh cups of tea, and I took a breath.

"A year later," Jean went on, "she showed back up at our parents' door with a baby." She raised her mug in a toast. "You."

I shook my head at her.

Jean went on. "My parents were terrified she'd leave again. They made her promise to stay with them. I think you were about two months old at the time. She wouldn't tell them anything about her life. But she did confess that she wasn't married and that the father had left her.

"It was a scandal, but your grandparents didn't care. They were just happy to have her back—and you. They took the two of you in for about a month before your mother got a letter from your father saying he missed her. That night she left a note of apology, took our dad's truck, and drove across the country to go back. And she left you behind."

I don't think Jean wanted to defend my mother, but she didn't seem to be able to stop herself. "She knew you were in good hands," she said. "Our parents were great with children."

I could feel a *"but"* coming. "But?" I said.

"But my mother was sick with rheumatoid arthritis by then—like I have now, along with some other things we didn't know about yet. It was too much for her to handle."

Jean took a sip of tea.

"So they called me," she went on. "And Frank and I moved back here. Neither of us wanted to come. We both had big dreams, and Atwater, Texas, didn't seem like the place to follow them. But we told ourselves it would only be for a little while. Frank said he just wanted to be wherever I was, which was sweet.

"And then we met you, and we fell in love. You really were way too much for my parents at their age, so you became mine. Frank took odd jobs around town—he was a painter by training, but he was handy, too. Taking you on seemed to cure my wildness. We settled down. We started saving money. We became responsible and thoughtful. We became better people."

I tucked my hair behind my ears. "And my mother?"

"Postcards," Jean said. "No return address."

"Did she come to visit?"

Jean looked at me a good while before she said, "No."

I looked down at my hands.

"It was just as well," Jean said. "We didn't want her to visit. As far as we were concerned, you were ours. When you were about two, our pal Russ, a lawyer, suggested we start adoption proceedings so she couldn't take you away from us."

"Russ?" I interrupted. "Your Russ?"

"Yes," Jean said, as if she'd forgotten I knew him. "Of course. My Russ." Then she went on. "But because Frank and I weren't married, we couldn't make that work."

"You couldn't just get married?" I asked.

"Well," Jean said, "that was complicated. Frank was married to someone else."

It really was too much. But there was no stopping it now.

"She wouldn't divorce him," Jean said. "Even though they'd been apart for years. He begged for a divorce, but she wouldn't give in."

Jean rubbed her eyes. She looked tired.

"And then one day, the week after your fourth birthday, your mother showed back up. She was getting married, she said, and she wanted you back.

"We told her she couldn't have you. We told her she'd given up her rights to you. We actually locked her out of the house and ourselves in. But she came back with the sheriff, and they took you from us."

Jean walked over to the sink. "I should have told them you were mine. I should have forged a birth certificate. I've thought about it so many times. Everyone in town had watched us raising you. They all assumed you were ours."

Jean turned back to me.

"My mother died not long after that. And my father—a month later, to the day. Frank and I used up our savings fighting for you in court, but we lost. After a while he wanted to try for a baby of our own. But I couldn't. I didn't want 'a baby.' I wanted you.

Nothing short of you would work. That's when he started building this house. We walked the path every day, and Frank imagined this place for us while I followed him in silence. I hated those walks. But I think they really saved me."

"Why didn't you leave town?" I asked.

She gave a quiet shrug. "I kept thinking she'd give up and bring you back."

"You were waiting for me?"

Jean looked up and nodded. "We had to stay. Just in case." She tucked her hair behind her ears. "Later, we did try to have a baby. But it never took. Many miscarriages later, we gave up."

"Jean," I said, "you're killing me."

"It's terrible, isn't it?" she said, laughing the way you do sometimes with sadness.

"And that's the fight between you and my mother?" I asked.

Jean nodded. "Though '*fight*' is too puny a word. The things you feel about the person who took your child from you—there are no words for that. The way she ripped you from us was so incomprehensibly cruel. To me, but especially to you. This total stranger showed up at our house one day with the sheriff and took you away from everyone who loved you. The terror on your face . . . I can't even think about it without feeling sick."

She paced the kitchen.

I said, "We lived in Hawaii for a while. Then San Diego. Then we followed a guy named Phil to Schenectady. Then Tulsa, Miami, Little Rock." My head was starting to hurt. It wasn't the moving that had been so bad. It just meant that I never had anyone to depend on besides that one crazy woman. The husbands and boyfriends didn't last, and the friendships I made got broken every time we moved. And now, with the pictures in the photo albums ticking through my head like a flip book, the idea of growing up in a real family, with Jean and Frank and two grandparents—the idea that this could have been my life . . . It was too much.

I stood up. "It's time to get the kids."

"I'll go," Jean said, and picked up her keys.

"Jean," I said, stopping her at the door. "Why didn't you tell me before?"

She rubbed her eyes. "I always meant to," she said. "I've written countless letters that I never mailed. As soon as you were old enough, I meant to—on your sixteenth birthday, I thought. Or your graduation. But what would you have thought, getting a letter like that from a crazy old lady? I was a stranger to you by then. I didn't want to mess with your life, or confuse you. And I was afraid," she went on, "that if I did it the wrong way, I might frighten you off forever. So I just kept waiting for the right moment. Which never came."

"And since I've been here? This is the secret you've been not telling me?"

She nodded. "I was letting you get settled in at first," she said. "And then I didn't know how to bring it up. It's all so ugly and so sad. After your mother showed up here, I was amazed at how it felt to see her again. I was just overcome with . . ." She shook her head, like she couldn't even come up with a word.

"Hatred," I said.

Jean nodded. Her eyes looked tired. "That's probably it. And it made it harder to bring it up, not easier."

Jean glanced at the clock. She was late for carpool.

"Go," I said. "It's okay."

We both stood up, and then she was hugging me with that familiar hug. "I'm so sorry I lost you," she said into my ear. And then she was out the door.

Chapter 21

The screen door slapped closed, and I looked back down at the open album on the table. I had work to do in the cheese kitchen, but as soon as I was alone, I knew it would have to wait. I turned and followed Jean out.

"Wait!" I shouted across the farmyard.

Jean turned around.

"There's something I need to do," I said.

"What?" she said, but I think she knew.

"I need to go see my mother."

Jean took a few steps toward me. She was assessing me, I could tell. Deciding exactly how crazy our conversation had made me. "Okay," she said next. "I get that."

"Can you put the kids to bed?"

"Of course."

"And can Sunshine do the evening milking?"

"Yes," Jean said. "She can." She studied me for a second. "Are you sure you want to go?"

My whole body felt like television static. I nodded.

She peered at me. "What are you hoping to gain from seeing her?"

"I don't know," I said. "But I have to go."

"Just be careful about your expectations."

Something about her tone made me hesitate. Maybe a confrontation wasn't the best idea after all. Maybe it would just make things worse. "Is it pointless to even go?" I asked.

"No," Jean said. "Not as long as you know what you want."

"I want a different mother."

"Not going to happen."

"I want her to see how wrong she was and collapse on the floor in regret."

Jean shook her head at me.

"I want her to apologize."

"Sweetheart," Jean said, "your mother is never going to apologize for anything."

A good reminder. "That's true," I said.

"So," Jean said, "go see her if you need to. But remember who she is. Going to your mother for understanding is like going to the hardware store for bread."

I went. There were an infinite number of things about my life that I'd never be able to change. But at the very least I had to stand up for myself—and after a lifetime of compensating for and apologizing about my mother, that felt like a change in itself. I had to say that I'd been wronged. Out loud. If for no ears other than my own.

Everything Jean had just told me swirled in my head, and it all seemed related. It was like I'd loaded every important thing in my life into the spin cycle. I thought about how often I'd worried that the loss of Danny would haunt my own kids in some inescapable way. But I was the one who was haunted. My kids had lost their dad, but they'd gained Jean, Russ, Sunshine—and even O'Connor as a fishing buddy and martial arts expert. Most important, they had never lost me.

It made me feel terribly sorry for myself, but it made me feel vastly better about my kids. The empathy I'd been using to imagine how life had impacted them had come from my own experience—but my own experience had been so much worse than theirs. I had assumed that losing Danny would leave them with the same kind of permanent homesickness that I carried with me wherever I went. But I suddenly realized that it wouldn't. And then I realized something else: I hadn't felt homesick in a long time.

When I got to my mother's condo, I beat on the door with my fists until I heard the locks start to click. Thirty years of disappointment and anger churned in my body like an inner tsunami, and I fully intended to unleash it all on my mother as soon as she opened the door.

But it wasn't my mother who opened the door. Instead, it was a man I'd never seen before.

"Can I help you?" he asked.

He smelled like cologne, and he wore a T-shirt under his blazer, Don Johnson style.

"I need to see Marsha," I said, pushing right past him.

"She's getting dressed," he said, following me across the living room, unsure if he should stop me. "We have a date."

I left him behind, bursting through my mother's bedroom door and slamming it behind me.

She caught my eyes in the mirror and waited with her eye shadow brush to her lid.

"What?" she said, already irritated.

I just glared.

"She told you," my mother said then, turning around.

I nodded as meanly as I could.

My mother shook her head. "And you hate me now, and I'm a terrible person, and blah blah blah." She didn't wait for a response, but went back to work on the eye shadow.

"It's not funny," I said. "It's not trivial."

"And? What? You're here to tell me I'm the root of all your troubles?"

I gave a fierce nod. "Something like that."

"Please." She unscrewed the cap of her mascara.

"Why did you take me from them?" I said. "I was happy! I was loved!"

"You were my child," she said, self-righteous as ever. "You belonged to me."

"No," I said. "I stopped belonging to you when you left me behind."

My mother sighed and set down her makeup. "Libby, what can I tell you? I was practically a child myself."

"I'm not mad at you for leaving, Marsha," I said, resolving not to call her "Mom" again. "I'm mad at you for coming back."

"For coming back to my own daughter?"

"Why did you do that?" I asked. "What were you thinking?"

My mother turned around then to face me. "I wanted you," she said, as if that explained everything.

I ran my hand into my hair. A whole lifetime of that woman dragging me along behind her without looking back flashed through my memory. "But you didn't!" I said. "You didn't want me."

"That's ridiculous," she said, as if it were actually ridiculous.

"You took me away in a squad car."

"That's not my fault! Jean and Frank were the ones who wanted a standoff at the OK Corral."

"You just wanted someone to love you," I said then, realizing as I spoke the words how true they were. "Someone who didn't have a choice."

I'd hit too close to the mark. "That's fine," she said. "You can believe that if you want to."

"I don't *want* to believe it," I said. "There's no other option!"

"Jean is perfect, and I am a monster," my mother said. "That's fine. But didn't I get you out of that shitty little town? We went places. We saw things!"

"*You* went places," I said. "*You* saw things." I was stuck at home—usually with a twelve-year-old babysitter. Or alone.

"Fine," she said. "I'm a terrible person. Can we move on?"

I shook my head. It was time to do something different. "I'm not sure that we can."

She evaded me with ease, the way she always did—as if she were just delivering the lines of her life. "Libby, Libby, Libby," she said, popping on her shoes. "We can't change the past. Was it the best decision I've ever made? Probably not. But obsessing over it and stomping around yelling about it certainly won't give us the answer. I don't know why you want to spend your whole life looking backward. *I* am looking forward at what's ahead." Before I knew it, she was at the door with her hand on the knob. "And what's ahead tonight is a date. With a man who drives a Ferrari."

Then she opened the door and slipped out, moving into another room and a different setting, expecting that once we were with company, politeness would compel me to drop it.

I caught up with her in the living room as she said, "Tony, this is my daughter, Libby."

"We just met," he said, a little wary.

I hadn't come for revenge. But suddenly the opportunity was there. Because the truest thing about my mother was that she needed the approval of strangers. Male strangers, in particular. She needed to impress them. She needed to dazzle and charm and seduce them. She needed to see herself reflected in their eyes exactly the way she wanted to be. It was why she never stayed with anyone. Once they got to know her well enough to see her faults, they couldn't give her the only thing she wanted: admiration. And nobody knew her faults better than I did. Which is why I was such a drag.

"We didn't meet, exactly," I said to my mother. "I barged past him on my way to confront you for abandoning me as a baby."

My mother's face stiffened into a smile. "Very funny," she said.

"And then for changing your mind," I went on, "and coming back to rip me from my adoptive family. In a squad car."

I was ready to go on and on. I was ready to expose all of her weaknesses and imperfections in front of this new man. It was the perfect chance to humiliate her and get her in the one place it would really hurt. I pulled in a breath. *Go home,* I was about to say to him. *This woman is hopeless.*

In that instant, however, my mother's composure broke. She leaned in to point at me. "Don't you dare make fun of me!" Her voice came out in a rush like I'd never heard before. "I never wanted to be a mother. But it happened. And after I left, I could have stayed away forever. But I forced myself to come back for you. I did the right thing, damn it—and you can't make me regret that."

The room was dead quiet. It felt like the first true thing she'd ever said to me.

I took a real look at my mother for the first time in years. Suddenly I noticed that her hair had gotten thinner. Her mascara was a little smudged under one eye. She was smaller than I remembered, too. The word that came to mind was *frail*.

I found myself thinking about how parents always seem like giants to their kids. They seem to control the whole world. But of course that's just perspective. It's not that parents are big, it's that kids are small. It's not that parents are powerful, it's that kids are powerless. My kids made the mistake all the time of thinking I should know things that I didn't, or that I should be able to solve things that I couldn't. There was no way for them to understand that I was just me—just a former child myself. And for the first time it hit me that my mother, in this way at least, was exactly the same.

I thought about how she had spent a whole lifetime looking for something she couldn't find. And I knew right then something about her life that she didn't: She was never going to find it. Not just because she was looking in the wrong places. Because whatever it was she wanted so badly just wasn't out there.

And with that, I felt something new for my mother: compassion.

"Well," my mother said then, lifting her chin to step back into her persona. "If you're finished with your little outburst, we've got dinner reservations."

I nodded. My voice was quiet now, all the urgency drained away. "I am finished with my little outburst."

I'd never turn her into a different person. I'd never make her see what she'd done wrong, or make her regret it, or even make her apologize. I would never have the mother I wanted, but she would never have what she wanted, either. And that wasn't just sad for me. It was sad for both of us. As thoroughly as my mother had ruined my life, she'd done a far more thorough job of ruining her own.

My mother stood up taller. "Good," she mustered at last.

"I'm going home now," I said, and suddenly I knew the only words in the world that had a chance to make things better instead of worse. I spoke them with care, fully aware that the person who really needed to hear them was me.

I turned back at the door and met her eyes. "And by the way," I said, "I forgive you."

Ten blurry minutes later, I was parked in front of the house I'd lived in with Danny and the kids. It was a 1940s *Leave It to Beaver* two-story with honeysuckle growing on the fence and a barn-red front door. Although, looking more closely now, the new owners appeared to have repainted the door black. Which looked terrible.

It was dark outside by now. The lights were on inside the house, and I could see the new family sitting down to dinner. The mom finished up in the kitchen as the father worked to keep three little boys in their chairs.

Back when we were living with my mother, it had soothed me to watch them. I'd still felt like a part of that place, like I belonged there—like I had every right to be there. That night, though, whatever magic watching these strangers inhabit my old house had held was gone. I used to be endlessly fascinated by them—not because of anything about who they were but because of where they were. That was *my driveway* they'd parked on. They slept in *my bedroom*. They ate in *my dining room*.

I hadn't been back since we'd moved away. Now it felt creepy and stalkerish. I felt like a police car would pull up at any moment and the officer would tell me to move along.

That night I didn't know them. Nor did I particularly care. They were suddenly strangers—as, of course, they'd been all along. Their lives were irrelevant to my own. The house they lived in, I realized then, no longer felt like my home. And next I realized something else: That house was no longer my home because, at last, I had settled into another one.

Chapter 22

A few nights later, at dinner on an unseasonably warm late April evening, Abby told us a new joke. "Why did the cow cross the road?"

"Why?" we all asked—especially Tank, who actually wanted to know.

"To go to the *moo*vies."

We gave her a good laugh, and then she said, "Got that from the kid next to me at lunch."

"Sarah B.," I said, nodding. I had the seating chart memorized.

Abby shook her head. "No, we had free seating today."

"It wasn't Sarah B.?"

"No," Abby said. "It was PeePants Gaveski." She took a gulp of water. "Except everybody calls him Jimmy now."

If I hadn't been so busy gaping, I might have shared an appreciative glance with Jean over the idea that "Jimmy" was somehow PeePants's nickname.

But I was too busy staring at Abby. "What was he doing sitting next to you?" I asked, forgetting the don't-ask-what-you-want-to-know rule.

Abby shrugged.

"Was he bothering you?"

She shook her head. "Nope."

I was too shocked to appreciate the triumph of the way that Abby was looking at me. Like: *There was an empty seat. Why wouldn't he take it?*

Later that night, though, after the kids were asleep, I replayed the moment over and over. Because the expression on her face told me exactly what I'd been wanting to hear all this time. That things were better. That PeePants had stopped teasing her. And that Abby, in that beautiful way kids do, had carried on with her life.

Jean had even extracted the information from Abby that PeePants had moved on to another kid—a "really, really, really small boy" in her class named George.

"How small is he?" Tank wanted to know. "Mouse-sized?"

"No," Abby answered, considering the question. "Bigger than a mouse. Maybe the size of a goat."

"Without the hooves," Tank added.

"That's right," Abby said. "He's the shape of a person, but the height of a goat."

Once that was settled, Abby admitted that she'd been teaching George some martial arts on the playground so he could protect himself from PeePants if the need arose.

"If O'Connor ever comes back, maybe I can invite George over for a lesson," Abby suggested. "From a professional sensei."

"Maybe," I said, not wanting to get anyone's hopes up.

But even as my worries about Abby waned, others cropped up

to keep me busy. I discussed it with Sunshine on what were becoming weekly trips up to the haunted house for séances: the way troubles seemed to resolve themselves only to make room for new ones.

Though I shouldn't even call those nights by the bonfire "séances." Aside from a few perfunctory calling-up-the-dead opening activities, there was nothing otherworldly about them. The haunted house seemed significantly less haunted now that I knew it was my childhood home, and the séances seemed significantly more like marshmallow-and-beer picnics now that Sunshine had become my friend.

She always listened carefully, and even though she didn't have any more answers than I did, she had a way of asking questions that got me thinking in new ways. She told me frankly about her struggles to resist the addictive pull of her old life (which had surfaced most recently when her ex-manager called with an offer to do a reality TV show called *Where Are They Now?*) and to figure out who she really was and what she loved to do.

I told her about my struggles, too: my worries about Abby, how I was trying to comprehend the truth about my childhood, and even my crush on O'Connor—and the temptation I kept feeling to feign a reason to drop by his house and check on him. Something about him being gone made it feel like I was holding my breath underwater. And I really, really wanted some air.

"Go see him," Sunshine said, as if it were the most obvious answer in the world.

"I can't," I said. "I'd be intruding."

"He wants you to intrude."

"There's no way to know that."

"I saw you two at Jean's party. I saw how he was looking at you."

That got my attention. "How was he looking at me?"

"The way cops look at doughnuts," Sunshine said, wiggling her eyebrows.

I felt embarrassed then. I put my hands over my face.

But Sunshine was having fun. "The way smokers look at cigarettes," she went on. "The way chocoholics look at Ding Dongs."

"Okay, okay," I said, waving at her to stop.

"It's tragic, really," she said. "That he's not free."

"It's not *tragic*," I said, wanting to be precise. "It just sucks."

"Maybe I could stop by his house for a visit," Sunshine suggested, "and leave my phone by accident, and then ask you to go get it for me. Or maybe we could break something at the farm and call him to come fix it."

"Nah," I said. "I'm not that desperate."

"Okay," Sunshine said. "We'll just wait until you are." Then she took a big swig of her organic beer, looked me up and down, and said, "Shouldn't be too long now."

And, in fact, it wasn't.

Not even a full day later, as Jean and the kids and I were finishing dinner, O'Connor showed up at the screen door and stood outside without speaking or coming in. When Jean noticed him, she set her fork down.

"What is it?" she asked.

O'Connor's voice was all gravel as he answered, "She's gone."

Nobody knew exactly what he meant, but even the kids could read that voice. They didn't shout his name or run toward him to beg for airplane rides. They held still, and we all watched Jean stand up and step out onto the porch.

The moment felt so important that the kids and I tiptoed up

the stairs without a word and talked in a whisper all through bathtime. I didn't know what "gone" meant, and all I could do was judge from his face that it was not a good thing. Had she died? Had she gotten lost somehow? What the hell was he talking about?

But I would have to wait to find out until after the bubble bath and the pajamas and the bedtime story. Though I couldn't tell you which bedtime story we read. My head was entirely elsewhere.

As soon as the kids' light was out, I tiptoed back down and eavesdropped. There at the foot of the stairs, I felt a swell of gratitude for Jean's love of fresh air. With the windows open all around the house, I could hear the conversation perfectly.

They were on the porch swing, and the extra length of chain clinked against itself as they swung back and forth.

"You did the right thing," Jean was saying.

"I'm not sure," O'Connor said.

"I can't believe she just showed up at your place without calling."

"Actually, she did call. She left a bunch of messages."

"Messages you didn't return?"

"That's right."

"Becky can take better care of Erin than you can," Jean said.

O'Connor sounded like his jaw was tight. "Erin hated Becky," he said. "She really hated her."

"Things were different back then," Jean said.

"She thought she was prissy, and anal, and perfectionistic. . ." O'Connor went on.

"That's right," Jean interrupted. "All qualities that make her a perfect caretaker now."

"Erin would never have wanted to live with her," O'Connor said. "If she could understand what's happening, she'd never forgive me."

"But she can't," Jean said.

"You don't know that," O'Connor said. "Maybe she can understand but just can't express it. Maybe she watched me hand her over to Becky and couldn't even beg me not to."

"Is that what you're torturing yourself with?"

O'Connor's voice seemed to trip over itself. "I promised to take care of her in sickness and in health."

"A lot has changed since that day," Jean said. "A whole lot."

They got quiet. The swing creaked back and forth.

"Even if she did understand what was happening," Jean went on then, "she'd know it's the best option."

"You don't know that, either," O'Connor said.

"I do know it," Jean said. "And you will, too, when you've had some rest."

He took a deep breath and let it out.

"Becky has money," Jean continued. "She has time, an empty nest, and a busy husband. She wants to help, now that they're back to stay, and she'll be good at it. She needs a project."

"Erin is not a project," O'Connor said.

"You know what I mean."

"If I sign over guardianship," O'Connor said, "Becky could put her in a facility."

"But she won't," Jean said. "She said she won't."

"But she could."

"I suppose she could," Jean said. "But that's a risk you have to take."

"Why?" O'Connor said.

"Because you need your life back."

It was quiet then. Just the squeak and clink of the swing.

"I'm selling the house," O'Connor said next.

"Are you sure you want to do that?"

"It's too empty there now that she's gone," he said. "I've slept in the Airstream the past two nights."

"Is she all settled in?" Jean asked.

"Becky says so," he said.

"But you haven't been up to visit?"

"No."

"Maybe you should go," Jean suggested.

"Maybe," O'Connor said, as though he didn't for a second believe it. "Becky's convinced it'll give me peace of mind."

"But?"

"But I don't see peace of mind in my future."

"You're more likely to see a thing," Jean said, "if you look for it."

"I'm fine."

"You're not," Jean said. "But I'm not going to be the one to tell you that."

"Okay," he said. "Don't tell me."

"You'll figure it out," Jean said. "You should come back to work. Libby's killing herself with only Sunshine for help."

"How is Libby?" he asked, and I tried to read his voice, but I couldn't.

"She's probably been better," Jean said.

"You told her about her mom, didn't you?"

"I did."

"How's she doing with all that?"

"How do you think?"

There was a pause, when even the porch swing got quiet, and then O'Connor said, "I'll be back to work in the morning."

In the morning, when I found O'Connor milking Pocahontas in the barn, just like old times, I said by way of greeting, "What are you doing here?"

"Getting back to work," O'Connor said, extra casually, as if it hadn't been more than a month since we'd seen each other. And then I couldn't decide if he was acting super casual because he really felt that way or because he *didn't*. I myself was acting extra super casual. But only because everything I felt was the opposite.

"Where's Sunshine?" I asked.

"I kicked her out," he said, glancing up.

I still couldn't believe he was really there. But I could see the proof. His Airstream trailer was parked out on the lawn like a space-age flying machine. I'd seen it through the window at breakfast and caught my breath.

"You're back, then?" I asked.

O'Connor kept milking. "Yup."

"And is that your spaceship out there?"

"Yes, it is."

"Tank would like to go flying in it after school," I said.

"Who wouldn't?"

"You own that thing?" I asked.

"It's not a 'thing,'" he said. "It's a 1973 Overlander. You should come for the tour."

"Are you going to be—" I hesitated. "Living there?"

"Yup," he said, as if no further explanation were needed. Which it wasn't, because I'd eavesdropped and heard everything I needed to know. But he didn't know that. . . . Or at least I hoped he didn't.

I was still standing there, watching him. He turned and met my eyes for the first time. "Jean is worried about you," he said.

"I'm fine," I said.

"Jean doesn't think so."

"Jean doesn't think you're fine, either."

"You didn't answer my question," he said.

"Did you ask me a question?" I asked. He was still holding my gaze, and it made me a little woozy.

He stood up so we were face-to-face. "My question is, 'Are you okay?' "

I nodded a little before I spoke. "I'm okay."

"Good," he said, as though he really meant it. There was a pause, and we both seemed to be resisting a magnetic pull to step closer. O'Connor looked away first. "Now get yourself to work," he said, nodding at my milking stool. "Mary Todd Lincoln's not going to milk herself."

That night, kids asleep and dishes done, I decided to take O'Connor up on his trailer tour. And here's why: He had a television, which I could see through his window, and it was on.

I slipped out the back door and crossed the yard in the moonlight, like a moth fluttering toward a porch light. Then I stood a few feet away from the Airstream for a minute, debating if I really wanted to knock.

Before I'd decided, O'Connor opened the door.

"Need something?" he asked.

"Um," I said, "I was just wondering what you were watching in here."

He glanced back at the TV, like he didn't understand.

"Because Jean doesn't have a TV," I rushed to explain. "She doesn't even approve of them. So it's been months since I've seen any TV at all. And I've kind of been in withdrawal. You know, like getting the shakes and all."

"You're here to watch TV?" he asked.

"If you don't mind," I said, suddenly feeling shy.

"I don't mind," he said, opening the door wider.

I slid past him to climb in.

The trailer looked larger from the outside. The sofa, in fact, doubled as O'Connor's bed, which was still—or perhaps perpetually—unmade. He pulled the covers a little straighter, and I sat down primly, pausing only to notice that his sheets were a blue chambray and a much higher thread count than I would have expected.

I looked up to see O'Connor watching me.

"What?" I asked.

"I'm just wondering what we're about to watch."

I shrugged. "Anything. I'm not picky."

He nodded.

"Except," I went on, "I probably won't want to watch shows with corpses in them. Or body parts. Or forensic pathologists."

"Okay," O'Connor said.

"Or war, either," I added. "Or explosions, or bombs, or severed limbs flying through the air."

"Okay," he said, starting to look amused.

"And no serial killers," I went on. "No rapists or child murderers. Nothing to do with death or destruction."

"So, not picky at all."

"Other than that stuff," I said, standing my ground. "Does that surprise you?"

"No."

"Good," I said in my own defense. "Because I am a mom."

"Moms can't enjoy death and destruction?"

"No," I said. "At least I can't."

He waited for an explanation.

"Because," I went on, "here I am, busting my ass to raise these two little people and teach them how to make the right choices and do the right things and be kind to each other. I'm, like, pouring my own life into them and really giving it everything I have in the belief that I am doing something—you know—critically, vastly, staggeringly important." I didn't know how to explain it better than that. "And I don't want to see Rambo or somebody come along and kill them."

O'Connor thought that this was funny. "You don't want Rambo to kill your children?"

"Anyone's children," I corrected. "I don't want Rambo killing anyone's children. Right? All those people he kills were once babies. They had mothers who changed their diapers and stayed up all night with them when they had fevers and loved them so, so desperately. And then Rambo just walks in with a big old blaster, and—*boom*—all of it was for nothing."

"A big old blaster," O'Connor said, shaking his head a little.

"It's insulting," I said.

"You realize they're just actors," he said. "They're not really dying in those movies."

"Irrelevant!" I said. "And patronizing."

"Sorry."

"I like shows about good things. Hopeful things."

"Like?"

"I don't know," I said. "Like people taking care of each other."

O'Connor wrinkled his nose, like such an idea was too cheesy for comment.

"Isn't there enough misery in the world?" I said. "Do I really have to spend my leisure time absorbing more of it?"

"Valid point," he said.

"I don't know why we all think war and dismemberment are the only important topics—"

"I think that's a book, actually: *War and Dismemberment*."

"What about kindness? What about resilience? What about bravery?"

O'Connor nodded, and then shrugged. "Well," he said, "it doesn't really matter anyway."

"It matters to me!" I said.

"I mean," he clarified, "in terms of watching television here."

"Why not?"

"My TV only gets two channels."

My shoulders slumped.

"Two and a half, actually," he corrected.

I glanced with disappointment at the TV.

"But between those channels," he said, handing me the remote, "it's totally your call."

He sat down next to me on the bed-sofa and picked up a library book that had been half hidden in the sheets.

"What are you going to do?" I asked, looking at the book.

He held it up. "I'm going to read."

"What are you reading?" I asked, surprised to see how thick it was.

"Oh, it's a war story," he said. "You'd find it insulting. And patronizing."

"Fair enough."

Two hours later, I was still there, clicking happily between the two and a half available channels. O'Connor had started yawning loudly, but I was ignoring his hints.

Finally he leaned over and knocked on my head.

"It's eleven o'clock, crazy person," he said. "Dubbie crows at five in the morning."

I ignored him.

He shifted positions so he blocked my view of the TV, but I just leaned to the side and kept watching.

"Okay," he said, "if that's the way you want to play it." He started taking off his boots.

"What are you doing?"

"I'm getting ready for bed," he said, pulling off his socks and dropping them on the floor. "I'm tired. Scram."

"Five more minutes," I said, glancing back at the TV.

"Nope," O'Connor said, starting to unbuckle his belt.

"I just want to finish this—"

But he wasn't kidding.

Next thing I knew, he'd unbuttoned his jeans and dropped them to his ankles.

"Hello!" I said, jumping up and stumbling back toward the door. "Unnecessary!"

O'Connor, in his boxers, gave a big grin. "Lucky for you I've got on underwear."

I put my hand over my eyes. "Jesus, O'Connor!"

"Wasn't entirely sure if I did or not," he went on, looking down for confirmation.

And with that, I rattled open the door, darted down the steps, and fled into the black night.

"Don't let the panther get you!" he called after me.

"Don't let the underpants police get you!" I called right back. And I scampered across the yard to the house.

After that, I started showing up at O'Connor's trailer door after bedtime every night, hoping for a TV fix. It was so blissful to space out in that particular way, and to mute all the worries that followed me like theme music, even if the only offerings on those two channels were *Seinfeld* reruns or the local news. I'd take it. I'd take it and be grateful.

Every night O'Connor read his book while I manned the remote. Every night around eleven he kicked me out against my will. And every night I skittered back across the yard to the house, worrying like hell about the infinitesimally small odds of a panther attack. Because that's how I roll.

I kept deciding I was going to hold back from going over there—that it was time to stop the insanity—but then I kept doing it anyway. Once I saw that flickering blue light, I was pretty much lost.

Jean swore she didn't mind losing me as her weeknight partner for Scrabble, dominoes, and gin rummy. She was reading a new series about a time-traveling zombie that she simply could not put down, and she actually seemed pleased to see me go. Even Russ was on pause until she got to the end of book seven.

"You'd rather read that book than hang out with me," I said one night on my way out the door.

She shrugged as though it couldn't be helped. "You have many great qualities," she said, "but you're not a time-traveling zombie."

———

hings went on like this for a good week until one night I looked out at O'Connor's trailer and found it dark. I walked over anyway and tried the door to the trailer, thinking I might just watch on my own until he got back from wherever he might be, but the handle was locked.

I took a seat in one of his woven lawn chairs and waited outside for a good while, feeling immensely disappointed, before giving up and heading home. Back at the house, I sat on the couch next to Jean and read a book of my own about a woman who planted an heirloom vegetable garden. We both turned in early, and I was pleased—as I mentioned several times—at the idea of how refreshed I'd be after a really good night's sleep. After multiple glances through the kitchen window at the still-dark Airstream, I was down for the count by nine-thirty.

But at midnight I was up again.

Someone was banging on the back door, and after I flew down the hall to the kitchen, I saw it was O'Connor—leaning against it with his head and pounding it with his fist.

I turned the handle, and he stumbled over the threshold, catching himself on my shoulders.

"Shut up!" I hissed. "Everybody's sleeping."

O'Connor looked around as though it hadn't occurred to him anyone might be asleep. "Sorry," he said.

His hands were still on my shoulders, using them for balance, thumbs against my collarbone.

"You smell like beer," I said.

He nodded. "That sounds about right," he said. "It's what I had for dinner."

"You're drunk."

"You're correct."

"Are you looking for Jean?" I asked. It occurred to me he might be in crisis and need a professional. "I can wake her."

"I'm not looking for Jean," he said. "I'm looking for you."

"Why?" I asked.

The question seemed to flummox him. "In case," he said after a minute, "you wanted to watch TV."

"Not at midnight, I don't," I said.

"Is it midnight already?"

"Yes, it's midnight," I said, getting all motherly and businesslike. "You have to be up early, I have to be up early. Let's put you to bed."

I turned him around to steer him out onto the lawn, and he said, "You're wearing that damned nightgown again."

I led him down the porch steps. "What's wrong with it?"

"It's too thin. It's like tissue paper."

"Well," I said, steering us across the yard, "if I were in my bed under the quilt, it really wouldn't matter." I hadn't stopped for shoes, so I was going slowly through the grass, hoping not to step on anything prickly.

"It's been a long time since I saw a drunk person," I added.

"Me too," he said.

I gave him a look that said, *"Please."*

"Really," he insisted. "I never do this."

I kept walking.

"I couldn't, could I?" he went on. "I had to stay alert and capable. I had responsibilities. But tonight it suddenly occurred to me: I can do anything I want. And I wanted to get drunk."

"And how is it?"

"It's awesome."

Just then I got a sticker-burr in my big toe. I let go of O'Connor and he tumbled onto the grass.

"Hey!" he said, as though I'd fallen down on the job.

"Shh!" I said.

I pulled the burr out and tossed it at O'Connor, who by now was lying on his back with his hands behind his head, gazing at the stars. "I know all the constellations," he said. "Did you know that?"

I held out my hand to help him up. "That's great, Copernicus. Let's go."

Instead of me pulling him up, however, he somehow pulled me down, and I landed with an "oof" on his chest.

"Watch out!" he said to me, as if I had been clumsy.

I scrambled back up and dusted grass off my nightgown.

He thought it was terribly funny, but I put my hands on my hips. "Do you want me to help you or not? Because I could be sleeping right now."

He got serious. "I want you to help me. I do."

"Then get up, man. You're wasting my time."

When we got to the Airstream, there were beer cans littered around the lawn chairs.

"These weren't here before."

"Before?"

It felt like I was really admitting to something as I said, "I came over after I put the kids to bed."

"That was a long time ago," he pointed out.

It clearly was. "Are these cans all yours?"

"I never do anything half-assed," he said.

It took him at least five minutes to unlock the door—and he wouldn't let me help. Once we were up the steps, he sat on the bed-sofa, and I said, "I'm going to get you some water and aspirin. Then I'm going back to bed."

"Okay," he said, holding himself upright.

I found a bottle of water in his mini-fridge and hunted down the aspirin in the medicine cabinet—noting that we used the same toothpaste. I brought him two pills and said, "Take these. And finish off the water." Then I knelt in front of him to pull off his boots, which somehow seemed like the right thing to do. He did as he was told and glugged the water, finishing off the bottle and lowering his head just as I finished with his second boot and raised mine—and suddenly we were nose to nose.

"Do you want to know what else I wanted to do when I realized I could do anything?" he asked then, his mouth just inches away.

I shook my head.

He looked down at my mouth, then back up at my eyes. The whole room felt completely still except for the two of us breathing. "I wanted to see you," he said.

In any other situation I'd have leaned in to kiss him just then. But he was wrong when he'd said he'd realized he could do anything. He couldn't really do anything. Because he was still married, no matter how agonizing or tragic or hopeless the circumstances. And knowing that was just enough to hold me back from the pull of longing that was tugging at me like a tide. I didn't lean in, though every cell in my body wanted to. Instead, I did the only thing I could. I stood up and shoved him sideways until he tumped over on his bed.

"Go to sleep," I said. "I'm putting a trash can here in case you have to barf."

And then, with the moment officially ruined and the right thing officially done, there was nothing left to do but take myself back to my bed and regret it.

Chapter 23

The next morning, I woke up wondering about seeing O'Connor at milking time once he was sober again.

There had been so much longing the night before, right on the surface of things in a totally new way. Sometimes alcohol can work like a truth serum, but sometimes it'll just make people say anything at all. I wasn't totally sure which effect all that beer had had on O'Connor, but I knew I would read the answer on his face when he saw me again without his beer goggles on—and I was dreading finding out. I confess to breaking down and putting on some lip gloss before starting the morning chores.

But he wasn't in the barn when I got there. He slept through the morning milking, his trailer silent until long after I'd milked every goat and fed every animal on the farm. Jean had left early for her Tuesday morning coffee-and-crafting meeting, and with Sunshine gone and the kids at school, I had no one at all to distract me from the crackly sense of anticlimax I carried all morning.

At some point, I kept thinking, he'd have to wake up.

But before he did, I got a phone call. About Abby. From the nurse at school.

"I don't want you to panic," she said, catapulting me at light speed into a state of panic, "but Abby's here in my office."

"What happened?" I asked.

"She has a head injury, and you need to come pick her up."

"What kind of a head injury?" I asked, every muscle now tensed for action.

"Not a terrible one," the nurse assured me. "It appears she fell down on the playground and scraped her head on the fence."

It was the weirdest injury I'd ever heard of. "She scraped her head on the fence?"

The nurse went on. "She's here in my office with an ice pack. She's in good spirits. But she should take it easy today."

"I'll be there in ten minutes," I said, grabbing my purse and idling next to the phone. If Jean had had a cordless, I'd have walked it out into the yard.

"One more thing," the nurse said. "When the head bleeds, it bleeds a lot."

"Okay," I said.

"It's stopped now," she said. "But Abby's clothes are pretty well drenched."

"Drenched?"

"Just so you can prepare yourself for the sight of it."

That morning Abby had worn a pink T-shirt that she and Jean had decorated with little white ribbon flowers. I tried to imagine it drenched in blood.

"I'm on my way," I said, just about to hang up.

"One more thing," the nurse added. "Abby's explaining to me now that she didn't trip on the playground. She was pushed."

My heart turned into a brick. "Who pushed her?"

I could hear the nurse turn to Abby and say, "Who pushed you, darlin'?"

And I didn't even need the nurse to report back the answer. Because through the phone, from across the room, I could hear Abby's clear voice say, "Jimmy Gaveski."

As I was racing across the yard, O'Connor chose that exact moment to emerge from his trailer, hung over, his eyelids at half-mast.

I slowed for just a second as he sauntered toward me, but I didn't even really focus on him. He'd gone from filling the entire frame of my mind to the size of a tiny speck of dust on the corner.

"Hey," he said as we both paused a few feet apart. And in that moment, reading his uncomfortable face, I had my answer about the night before. The way he'd looked at me . . . it had been beer goggles.

It was my worst-case scenario for seeing him again, but it paled in comparison to the worst-case scenario of my sweet child waiting for me in the nurse's office at school. I edged toward the car.

"I just want to apologize for last night," he said. He looked physically uncomfortable, the way a person would if he were, say, standing barefoot on a hot summer sidewalk. Or deeply embarrassed.

"No need," I said, still edging.

"Can we talk for a minute?" he said. "There's something I need to tell you."

But I didn't have time for that conversation. The whole thing flashed through my mind in a millisecond. He was sorry, it had been a mistake to go out drinking, he didn't know what he'd been thinking, he didn't think of me that way. Blah, blah, blah.

"You don't have to tell me anything," I said. "And I really have to go."

I turned and walked fast toward the car.

O'Connor followed me. "Where?"

"The school just called," I said over my shoulder. "PeePants Gaveski pushed Abby down on the playground and gashed open her head."

"Pushed her down?"

"The nurse warned me to expect a lot of blood."

I'd reached the car door and was moving fast. I swung in, buckled up, and hit the ignition before I noticed that O'Connor was buckling up right next to me in the passenger seat, all traces of hangover removed from his demeanor. He sat straight up and leaned forward, as if willing the minivan to gallop away.

"What are you doing?"

"I'm coming with you," he said.

There wasn't time to argue. I floored it, and the wheels of the minivan skidded on the gravel road as we fishtailed out onto the highway. The school was fifteen minutes away, but we made it in ten. On the drive, I told him everything I knew.

As we screeched up to the front steps, the principal was waiting at the entrance. We were well into May, but she looked so frazzled, I wondered if she'd make it to the end of the school year.

"It's not as bad as it looks," she promised as we coursed through the hallways. Class was in session, and the place felt deserted. "And Abby is alert and cheerful," she added. Even though my endless frustration over this PeePants problem was crystallizing into rage at the same moment, it did make me feel a little better to hear that.

But only until we reached the nurse's office.

The sight of Abby—lying so still with closed eyes, the hair on one entire side of her head matted and her T-shirt crimson with blood—made me literally dizzy. It's the kind of nightmare image you don't even let yourself prepare to see. She looked dead. In that instant I was transported back to the moment the ER nurse had pulled the curtain back on Danny.

My knees seemed to disappear.

I buckled, but O'Connor, who I'd forgotten was even there, caught me before I hit the floor. He pulled me back up, put his arm around my waist, and held me steady. I took a big, slow breath, and then I remembered who I needed to be in that moment, and I kneeled down beside Abby.

She opened her eyes. "Hi, Mom."

"Hey, ladybug," I said. "How are ya?"

"Good," Abby said.

"Does it hurt?"

"Not really," Abby said. "Just the blood, you know, kind of freaked me out."

"What happened, sweetheart?" I asked.

"Jimmy Gaveski pushed me," Abby said.

"That little shit," I said.

"Mom," Abby said, glancing over at the nurse. Then, in a whisper: " '*Shit*' is a curse word."

"I thought Jimmy Gaveski wasn't bothering you anymore," I said. "I thought he was picking on some other kid."

"He wasn't bothering me," Abby said. "That was the problem. He was bothering George."

"What do you mean?"

Abby sat up, to better explain. I tried to stop her at first, but the nurse said it was okay if she felt up to it—and Abby clearly did. She swung her feet off the side of the cot and gestured with her arms. "Jimmy kept pushing George down. You know that section of the playground with all those big tree roots everywhere?"

I didn't, but I nodded anyway.

"He pushed him into the tree roots. He kept saying, 'Stop stumbling! Stop stumbling!' But then he'd push him and make him stumble. George's knees were all bloody and everything." With that, she pointed across the room, and for the first time I noticed a second cot, this one with a kindergarten-sized boy lying on it. His knees were bandaged, and so were the heels of his palms.

"Hi, George," I said.

"Hello," he said, lifting a bandaged hand to wave.

I turned back to Abby. "That's why PeePants Gaveski shoved you? You were standing up for George?"

Abby nodded emphatically. "That's right. I said, 'Knock it off, Jimmy. That's not cool.'" She turned toward O'Connor, and from the look that passed between them, I could tell he'd taught her the phrase.

The rest of what she had to say was for O'Connor, too. "I was about to use Crouching Chicken on him," Abby went on. "Or maybe the Ice Fist. But he fought dirty and slammed me into the fence while I was still helping George to his feet."

"But why, sweetheart?" I asked. I could feel all my old worries about Abby rushing back into my body like icy water into the *Titanic*. "He was finally leaving you alone! He'd moved on. Why on earth would you step in like that and get it started all over again?"

It was a cowardly question; I knew it even as I spoke the words. And cowardly wasn't Abby's style.

"Mom," she said to me, as if the answer were so obvious she couldn't believe she had to say it, "somebody had to help George."

I t was agreed that Abby should go home—and get an ice cream cone for bravery on the way. The nurse rooted around in Abby's hair with her fingers to show me the cut on the scalp, which really didn't look that bad for such a gusher. It was maybe an inch long, but it was thin, clean, and already scabbing over. The nurse said we could go get stitches if we wanted to, but she thought it would heal up just fine without them.

"No one will see the scar under all that pretty hair," the nurse said.

From across the room, George added, "Plus, scars are awesome."

Through it all, O'Connor was absolutely silent. He stood next to me as if poised to catch me again, and didn't say a word. That is, until we were walking out past the principal's office and saw the newly suspended PeePants sitting on a bench waiting to be picked up and driven home.

"That's him," Abby said as we approached, stopping to point. "That's PeePants Gaveski."

We all stopped, turned, and stared at him. He glanced at us and then turned his head away.

For some reason I'd been expecting a redhead. In my mind, he was an iconic TV-style sitcom bully—a tall, mean, freckled kid with a pug nose and a sneer. But that wasn't what I saw on the bench. The real PeePants had mousy hair and totally nondescript features. He had a nose and eyes and a mouth and ears, but I couldn't tell you much else about them. If he was heading for a life of crime, he'd chosen the right profession. You could never pick this kid out of a lineup.

"This is the kid who pushed you?" O'Connor asked Abby, speaking up for the first time since we'd arrived at the school.

"Yes," Abby said.

"This is the kid who's been calling you names all year and taunting you?"

"Yes."

Without another word, O'Connor made it over to PeePants in one step, grabbed him by one arm and the back of the collar, and dragged him right out the set of doors that led to the playground. As the doors clanked closed behind them, Abby and I turned to each other for a reality check—and then hustled to follow.

O'Connor and PeePants were several steps ahead, and when O'Connor let go, the poor kid stumbled and hit the ground.

O'Connor turned around and found Abby's eyes. "Is this your class?" he asked.

Abby nodded.

"Second graders!" O'Connor shouted then, in a voice so loud it shocked even the teachers into silence. "Listen up!"

O'Connor waited for everyone's attention. PeePants, too petrified to escape, waited for O'Connor's next move.

"This kid," O'Connor announced, "has been bullying my friend Abby Moran all year. And I'm here to tell you that the bullying is over." O'Connor turned to PeePants but continued to yell. "If you touch Abby again, even by accident, or call her a name, or even dare to speak to her, I will come and find you. I haven't decided yet if I'll break your arm, or your neck, or maybe even poke out your eyeballs. But I guarantee that you will spend every minute of every day of the rest of your life regretting that you even thought about messing with my friend. And if that doesn't stop you, I'll come back for your parents, and your brother, and your dog, and your pet hamster. Do you hear me?"

PeePants gave the tiniest nod.

"And that goes for all of you," O'Connor went on, gesturing around. "If you see this little shit hurting someone or teasing someone, you stand up and stop him. Be brave! Do the right thing! And then tell Abby to tell me. And I will come after this kid like a bolt of fire."

The teachers were onto O'Connor now. There was so much wrong with what he was doing that I was sure that he'd wind up in jail. The teacher nearest to us started marching toward him, saying in her teacher voice, "Sir, you can't—"

"And these teachers can't protect you," O'Connor roared over her, turning back to PeePants. "I will ram this playground fence with my truck if I have to. I will run over your pets and haunt your dreams. I will make you wish you'd never been born."

"Sir!" the teacher said, totally outraged. "I'm calling the sheriff!" She shook her cellphone at O'Connor like it was a weapon.

"Go ahead," O'Connor dared. "He's my cousin."

Who knew if it was true or not? It shut her right down.

"Do your job," O'Connor said, pointing at her. "Or I'll do it for you."

I was sure no parenting book in the world would tell you to march into your kid's school and threaten to maim her bully, and I was equally sure that if they could find a way to do it, these teachers would slap charges and a restraining order on O'Connor before the day was out.

But in that moment, if only to myself, I made it official: I loved him.

And so when O'Connor stormed past us and blasted back

through the double doors and down the hallway, leaving PeePants and an entire slack-jawed class of seven- and eight-year-olds staring behind him, Abby and I joined hands and followed.

But not before Abby turned back to PeePants, still on the ground, and said, in a moment I will remember for the rest of my life: "Take that, you little shit."

On the drive home, with Abby in the back and O'Connor in the passenger seat still breathing like an angry bull, something hit me.

"Abby," I said, "PeePants Gaveski never totally left you alone, did he?"

Abby waited a minute before she admitted, "Not completely."

I hadn't wanted to be right. "Seriously?"

"He mostly stopped," Abby said, clarifying. "But he still calls me 'Limper.'"

"Why didn't you tell me?"

She shrugged.

"Abby," I said again. "Why didn't you tell me about it?"

She looked out the window for a second, and then she said, "I don't know. I guess I didn't want you to feel like a bad mom."

"Why would that make me feel like a bad mom?"

"I don't know," Abby said, turning her eyes back to the window. "I guess because you couldn't protect me."

I pulled in a breath and felt the sting of tears rising.

"You know what, babe?" I said. "I could never feel like a bad mom. I am an awesome mom. And do you know what makes me awesome?"

Abby shook her head.

"Because I try so hard," I said. "I let you down sometimes, and

I forget your lunch sometimes, and I certainly can't protect you from everything. But I don't give up. Even though I make mistakes, and even though I'm nowhere even close to the perfect mother that I'd give anything for you and Tank to have, I pick myself up after every stumble and I get back after it and I keep trying—harder than I've ever tried at anything in my life. Because"—and here another true thing hit me for the first time—"raising you and Tank is the most important thing I will ever do."

"You really do try, Mama," Abby said.

I nodded, feeling like I was giving her a terrific life lesson. "And that's what makes anybody great at anything. Just trying like hell."

Abby took that in.

"You hear that, right?" I asked. "Because I think that's probably the smartest thing I will ever say to you."

"I hear it," she said.

"Good," I said.

"But Mom?"

"Yes?"

"You have *got* to quit cursing."

When we got home, I paused in the yard to thank O'Connor, but then I wasn't sure what to say.

"Is the sheriff really your cousin?" I asked.

O'Connor nodded. "But I was bluffing. He'd actually love to put me in jail."

I wanted to take his hand and squeeze it and look up into his eyes and tell him how very grateful I was for what he'd just done. But I hesitated, and in that moment, he caught sight of Abby, who was clearly feeling better and making a break for the tire swings.

He nodded in her direction. "Better catch her. You don't want that scrape to start bleeding again."

I definitely did not.

I turned to corral her just as Jean came down the back steps and saw Abby.

To her credit, she did not freak out. "Got a little scrape there?"

Abby nodded.

"You know what that means," Jean said.

Abby shook her head.

Jean pointed at her. "Ice cream for dinner."

Abby checked my expression. "Really?"

I looked at Jean like she was totally crazy. "I guess so," I said. I turned back toward O'Connor to see if he might like ice cream for dinner, too—but he had already left the yard.

Jean went to pick up Tank while Abby and I went upstairs and spent the rest of the afternoon reading, playing Go Fish, and adding soaps to a luxury bath.

After bedtime, I creaked back down the stairs to the kitchen and let all my rage bubble over to Jean as I paced around barefoot.

"Did you see her shirt?" I demanded. "She must have lost half the blood in her body."

Jean had made me a cup of tea, but it had gone cold while I ranted.

"The shirt looked bad," Jean agreed. "But at least it wasn't unprovoked."

"Unprovoked?"

"What I mean is," Jean said, moving to start another teakettle, "at least it was a playground fight. At least Abby wasn't a hapless victim."

"She *was* a victim!"

Jean nodded. "But he wasn't just bullying her. They were adversaries."

"Who cares?" I said. "He pushed her into a fence."

"But," Jean said slowly, so I could take a breath, "she was standing up to him when he did that. And not even for herself—for someone else. She chose to pit herself against him."

"And now she's got a gash in her head to show for it."

"What I mean is," Jean went on, all patience, "the fact that she stood up for George tells me she's not afraid. She saw herself as strong enough to protect him."

"But she wasn't."

"It doesn't matter. What matters is that she tried."

"Hasn't she just learned now that standing up for others gets your head bashed in?"

Jean shook her head. "No," she said. "She's learned that standing up for others makes you feel braver. She's learned that it feels good to do the right thing. And she's learned that even getting a gashed head is not going to break her."

I considered this.

"Didn't you see her face tonight?" Jean said. "Didn't you hear her telling the story over and over? She's proud of herself. And not because we told her she did a good thing. Because she knows in her bones that she did a good thing. She's proud from the inside out."

Abby *had* seemed awfully happy that afternoon, I thought. I'd chalked it up to leftover adrenaline.

Jean's eyes were shining. "You couldn't stop the bully, even though you wanted to. I wanted to, too. But something better has happened. Abby stopped him herself. She showed us all."

"Do you think he's really stopped?" I asked, afraid to even hope for it.

"It doesn't matter what he does," Jean said. "Maybe O'Connor scared him into changing his ways, or maybe he just made him worse. Either way, he's not going to bully Abby. Because she's not a victim anymore."

I wanted to believe that too much to actually let myself believe it.

But I stopped pacing at last and sat down and put my head in my hands. All the tension of the day had emptied me out, and I suddenly felt like a human version of a rubber chicken. I couldn't even answer when Jean said the new tea was boiling.

She looked over and eyed me at the table. "Go to bed," she said, adding, "You look like a rubber chicken."

I sat up in amazement. "I was just thinking—*just thinking*—that's exactly what I felt like."

Jean shrugged. "It shows."

She dried off the last clean pot with a dish towel while I watched. When I finally rose to take my untouched tea to the sink, I had a Pavlovian response to look for O'Connor's trailer at the kitchen window. But it wasn't there.

"Where's the Airstream?" I said.

"O'Connor took it," Jean said. She was doing a little sweeping now.

"Took it where?" I asked, looking back to double-check.

Jean didn't seem sure of what to say. "He wanted to talk to you about it," she said. "He waited down here for a long time this afternoon, hoping to see you."

"But?"

"When it started getting late, he had to go."

"Go where?" I asked, feeling a hitch in my chest.

"I really can't say," she said with a sigh. "He wanted to talk to you himself."

Jean truly was a vault, and I loved that about her—usually. "You can't know and not tell me!" I said.

She shook her head. "He specifically asked me to let him handle it."

"Handle what?"

Jean put the broom away. "It's not my place to have O'Connor's conversations for him. Especially ones like this."

"Jean," I said, "you're killing me."

"He'll explain everything when he can."

"Just tell me where he went," I said, feeling like that one decent piece of information would be enough.

And so Jean, finally taking pity on my tired face—while knowing full well that one piece of information would not even remotely be enough—set a record for the most information she'd ever let slip about another person's life: "He went to Austin."

A ustin's not good," Sunshine said in the milking barn the next day. She was back now as a kind of substitute milker.

"Why not?" I asked.

"One, his wife is in Austin with her sister now." Sunshine counted on her fingers, as if she were piecing together a great mystery. "Two, he's got their house here listed for sale. And three: Russell just told me that a buddy of O'Connor's at the Austin Fire Department got him a really awesome job there." Sunshine turned to give me a shrug. "So it looks like maybe he just moved away."

I stood straight up and almost knocked over my milking bucket.

"What?" Sunshine asked.

"Why would he move away?"

"Maybe he wanted to be near his wife. Maybe he wanted a real job."

I gestured at Betsy Ross, up on the milking stand. "This is a real job."

"No, it isn't," Sunshine said. "You said so yourself."

"But he wouldn't just disappear like that."

"Jean said he waited around all afternoon to talk to you," Sunshine said. "Maybe he was waiting to say goodbye."

The situation was so backward: Jean couldn't tell me what was going on with O'Connor because she *did* know, but Sunshine could go on and on about it because she *didn't*. But the more I thought about it, the more the pieces came together. Try as I might to assemble them another way, they only really seemed to fit one scenario: that Sunshine was right. O'Connor was gone. He had hitched up that Airstream and left us all in the dust.

Chapter 24

In the days that followed, I watched Abby closely. And Jean, for her part, watched me.

"You look a little tense," Jean told me one morning.

I thought about it. "I am tense."

Jean studied me for another moment. "Because Russ and I were just thinking about how fun it would be to take the kids camping this weekend."

"Camping?" I asked, like I didn't know what it was.

"Sure," Jean said. "They could use an adventure. And you could use a break."

"I don't know," I said. "What about Abby's head?" Camping didn't seem very sterile.

"The cut is all scabbed over," Jean said. "We just won't go swimming."

I did not want to let Abby go camping. I just wanted to keep her in the house and stare at her until she was healed up good as new. But Jean wasn't about to let me get away with that.

"So it's settled," she said. The four of them would go to Enchanted Rock with Russ's family-sized tent, and I would stay home and have a glass of wine. Or several.

"Maybe I should come along," I said, frowning at Jean.

"You," Jean said with a smile, "are not invited."

In the end, I let them go. I did need a break. I needed some sleep, too, after so many nights of thrashing around. Jean wanted me to have a nice dinner, soak in a hot bubble bath, and read a book—preferably all at the same time. But I didn't do any of those things. The day they left, I was so tired, I was fast asleep by seven-thirty.

In the morning, I woke up before Dubbie crowed. Sunshine never showed up, and so I spent the sunrise hours alone—milking by myself and packing up the truck for the farmers' market, my feet rustling through the long grass as I went. I moved so quietly through the Saturday morning routine that all the lonesomeness I'd been too sleepy to notice the night before seemed to drizzle down on me like rain.

With everybody gone, I had no one to talk to but myself, and nothing to direct my thoughts but their own whims. What really bugged me that morning, as I drove the highway to Houston, was how very hard I kept trying to build a life for myself—a sturdy one I could count on—and how the universe kept getting in my way. I'd had Jean, but then my mother took me from her. I'd found Danny, but then he died. I'd found O'Connor—or at least I'd wanted to—but now, apparently, he'd moved away.

Jean had taught the kids, when they had trouble falling asleep at night, to count their blessings instead of counting sheep. She literally had them make lists of all the things they were grateful for. I spent my entire, silent morning at the farmers' market trying to talk myself into doing the same thing. But I didn't feel like counting my blessings that day. I just felt like moping.

The late afternoon was the same. Mostly I just walked restlessly out to the barn and back again, checked on the goats and the garden, and kept my body busy to try to distract my mind. At last, out of desperation, I went through the motions of the bath and book, but I hardly achieved the restorative bliss Jean had hoped for.

For dinner, I made a big, sensible salad with cucumbers and lettuce and carrots from the garden. I ate it by myself in the kitchen, listening to the clock ticking and the cars zooming past down on the highway.

I had just decided to go looking for the first volume of Jean's zombie book when the phone rang. I literally jumped up at the sound, things had been so quiet for so long. Then I walked over and spoke the first word I'd said all afternoon. "Hello?"

It was Sunshine. "What are you doing tonight?" she asked. "I've got some great gossip on O'Connor."

"Gossip?"

"Want to hear it?" she asked.

I only nodded, but she went ahead anyway.

"I talked to Russ yesterday, prodding him for the scoop, and even though he gave me no current information on what O'Connor's doing in Austin, I did get something else out of him."

"Why didn't you tell me this yesterday?"

"I had a date yesterday," she said. "Don't you want to know what he said?"

"What?"

"O'Connor isn't married."

I held my breath. "Isn't married?"

"Nope."

"But—" My mind was flickering like it might short out.

"I know!" Sunshine said, delighted to have the goods. "Check it out: They're divorced."

"But—"

"I know!" Sunshine said again. "And Russ knows for certain, because he drew up the papers."

"Why would they still be together if they're divorced?"

"Well," Sunshine said, winding up for the full story, "O'Connor didn't want the divorce. She was the one who left him. He signed the papers because she insisted, but then he tried to get her back. The night of the car accident, O'Connor had talked her into going on a date."

"Was she going to take him back?"

"Apparently she was thinking about it."

I took it all in. "And then, on the way home—"

"A kid on a cellphone breezed through a red light," Sunshine said. "And totally crushed Erin's side of the car."

"Shit," I said.

Sunshine nodded. "O'Connor spent months sleeping on a sofa in her hospital room. And when she was well enough to go home, she had nowhere to go. Her sister was out of the country and wanted to put her in a facility, but the insurance only covered three months."

"The sister didn't come home?" I asked.

"Nope," Sunshine said, "because of her husband's job. They had a contract to stay for three years."

"But now the contract is over and they're back," I said.

"Exactly," Sunshine said. "Plus Erin and her sister never liked each other much. So there was that."

Now the pieces all fit together. I said, "He didn't want the sister to take Erin, but after his neighbor had that stroke, he ran out of choices."

"He couldn't work," Sunshine chimed in. "He was draining all his savings. And he's not an indoor guy. You've seen how he gets indoors."

I had.

"So now he's let the sister take her," I said, "and he's moved to Austin to keep an eye on her."

"Looks that way," Sunshine said.

I let out a sigh.

"It's a lot to process," Sunshine said. "I'm free if you want company."

I absolutely wanted company. I was so sick of my mopey self I could have carried a sign: WILL WORK FOR COMPANY.

But Sunshine wasn't usually free on Saturday nights anymore. "Don't you have a date?"

"Not tonight," she said. "He's playing pool with the guys. We're meeting up later."

We agreed to meet at the haunted house. I was in charge of marshmallows, and she was in charge of beer. I felt overjoyed at the prospect of having someone to talk to. The last person in the world I wanted to spend the evening with was myself.

"Isn't it great?" Sunshine said before we hung up. "O'Connor's free. He's not tragically unavailable after all. He's been free this whole time."

But it wasn't great, actually. And the more I thought about it, as I sat by the bonfire with a bag of marshmallows on my lap waiting for Sunshine, the more I realized just how very not great it was.

My first reaction on hearing the story had been the same as Sunshine's—if he wasn't married, there was at least some hope of us maybe, possibly getting together. But then I started thinking that if we weren't together by now, despite multiple opportunities and my own overwhelming willingness, and if it wasn't a tragic obligation elsewhere that had been holding O'Connor back, then there must be another reason. And the only other reason I could imagine was that he just wasn't interested.

Which was worse than a tragic obstacle. Because it made me an idiot. Isn't that the rule about guys? If you think they don't seem interested, that's because they aren't.

I flipped back through my memories. Had I imagined everything? He'd seemed interested at the farmers' market when he'd given me the fake kiss, but maybe he was just putting on a great show. He'd seemed interested on the night of Jean's birthday party, but maybe he'd just felt sorry for me. And he'd seemed interested the night he drank his body weight in Budweiser and then banged on the door, but that, I'd already decided, had just been beer goggles.

The more I thought about it, the clearer it seemed that I'd been letting my own wish-fulfillment fantasies skew my perceptions. I'd developed a crush on this unsuspecting guy, and then I'd woven a tragic and fictitious story through every one of our interactions to make the crush seem viable.

I felt a warm flush of humiliation. I hadn't thrown myself at O'Connor, exactly, but I hadn't held myself back, either. I hadn't flirted, but I hadn't masked my feelings. My words were always appropriate, but my eyes, I knew, were kind of the opposite.

And that's the thought that hit me just as Sunshine pedaled up the gravel drive to the haunted house.

As I walked to meet her, I was primed to obsess over this new information and examine and theorize about every angle. But Sunshine was no longer in any condition to do that. Because, when I reached her, she'd let her bike tump over in the yard and she was crying.

"What?" I said, rushing closer. "What happened?"

But she didn't speak. She just wiped her cheeks and pushed past to stand beside the fire.

I followed. "What is it, Sunny?"

She stared at the flames and shook her head.

"I can't help you if you don't tell me," I said. It was something I'd told Abby a hundred times.

Finally, without turning to meet my eyes, she pulled a wadded-up piece of paper from her hip pocket and handed it sideways to me.

I took it and opened it up, fold after fold. But even before I was done, I knew what it was. It was the cover page of the tabloid.

"Where did this come from?" I asked, without looking at it.

And then the tears really came. "Marshall's mother has a subscription."

"I'm sorry," I said. "We tried to get them all."

Sunshine looked over. "You did?"

I nodded. "Jean and I went around town the morning they hit town and collected them all up to burn them in the trash pit."

She smiled a little and started crying harder at the same time. "You did?"

I nodded. Then I hugged her.

"I just can't escape," she said, all muffled into my shirt. "It's like my old life won't let me go."

"You've already escaped," I said, stroking her hair. "This stuff can't touch you."

"But it can haunt me," she said.

"Well," I said, "we're all haunted by something." And I was struck by how true that was.

Sunshine wiped her face with her T-shirt, took a few deep breaths, and then said, "I broke up with Marshall, by the way."

"What?" I said. "Why?"

"I don't know," she said. "Because!"

I held up the page. "How did you even get this?"

"I dropped by his place for a kiss on the way over here. And it was on his sofa."

"And that's why you broke up with him? Because this was in his house?"

"Because it was in his house. Because he didn't tell me about it. Because now he's seen it, and that makes it real, and things will never be the same."

"He's always known who you are," I said. "It's not like he didn't know."

"I'm just done with it all," she said. "I'm done with men. I'm done with love. I'm going to move to Antarctica."

"You realize no one actually lives in Antarctica," I said. "Just penguins."

"Fine," she said. "Perfect. I love penguins."

From her pocket came the muffled sound of her cellphone ringing: Aretha Franklin. She pulled it out and looked at the number.

"It's him," she said.

"Answer it."

But she stared at it as Aretha sang on.

I pointed at her. "Men may cause all sorts of trouble," I said.

"But they're better than penguins. And it's not his fault that his mother reads trash."

"Fine," she said, lifting the phone to her ear. She answered with: "Whatever."

She was quiet for a long time as she listened to Marshall. He had a lot to say, and she was going to hear him out. I watched her face soften as he went on and on, and then, after a while, she said the only word she contributed to the entire phone call—"Okay"—and hung up.

She looked up at me. "I have to go."

"What did he say?" I asked.

"He said he'll never look at a Snickers bar the same way again."

I grabbed her for a hug. "So you're better now?"

"What can I say?" she said. "He's persuasive."

Then Sunshine turned toward the fire, crumpled up the tabloid page, and threw it in.

We watched it ignite and burn, and I said, "Good girl."

Before she left, Sunshine paused, worried about leaving me alone. "What are you going to do?"

I shrugged. "Stay here and have a séance."

"Tell Danny I said hi."

"But you know what?" I went on. "I think it's going to be my last one."

Sunshine nodded, like she really got it. Like it was as clear to her as it was to me that everything had to change. Because we really didn't need those séances anymore, if we ever had. She leaned in to kiss my cheek.

"Thank you for being my friend," she said.

Long after she was gone, I stood by the fire, watching the flames and, without really meaning to, talking to Danny. "It is the last one, you know," I said out loud. "And you can't argue with me, because you're dead. In case you didn't know."

I missed him acutely right then. I felt as alone as I ever had. And figuring out that O'Connor didn't care for me in the way I'd thought made me absolutely long to run into the arms of someone who did. But those arms weren't there anymore, of course. There was no one to run to.

I crossed my own arms over my waist as a gesture of comfort. But when the wind kicked up, it blew right through me anyway.

And then I realized something: I would always miss Danny. No matter how full my life became, there would always be a hole where his living presence had been. But the truth was, I was already better. And not despite that hole—but because of it. His loss was now a part of the story of my life. And that was okay. The things I had weren't negated by the things I didn't have. In fact, missing things made having other things that much sweeter. And, what's more, the very worst thing I could possibly imagine had happened to me, but I was still okay. And not just okay, but standing by a gorgeous fire on a windy night, brave in a wild wilderness near my long-lost childhood home.

You can't just wish strength for yourself. Or wisdom. Or resilience. Those things have to be earned. I felt calm as I thought about it. I never would have traded Danny for those things. Now that I had them, though, I had no choice but to be grateful. And I was so lost in the idea, and the universe seemed so connected and gusty and magical at that moment, that when Sunshine returned and walked up behind me, snapping a twig with her shoe, I genuinely thought for half a second that it was Danny.

But it wasn't Danny. And it wasn't Sunshine, either.

It was O'Connor.

"Hey," he said, stopping in his tracks.

I was so surprised, I didn't speak. All my calmness completely disappeared the moment I saw his face. Only a second before, I had been at peace with all the loneliness and sorrow and tragedy of the universe. But one look at those blue eyes of his sent me right back to war.

"Where is everybody?" he asked.

"Camping at Enchanted Rock," I said. Then, "How did you find me?"

"Sunshine."

I nodded and then turned back to the fire. I was so unreasonably thrilled to see him, it made me want to slap him across the face.

He walked up beside me and we stood side by side watching the flames.

"How's Abby doing?" he asked.

"She's fine, actually," I said. "She's kind of become a second-grade celebrity."

O'Connor nodded. "As she should be."

"And, of course, she has George's undying devotion," I added. "If he could get a tattoo with her name on it, he would."

"The cut's healing up?"

"Yep," I said.

"Well, it must be," he said then, "if you let Jean and Russ take her camping."

I smiled in spite of myself. It felt good to be teased. "Yes," I said, "but they're keeping her in a germ-free tent, like the Bubble Boy."

"Of course," O'Connor said. There was a pause, and then he said, "I have a question for you."

A question for me. I held my breath. Against all logic and reason and basic common sense, against everything I knew and had figured out, I suddenly felt certain that this man I hadn't seen in days, who I had never even really kissed, and who wasn't interested in me at all, was going to ask me to marry him.

Maybe he'd just moved to Austin. Maybe he was still in love with his ex-wife. I'd been working for hours to accept that he'd never been crushed out on me the way I had been on him. But there's a testament to the way that hope can triumph over information. It was sad but true: My heart took flight with longing.

"What's the question?" I asked, and the words themselves felt like feathers.

O'Connor took a step closer, then another, and then another. He stopped close up and looked right into my eyes.

"Can I have your marshmallows?" he said. "I'm starving."

I had no idea what he was talking about. But I looked down and realized that I was, in fact, still holding a bag of marshmallows. Still, I stared at him like he'd spoken another language.

"The marshmallows you're holding?" he said, gesturing at them.

I looked down again, feeling all the misery and injustice and self-pity that I'd just foresworn taking back over.

"Take them!" I said, but I threw them on the ground. And before they even landed, I was striding back through the yard toward my car.

O'Connor followed me—to his credit, without stopping to pick up the marshmallows.

"Hey!" he said, catching up. "What's that about?"

"Nothing," I said.

"Where are you going?"

"Nowhere," I said. "I'm going nowhere."

And it was literally true. Because when I got to my car, O'Connor's truck, with its Airstream trailer still attached, was blocking it.

But that wasn't stopping me. I turned around without breaking stride.

He was right on my heels. "You're mad at me because I wanted your marshmallows?"

So literal. "No," I said.

"Keep them!" he said. "I don't care."

"This is not about marshmallows," I said. I knew where I was going now. The forest trail to Jean's house was on the other side of the clearing. If I couldn't drive away, then I'd walk.

"Then what *is* it about?" he demanded.

If he didn't know, then I couldn't tell him. And the fact that he didn't know—that he hadn't known all along—absolutely enveloped me with rage. Right about the time that this feeling hit, O'Connor caught up with me, grabbed my arm, and spun me around.

"You're not going into the woods," he said, his face determined.

"Yes, I am."

"I'm not asking," he said. "I'm telling. You are not going into the woods."

"You can't tell me what to do," I said, sounding like a four-year-old even to my own ears.

"You want to go in there in the pitch black and stumble down an unlit and unmarked path for half a mile downhill past brambles and poison ivy?"

"Yes!" I said. "That's exactly what I want to do."

O'Connor seemed at a loss. "What about the panther?" he said at last.

"The panther?" I said, like he was totally crazy. "Fuck the panther!"

I turned to keep going.

But there was his hand on my elbow again pulling me back, and this time, he didn't let go. He put his face right in mine. "Libby!" he said. "What the hell is going on?"

"I don't know!" I said. "You tell me. You show up at Jean's in the middle of the night falling-down drunk and drag me out into the yard, and then you march into Abby's school like a vigilante, and then you disappear with your crazy trailer and Jean won't even tell me where you've gone, and then you show up out of no-where and ask me for marshmallows! You tell *me* what's going on! Because I sure as hell have no idea."

He was a little out of breath from the chase and the arguing. He let go of my arm, and his voice got quieter. "I *have* been acting kind of bananas, huh?"

"Damn straight," I said, a little quieter myself.

"I think," he said then, studying my face, "if I'm really honest . . . I think it's because I'm in love with you."

Everything went quiet. We were both a little out of breath.

"You can't be," I said at last.

"I can't be?"

"What about Erin?"

"I was in love with Erin," he said, nodding, "when we were married. But when she cheated on me and then divorced me, that kind of killed it."

"She cheated on you?"

He nodded. "She did."

"And then you got divorced?"

"That's right."

"But you took care of her anyway."

He nodded, and he reminded me so much of Abby when he said, "Somebody had to."

"And now her sister's back," I said.

"Yes. In Austin."

"Is that where you went?"

"Yes. To check on her and to see the setup."

"And you've moved to Austin, too."

O'Connor frowned. "Who told you that?"

"Sunshine," I said.

He shook his head.

"Didn't you get a dream job?" I asked. "In the Austin Fire Department?"

"I got an *interview* for a dream job," he corrected. "But I didn't go."

"Why didn't you go?"

"Because Abby got hurt that day, and I went with you instead."

"You ditched your job interview to come with me?"

O'Connor nodded.

"Why?" I asked.

"Because it was time to open up a can of whup-ass on PeePants Gaveski," he said with a grin. "And because, like I said, I'm in love with you."

"You can't be," I said. "I've been throwing myself at you for months and you've been totally uninterested."

O'Connor blinked. "You haven't been throwing yourself at me."

"Yes, I have."

"No," he said. "You've been having séances to contact your dead husband."

He had me there. "But those weren't real."

"Sunshine thought they were real. She told me all about it. She was going to get him to come to you every night in your dreams. Because you'd never gotten over him and you never planned to."

"I did get over him," I said. "A while ago."

"Sunshine doesn't think so."

"Why does Sunshine get to be the expert?"

I had him there. "She sounded really certain."

"She's an actress."

"She was pretending?"

"She was just wrapped up in the whole story of it," I said, "and the romance of a lost husband who returns from the dead. So was I, a little, at first. But then we kind of moved on."

"Why?" he asked.

"I don't know," I said. "Because we had more fun drinking beer and goofing around. The séance stuff wasn't very interesting."

He looked at me like my answer was vitally important. "Why not?"

I thought about it. "Partly because it was pointless. And partly . . ." Despite everything he'd just confessed and the breathless way he was looking at me, I couldn't quite say out loud the words that were in my head.

Instead, I reached out to him and pulled the hem of his T-shirt until he stepped closer. But once he was there, I couldn't bring myself to look up. I twisted his shirt around my fingers.

He was waiting for an answer—even though, really, he already had it.

I thought about him, and me, and the human race in general—how brave and resilient and hopeless we all are. I felt so sorry for us, all broken and disheartened, but I admired us, too. We muddled through. We didn't give up. We found wisps of happiness snagged on brambles. We made all those ridiculous mistakes humans are so famous for. I'd tried so hard to make a perfect, untouchable life for myself. But trouble finds you. Tragedy finds you. And we keep trying anyway. We hope for the best. We believe we can make something for ourselves—something good that will last—even though, at the exact same time, we know we can't.

And there was O'Connor, living a life he'd never expected. And there I was, exactly the same. Both of us still alive, and both of us still trying to do the right thing. And I knew it was time to stop wasting time. Because all of this—everything around us—was slipping away, even as it happened.

His hands were on me now. They were warm and callused, and they'd found my hips under my shirt, just there above my jeans. He leaned in so close that I could feel his breath in my hair. I let my hands copy his and find their way under his T-shirt, too. It was time to be brave and confess.

But, before I could do it, he brought his head down to lean his forehead against mine. His hands left my hips as he brought them up to my face. He nudged my chin up, and I met his eyes, and when I did, he pressed his mouth against mine. A kiss different from any I'd ever had. Sadder. And more determined. We weren't some perfect picture book, I thought, and for the first time I understood the way that imperfection can make things better. Our lives hadn't played out the way we'd expected. Things we'd counted on had slipped away, and were still slipping away—which made this little kiss and whatever it might lead to that much more of a blessing. I didn't know what troubles waited ahead, but I knew that we'd found each other for now.

I tightened my hold on him at the same time the rest of me started to melt.

"Partly what?" he asked then, again, barely letting go of the kiss. "What's the second 'partly'?"

"I forgot what we were talking about," I said.

"No, you didn't," he said, and kissed me some more. "You said, 'Partly . . .'"

And so before we made our way back to the Airstream, and before we stumbled sideways up the steps, still kissing and fumbling for the bed, and before I could give myself over to the blissful relief of not being alone, and before O'Connor could make a barefoot midnight stumble out to the bonfire embers to retrieve that bag of marshmallows, I had to earn it all with the truth.

I put my hands up behind his neck, pulled his ear down close, and took a breath. "Partly," I said, "because of you."

Chapter 25

By lunch the next day, when Jean and the kids got back, O'Connor and I had spent a long morning tangled in the sheets in his Airstream, made it back home to milk some annoyed goats, and done a morning's worth of farm chores. As Russ's Mercedes rattled up the gravel drive, we posed ourselves on the front porch as innocently as we could manage.

The kids disappeared in the garden after a quick hello, but Jean stayed on the porch untangling the fishing poles while Russ unpacked the car. She eyed us over and over, and when Russ showed up to announce he was so dirty he'd need three showers in a row, Jean gestured at us and said to him, "You owe me fifty bucks."

"Why?" Russ said.

"Libby and O'Connor," she said, waving her hand at the two of us. "It worked."

"Oh," Russ said. "It did?"

"Can't you tell?" Jean said. "Look at them."

And it was easy to see that Russ could tell once he looked. Some things, like being happy, are hard to hide.

"What do you mean?" I asked then.

"We had a bet about you guys," Russ said. "Jean thought you were meant for each other, and we bet fifty bucks on it."

"You bet against her?" O'Connor asked.

I gave Russ a look. "Does that mean you didn't think we were meant for each other?"

"Actually," Russ said, "I thought you were meant for each other, too. But Jean likes me to antagonize her, so I try to oblige when I can."

I flipped back through all the times Jean had forced O'Connor to drive with me to the farmers' market. "Was it all a setup?" I asked. "All those Saturdays?"

"Not all of it," Jean said, looking pleased with herself. "The broken fridge door? You can't buy a setup like that."

"But," I said, "you *were* setting us up?"

"As often as possible," she said with a little nod.

I looked at O'Connor in disbelief, and he started to laugh.

"Can you blame me?" Jean asked.

Russ was counting bills out of his wallet. "Fifty bucks," he said to Jean. "You can buy me a steak."

There was nothing left to do then but give up and go sit close to O'Connor.

He put his arm around me as Jean took Russ back to his car to say goodbye, and they walked out arm in arm with the goats at their heels. As I shifted my gaze to the kids on the tire swings, then both packs of dogs lounging near them, then one of the kittens chasing after Dubbie the rooster, and then the long grass waving in the wind, my mind pulled back to see it all from a great distance. It seemed so clear now—the way we were all connected, the way *together* and *apart* pushed and pulled on each other, the way you had to lose one thing to find another. I couldn't help but think about Danny and the way losing him had led us here. And I knew there was no place I'd rather be.

Maybe it wouldn't last. Maybe things wouldn't always be exactly the same. Maybe O'Connor and I were meant for each other, or maybe we weren't. Maybe Tank would grow up to run the goat farm, and maybe Abby would grow up to run the country. Maybe Sunshine and Marshall would grow up, too, and stay together, and have ten little goth children in skull T-shirts. Maybe PeePants Gaveski would learn to regret all his meanness, or maybe he'd spend his whole life wondering what was wrong with everybody else, just like my mother.

And maybe Jean would live to be a hundred and we'd wind up with many more years together than we'd spent apart. Maybe she'd write a bestselling beef-and-butter cookbook and go on the *Today* show in her overalls. Or, more likely, maybe we'd never really make up all the years we'd lost.

Anything was possible. Everything was uncertain. But I knew one thing for sure: I'd bounced back before, and I would do it again and again and again. Because that's the only choice there is. And as many things as I still had to lose, I had just as many more left to find.

Acknowledgments

~~~~~~~~~~~~~~~~~~~~~~

For my first book, I thanked just about every person I'd ever met. This time around, I'm keeping things simpler. But believe me, I could write a book of thanks.

I need to thank my friends Christian and Lisa Seger out at Blue Heron Farm for letting me come visit them so many times and meet their goats and eat their phenomenal cheese. Their charming country life is very inspiring, and I'm so grateful they've been willing to share it with me. I'm also indebted to the lovely Gene Graham for letting me spend time writing at her divine house in the Texas hill country.

I am truly thankful for my fantastic agent, Helen Breitwieser, and so lucky to have her help and guidance. And I am in awe of my editor Jen Smith's patient and savvy attention to this manuscript through draft after draft.

I am also always grateful to my family: my awesome husband, Gordon, and my amazing mom, Deborah Detering, share the first shout-out for encouraging me, reading drafts, watching the kids, listening to me worry, and always, always doing everything they can to help me get my writing done. It's a profound gift to have two such phenomenal people in my life, and not a minute goes by that I don't know it. Many thanks, also, to my sisters, Shelley Stein and Lizzie Fletcher, who always encourage me, and to my dad, Bill Pannill, an editing ninja who genuinely loves to talk about words and language and grammar. And of course, of course: to my kids, Anna and Thomas, who are the sweetest, cutest, most delightful people I could ever have wished for.

KATHERINE CENTER is the author of four novels about love and family: *The Bright Side of Disaster, Everyone Is Beautiful, Get Lucky,* and *The Lost Husband.* Her work has appeared in *Redbook, People, USA Today, Vanity Fair, Real Simple,* the *Dallas Morning News,* and the *Houston Chronicle,* as well as in the anthologies *Because I Love Her, CRUSH,* and *My Parents Were Awesome.* Katherine has degrees from Vassar College and the University of Houston's Creative Writing Program. She lives in Texas with her husband and two children.

www.KatherineCenter.com.